# Sloth

## Love is Cure, Vol. 1 - Vices & Virtues

### Book Seven

## Brookelyn Mosley

85 Media LLC

# MORE BY BROOKLYN MOSLEY

*Novels/Novellas/Novelettes/Series*

No Fraternizing, Pt. 1

No Fraternizing, Pt 2

No Fraternizing, Pt. 3

First Came Love: The Love, Hate & Revenge Prequel

Love, Hate & Revenge, Pt. 1

Love, Hate & Revenge, Pt. 2

Love, Hate, & Revenge, Pt. 3

Girl Code

Mr. & Mrs. Jones

Forbidden: An Anthology

They Call Me Mello

A Love Deferred

Indecent Arrangement

Last Comes Love

Ebb & Flow

PRIDE

Meant To Be

LUST

Loveless

GREED

Rekindled

My First, My Last

ENVY

Ready or Not

So This is Love

Home Before Midnight

GLUTTONY

When Luke Met Juliette

When Life Gives You Sunsets

In Love, I Trust

WRATH

***Short Stories***

Just Friends

Chateau Luxure

Lena's Ex-File

Dream Boss

Unsilent Knight

Twice In Love

Home For Christmas

# ByBK Exclusives

Bed Bully
Stuck
LHR Rewind Series
Home Before Midnight
Maybe This Time Will Be Different
Lovekilla
Incoming Call
Rough
WYD
Drinks on Me
Cali & Lee
Ray & Jay
Living Out a Love Song
Glimpses
One Mic

Click Here to see if new exclusive shorts have been added to ByBK
(Copy + paste this link if the above link doesn't work: https://
bybrookelynmosley.com/collections/ebooks)

# Message from the Author

Thank you for purchasing your copy of *Sloth*.

*Sloth* is the final chapter in *Love is Cure, Vol. 1 – Vices & Virtues*, marking the seventh book in the series. Although it's part of a series, *Sloth*, like books 1–6, can be read as a standalone. If this is the first book you've come across in the series, feel free to start here—you won't get lost in the story.

You'll find references to characters from earlier books in the series, as well as characters from other stories in my catalog. To enhance your reading experience, I've included a cameo list at the end of the book, complete with links to the stories where these characters originally appeared, so you can explore more of my book world.

**Content Warning: This story explores themes of emotional trauma, loss, and difficult decisions that may be triggering for some readers. Please take care while reading.**

Thank you again for joining me on the final leg of this journey. I hope you enjoy!

Love,
BK

# ACKNOWLEDGMENTS

As always, and in every book acknowledgment, the first shoutout must go to my husband. From story ideas I ask you about to debating the direction of my stories, you're always all ears and honest. I appreciate you not only as my husband but as my homie, lover, and friend.

To my children—when I started this journey, there was only one of you, and now there are two amazing souls to balance while I write. Thank you for your patience and understanding. I get up at the craziest hours to get words down, but sometimes I cut into your time to do a little of this or that. You two inspire me in ways you may never fully know. I am blessed.

To my reading family: So many of you have been reading these books in the order they were released, waiting patiently with each one—not rushing me, but reminding me that you were waiting every chance you got! I thank you for your support and kind words. This series was for both me and you, and I'm so grateful you enjoyed it as much as I enjoyed creating it.

To my ARC reading community, bookstagrammers, book clubs, book bloggers, and book reviewers who read and review my stories—especially the ones in this series: You have made this experience something I've looked forward to from book one to book seven. I know we all have busy lives outside of these pages and all the other books you read, but I appreciate you so much for fitting my work into your life. You are beyond appreciated.

To my BK Insiders and Brookelynite Daily subscribers, thank you for your emails and the conversations we share in my inbox. They always come at the right time and remind me exactly why I started all of this.

And finally, to me! I'm very proud of me. This journey has not been the easiest to travel. It's been filled with a lot of emotions, conflicting feelings, wins, and losses that I've had to work through to keep creating. Despite the roadblocks and disappointments, nothing compares to the love I have for storytelling. I'm forever a student of the craft, and as of this writing, I'm grateful to have spent nine years as a pupil.

Thank you to everyone who has ever purchased one of my books, mentioned me in a room I wasn't in, or even one I may never step into. Thank you for speaking light and love whenever our paths cross, whether online or in person. You are valued, you are appreciated, and you are very much a part of my process. Thank you!

*Dedicated to the saints and the sinners...*

# One

## Los Angeles, California - May 2023

**ERYN**

"I know that ain't..." I mumbled, my words trailing off. My fingers froze, hovering over the computer's keyboard. My eyes locked onto shiny black curls bouncing over the narrow shoulders of a woman I thought I'd never see again.

When she moved out of sight, I blinked myself out of my daze and immediately pushed my office chair back on its wheels to stand to my feet.

My blowout feathered the air as I made my way to my office's front door. I poked my head out of it and homed my eyes down the hall, watching as the curls and the woman disappeared into the nearest conference room.

"Ain't no way." I shook my head, stepping out and making my way toward the front desk.

Opal Sands Marketing Agency was my home away from home. I'd been working there for four years, originally starting as a public relations assistant and sleeping my way to a public relations manager position.

Yes, you read that correctly.

More on that in a bit, though.

"Gina," I said to our receptionist before I arrived at her desk.

The office was quiet at the present hour. It was 9am local time. Most of Opal Sands' employees didn't report to the office until late morning. Often following around our clients on press junkets, media interviews, and other media related assignments. Only entry-level employees were typing away in their cubicles, the rattling of the keys drowned out by the sound of my heart pounding in my ears.

When I had Gina's brown eyes on me, I pointed behind me toward the conference room with my thumb. "Who just walked in?"

Gina shrugged. "I don't know. She didn't even greet me when I said good morning to her."

I rested my forearm on the ledge of her L-shape reception desk. "I know there's a meeting scheduled for today at 9:30am. Who all gon' be there?"

Gina giggled as she peeked down at her laptop and began moving her fingertips along the laptop's touchpad.

I already knew there was a meeting today. My human ticket to the top, better known as Richard Laine, had already revealed to me the meeting would discuss the year's quarterly promotions.

A promotion he promised I would get while I was up under him in the missionary position.

"Richard will be present," Gina answered. "Along with the other senior executives..."

I peeked behind me and towards the conference room.

"That's all I see listed here," she confirmed. "Everyone added to the calendar for the meeting are our usual attendees."

"But that woman who walked in, isn't?" I blinked erratically. "You don't see a woman's name on the calendar today that you've never seen on there before?"

"Yeah, no. I don't see any unfamiliar names here. *Hmm.*" Gina focused down on her laptop's screen again. "That's weird."

"What's weirder," I uttered low, "is that I think I saw my brother's ex."

"Eryn," Richard called from down the hall.

When I glanced in that direction, I saw he had one foot out of the conference room and the other still inside of it.

A few feet ahead of him were two of the building's security guards stationed opposite him, on either side of another conference room door.

Richard gestured with his head for me to approach.

I looked at Gina and arched both brows, then winked. "Let me go see what's going on."

"Okay, girl," she replied, attention back on her laptop's screen. "Keep me updated, please."

Richard stepped out from the conference room and waited for me up the hall. He wore an expression that for the life of me, I couldn't read.

Richard was your standard edition black guy. Average and regular as hell. But he looked great on paper. Never married, no kids, great job. He was Opal Sands' PR Director... and who I'd been using to climb my way to the top, via, what we can call, an express ladder.

"Hey Kev," I greeted one of the security guards. "Liam," I said to the other.

Richard walked up to me as I sauntered closer.

"What's going on?" I asked when I was near.

He scratched his head and looked away.

That gave me pause.

I held up a hand and stopped in front of him, then pointed toward the conference room behind him. "What's happening?"

"Let me start by saying," he whispered, "this was out of my control."

I leaned forward a little to peek through the conference room's glass wall and damn near swallowed my tongue.

"What in the actual hell?"

I pushed past him, feeling as he tried to grab my hand to stop me, but he was too slow.

"What the hell are you doing here?" Were the first words out of my mouth.

Brielle Chadwick sat at the head of the conference room table wearing the most annoying grin on her lips.

I hated that fucking grin. It was so maniacal. So untrusting. It begged for me to slap it right off her lying ass face.

"Eryn," she greeted, gesturing at a nearby chair. "Please, have a seat."

"I'd rather not." I turned to see Richard closing the conference room door.

I recalled Gina saying there would be senior executives in the meeting, but there was no one else in the conference room. They'd likely be here by 9:30am, as stated in the meeting's calendar time. So, it was only me, Richard, and Brielle... my brother's ex-girlfriend and *almost* fiancée.

Brielle was my brother's ex and *almost* fiancée because she was a lying, conniving, cheating ass bitch who broke his heart. And I still owed her ass a good ol' Brooklyn beat down for it.

I watched as Richard made his way around me to take a seat in one of the several conference room chairs.

"What's going on?" I asked, more so to Richard, who I kept my eyes locked on.

Brielle snapped her fingers, the sound traveling throughout the room. "Over here."

I jerked my head back as I shot my eyes over to hers. "Who the fuck are you snapping at?"

"Language," she replied, fluttering her eyelashes as she batted them at me. "That's not a very nice way to talk to your boss."

"My..." I blinked so hard I saw colors with my eyes closed. I pressed my hand to my black halter top's high neck next. "My, what?"

Richard cleared his throat. "Chadwick Capital, the private equity firm owned by Brielle's father, Julian Chadwick, bought Opal Sands. That is what today's meeting later is about. The official signing over of the company."

"And restructuring," Brielle chimed in.

"Excuse me?" My hands were up in front of me. "I thought your father was into sports media."

"My dad is into *everything* that's lucrative, including Opal Sands." Brielle smirked. "As such, Opal Sands is now my father's company," Brielle added. "And he has made me COO. As of today."

I focused on Richard. "How long has this been in the works?"

He looked away.

"For the last four months," Brielle answered for him.

My jaw nearly hit the floor. "Four months?!"

"*Mm-hmm*," Brielle confirmed with a nod. "Around the time your brother announced his engagement to Ms. Muscle Butt."

I was way too shocked, too perturbed to give her comment a second thought. Too busy confused about how something like Opal Sands being bought out and the deal taking four months to complete, but I was only hearing about it that day. Especially when Richard and I slept together last night. And there was no sleeping going on.

So, yes, about that.

I was using Richard. He was my ticket to the top. Unproblematic. Easy to manipulate. He was a man led by his dick, respectfully. And that worked for me because I was willing to look past his inability to keep his dick up long enough to fully get mine. I was okay with when it *was* up, it barely being able to do much. Sleeping with Richard was not because I loved him or saw the potential to love him. I wasn't even all that attracted to him. He was simply my ticket. *Only* my ticket. Because I decided four years prior, after spending four of my good years at another agency slaving and getting nothing but my picture on the employees of the month wall, that my days of working hard just to get a pat on the back were over. I was voting myself off the modest, put-my-shoulder-to-the-wheel island.

Fucking my way to the top may not be the most celebrated way for me to accomplish my goals, but it was working for me.

At least I *thought* it was working for me.

Because if it *were* working for me, why was I just hearing about *this*?

I slowly guided my attention over to Richard, feeling my teeth clench behind my tight lips.

"Niggas," I whispered the moment we locked eyes.

"Back on topic though," Brielle continued, waiting for my eyes to meet hers. "With me as COO, I'm changing some things around here. Starting with you. Eryn, you're fired."

My breathing hitched.

My lips formed the shape to question her, but my voice was too stuck in my throat.

"Full transparency." She folded her hands over the conference room table. "You're only collateral. I know you've never liked me and, to be frank, I've never liked you either. And I'm willing to bet everything that you're partially the reason Everett refused to take me back."

"He refused to take you back because you were fucking and sucking other men on camera while you were in a relationship with my brother and keeping the tapes of you fucking and sucking, you dumbass."

Richard sat up in his seat. "Eryn—"

I pointed at him. "You shut the fuck up."

"Be that as it may." She smoothed her hand down the back of her neck. "I had my father buy this company specifically to get you out of it. So there. It's done."

"You sneaky, disloyal, conniving ass bitch—"

"Eryn," Richard cut in.

"Don't forget to mention smart." She smirked. "Because I know little about you, Eryn, since you've *never* made it a priority to have a relationship with me and you kept it no secret you didn't like me, but I know how much you *love* this job so." She shrugged like the spoiled daddy's girl she was. "All is fair in war, right?"

I considered using the toe of my suede mules to kick off the other shoe and throw it at her, but the urge within me wasn't willing to wait. I needed my fist in her face, without delay.

"That's it. I'm about to move furniture with your ass," I said, taking quick steps towards her. "Come here!"

I saw when her eyes ballooned, her hands gripped the arms of the chair she sat in, and when she pushed her chair back quickly in her attempt to get away. My legs were swallowing the distance between us as I drew my hand back, prepared to slap the malice out of her ass. My hand was within inches of her face when I felt Richard grab my arm, then looped his other arm around my waist, lifting me off the floor.

"You're insane!" Brielle shouted.

"Oh, you haven't seen insane yet," I shouted back, trying to get free of Richard's grip. "But you will after I beat some sense into you."

"Eryn, calm down," he tried.

"Let me go, Rich!"

Kev and Liam, the security guards I found waiting outside of the conference room, busted through the conference room door only a few seconds later.

Other PR assistants and entry-level employees were poking their heads out above their cubicles to get a glimpse of the action.

"Get her out of here right now," Brielle hollered over the commotion.

There were whispers as Richard literally pulled me away from the conference room, damn near dragging me to my office. Security, of course, not far behind.

"Get the fuck off of me," I said to Richard, shoving him away from me and pulling my arm free. "I can't *believe* you would do this to *me*."

He held his hands up in front of him in surrender.

"It was completely out of my control."

"Bullshit!" I screamed. "You *completely* blindsided me."

"Ms. Peters," one of the security guards, Liam, voiced at the threshold of my door. "Please. If you could gather your things and exit the premises—"

"Liam, you better give me a damn moment!" I yelled at him.

I couldn't believe this was happening to me. I was in disbelief.

"We were together last night," I said to Richard. "*Why* didn't you tell me any of this last night or any of the other nights we were together?"

"I didn't want to ruin our quality time," he whispered.

"Nigga." I pointed over his shoulder. "Me walking in and getting completely blindsided was better? Does this seem like a better alternative to you telling me what would happen today ahead of time?"

"I was bound by contract not to disclose."

"Was this before or after I rode your face last night?"

He coughed and glanced over his shoulder, moving closer to me. "Can we *not* do this right now?"

I scoffed. "When the fuck can we do it then, Richard? *Hmm*? When?"

Richard tried to take my hand, but I snatched it out of his reach.

"I did not know you two knew each other, okay?" he told me. "At our first meeting, shortly after the signing, when Brielle detailed her plans of wanting to let some employees go, and she mentioned you being the first of those people, I tried to explain to her you were an asset to Opal Sands but she wouldn't hear it. Now I know why?"

"Your realization is a little late," I said through my teeth. "Don't you think?"

He sighed.

"You should have told me." I stuttered an exhale. "You should have told me *something*, Rich."

"We can meet up later," he whispered. "And figure something out."

I tilted my head to one side.

"What's happened here doesn't have to change what we have," he promised.

To hell it didn't.

Richard was not my man and would never be. Our relationship was completely transactional. On my part, at least.

I considered our hooking up my work because I wasn't willing to do the actual work to move up at Opal Sands the legit way.

The moment I arrived at Opal Sands, I scoped out the higher-ups to see who my target would be. Who would take the bait? Because my whole reason for moving to L.A. was to work at Opal Sands. And when there were no positions available for me to apply to work in, when I first moved here, I got a job at a lesser-name agency hoping to build my name in the industry. It never happened. Too busy doing my work and everybody else's work while being severely underpaid. It was all a waste of time. So, when I reapplied and got an entry-level position at my dream agency, I decided on my course of action immediately, before starting my first day. The way I saw it, I was getting older, and I'd already wasted four years at the other PR agency.

And I would not do that at Opal Sands.

Opal Sands was my retirement plan. Managing PR for A and B-list celebrities and major corporations. Industry experts praised Opal Sands for its stellar media crisis management services.

*My* media crisis management services that I'd rebuilt and totally revamped. And my work earned Opal Sands its notoriety for putting out the nastiest media fires that showed no signs of hope until we took it under our wings. *My* wings. *My* ideas, *my* executions.

*Mine!*

Richard was only a piece on my game board. As soon as I got that head of communications promotion the following month, I would have ended things with him. I wouldn't have needed him anymore. We both would have been in senior roles, and I would have used that as my way out.

Not after that day.

*Damn.*

I turned around and snatched up my quilted designer shoulder bag and gave Richard a once-over.

"Have my things couriered to me," I snarled, shouldering past him on my way out. "Because if I stay another second on this floor, I'm gonna kill somebody—specifically you and Brielle."

"Eryn," he called.

I raised my arm and lifted my middle finger high overhead, flipping him the bird in response, being sure to add, "Fuck you, Rich."

"Eryn." Gina jumped to her feet. "What's going on? Where are you going?!"

"I'm out of here," I said to her as I stabbed at the elevator's call button. "I need to go right *now* before I catch a case."

"What?"

"Please have my things couriered to my condo, girl." I shook my head. Really trying to keep the tears back. "You know the address."

I moved my eyes off her for a moment to take a last glimpse of the place I swore I'd retire from and sighed in defeat.

I walked onto the elevator on Opal Sands' floor and then off the car when it reached the parking garage a few minutes later. Practically threw myself onto the leather seat inside my rose-gold Range and started the SUV, peeling out of my reserved parking spot I would likely never use again. Everything I did from stopping at red lights, making right then left turns. They were all a blur. A blur from the tears clouding my eyes that I cleared away before any could fall. A blur because I was just moving and closing the distance between myself and my bed.

When I got out of bed that morning, never did I imagine I would be returning to it with my dreams remaining just dreams.

"I knew I should've kept her sex tape and leaked that shit," I mumbled after I parked in my condo's parking spot and got out of my SUV.

The moment I slid my key into my condo's door and stepped inside, my eyes met the beautiful, clear view of North Hollywood straight ahead.

I'd perfectly tailored my life in L.A. to forget every and all the things I left behind in New York.

I promised myself I would have everything I wanted when I moved out here with my older brother.

I would be a big-time PR executive and live as fabulously as I wanted to, like Samantha Jones in Sex and the City. But the black woman living in Los Angeles, version.

"So much for that." I tsked softly as I dropped my keys in the empty bowl I kept by the front door.

I started going through my return home routine. Work blazer draped on the chair by my door, shoulder bag on the coat rack at the closest wall.

A routine I'd mastered that was supposed to keep me focused and organized. To fight procrastination and my natural inclination towards being lazy, which I couldn't be if I wanted what I wanted at Opal Sands. All so I could finally enter the big leagues at my dream job. All the girl boss manuals I consumed like candy when I first moved here suggested it. Every single book on leaning in and bossing up gave the how-to level up at work and at life.

*Always put things away. Keep your space neat and smelling fresh. Take your shoes off and place them on the rack. Everything in its place.*

*An orderly home leads to an orderly life. And an orderly life brings you closer to the life of your dreams.*

Yeah, fuck that.

Because at that moment, I wanted to do nothing besides fall face first on my pillow.

So instead of draping my blazer on the chair, I dropped my blazer on the floor. Instead of putting my shoes away, I kicked off my mules, allowing them to fall wherever gravity wanted them to fall.

I pulled my high-neck halter up over my head as I made my way towards the stairs to my bedroom. Stepped out of my cream trousers next. I left all that shit wherever I flung them.

Not giving a single fuck anymore.

Like old times.

# Two

## SIMEON

"Well, this is cozy," Hazel said across from me.

I peeked up from my meal to focus her way and allowed a smile to pull at my lips.

We were at a steakhouse in downtown Oakland, not too far from my place.

Hazel's idea.

The steakhouse, being only a mile from my home, was her reasoning for insisting we visit there after I asked her to have dinner with me.

And the only reason I asked her to eat dinner with me was because my friend and client Dallas insisted I do so.

*"We can stop at your place after,"* Hazel offered a week prior when I invited her out to dinner.

But we wouldn't be doing that.

She's never been to my home and... I liked it that way.

"It's cool," I replied, forking a piece of well-done steak into my mouth. "It's quiet, has good lighting. Your kind of spot."

"*Our* kind of spot." She winked.

I chuckled lowly.

This was technically *our* second date, even though we'd been seeing each other for over a year.

Hazel and I had met at a post-game press conference for the Oakland Flames last spring. She was press, a reporter for a struggling sports website that was relying more and more on gossip to maintain site traffic. Dallas was on the microphone answering questions and she kept on asking intrusive ones. Like when he was planning to set a wedding date for him and his fiancée's wedding and where they planned to wed. If they planned to have children. If so, how many?

I wanted to get a good read on her because while her questions weren't messy, they were personal. And as many times as Dallas tried to politely 'no comment' her into silence, I could tell she was getting under his skin.

And I refused to let her get him out of his element. Image was everything to me and she appeared to be a threat to it.

So, I approached her to see if she was a friend or foe. I invited her out to dinner that evening and we ended the night hooking up at her place a few hours after I asked for the check.

A year later, and I was still unsure if she was a friend or a foe of Dallas, but she was audacious and bold, albeit nosey as hell. And my healthy vice was finding audacious and bold women extremely attractive and irresistible.

But more than that, Hazel was interesting. Not exactly exciting—which I actually preferred in a woman—but still, she was interesting. And interesting was nice to be around when I had to be reliably predictable and the most responsible one in a group most of the time.

"I'm happy you could meet up with me tonight," she started. "*Off* a bed."

I snorted, then shook my head.

"Correct me if I'm wrong," I stated. "But isn't *on* a bed always because of your insistence."

"You never deny me."

"Now why would I do such an idiotic thing like that?"

Hazel smiled shyly, playing the part very well, I must add.

Because her cleavage spilling out of her red skintight dress was giving everything but shyness.

*Perhaps having her over at my place tonight wouldn't be such a bad idea.*

Relationships were the last thing on my mind, even though my parents kept insisting marriage should always be on my brain at my age.

*"Is 38 the year?" My mother asked during one of our recent phone calls. "Will this be the year I get at least a save the date in the mail, Simeon? At this rate, baby, I'd be okay with an elopement. I just really need something from you."*

Unfortunately for my mother, it was looking like a no across the board, if I was being honest.

My parents had been happily married for almost four decades and were perfect for each other. But to me, marriage wasn't going to happen.

I learned years ago marriage was not for me. And I don't think it ever will be. It thrilled me to know Hazel didn't prioritize talking about relationships, marriage, or any of those permanent things. That was another reason we'd been seeing each other, too.

My phone buzzed in my pinstriped trousers' pocket and I ignored it. I promised myself I wouldn't have my eyes on my phone tonight out of respect for Hazel.

I didn't do the dating thing often. Never, is a more appropriate way to say that. But I at least understood no phones at the dinner table would be best. Although I was sure Hazel wouldn't mind.

I got lucky with her.

She was a bit of a workaholic like myself, so her work hours inundated her time the way my work hours inundated mine.

I only had three clients on my roster at King Sports Management— KSM for short—but they were big clients. Managing their careers took up most of my time, leaving me with barely any time to vacation.

Finding a woman who was understanding of that and okay with the arrangement of maintaining something strictly physical was good.

Although, I wondered if insisting Hazel and I have dinner tonight gave her the wrong impression. I questioned if inviting her to dinner made her think I was looking for more.

*God, I hoped she didn't think that.*

My phone buzzed again, and that got my attention.

I smiled up at Hazel as I pulled my phone out of my pocket and pressed the side button to brighten the screen to steal a quick glance.

And I nearly swallowed my damn tongue when I read the bold headline.

"What the...?" I whispered.

I sat up straight in my seat, my thumbs flying over the device's screen to unlock my phone. It was an alert. Like all the other high-profile players I managed, I had my client Dallas's name set up for media monitoring. This included Google alerts and various search engine keyword tracking apps that worked around the clock, scouring every corner of the web—including social media sites—to find any mention of their names or brands. This was especially critical for Dallas, who was not only my first *and* biggest client at my company, KSM, but also my friend. Whether it was a simple sentence in a news article or a major feature, I needed to ensure every mention of Dallas left a positive mark.

Like I said, image was everything to me with my clients and their brands... both personally and professionally.

It seemed he was the topic of the hour. Of the night.

And not for reasons that were good like I preferred it to be.

**Breaking: Dallas Roque's Brother Rapper Da Dom Is Threatening to Release Nudes Of Dallas' Fiancée Ayanna Dale. Claims Ayanna Cheated with Dallas When She Was Still Dating Da Dom.**

My long legs were pushing my chair back before I could think to stop them.

"I... *um*... shit." I cleared my throat as I reached for the dinner napkin to clean my mouth. "Something has come up and I have to go."

I looked up long enough to see Hazel's phone in her hand.

"Does it have anything to do with these nudes I got an alert about a second ago?"

"*Fuuuck*," I drawled low, standing to my feet. "I mean… *stay* as long as you want and order whatever else you're interested in having."

"What I'm interested in having most is a comment from a source close to Dallas and Ayanna, and that's you." Hazel smirked. "But you knew that, huh?"

I released a nervous laugh while wagging my finger at her. "You."

She batted her eyelashes; her smile growing more maniacal. "Me."

"Hazel?"

"Simeon."

"Anything you want."

She parted her lips when I lifted a hand to stop her.

"You can have whatever you want *off* the menu." I lowered my chin to look at her under my lashes. "*Only* off the menu. On me. I'll call you."

"With a comment, I hope," she tried again.

"I'll call you."

I was walking away from the table before we could exchange another word.

———

I couldn't get to Dallas and Ayanna's house fast enough. I practically threw my tip at the valet driver when he brought my BMW around. I hightailed down the streets of downtown Oakland, doing more than the speed limit towards their home on the hills, feeling as Oakland's Mediterranean climate cooled the sweat beads forming on my brows.

I was freaking the hell out. But I couldn't show that. I never showed it.

"Hard times always lead to something great," I quoted as I turned onto the path that led to Dallas and Ayanna's driveway. "My strength is greater than my struggle."

I parked my car and sat in the driveway for a moment to collect myself.

For the past five years, Dallas has kept a spotless image. The most they knew about the man is he played for the Flames, was engaged, and had a sports nutrition line. He didn't partake in the celebrity lifestyle like other players on his team. Dallas barely left his house besides to go to practice or to travel for away games. Dallas lived quietly.

Something told me that was about to change.

All the lights were on in their property. Not unusual for the 9pm hour.

I considered calling Dallas before driving to his house. I always called. But tonight I had to make the exception.

"Hard times always lead to something great," I repeated as I pushed opened the door and stepped out.

I figured if they hadn't heard the news, it would be best they hear it from me first. If they had heard about it, there was no way I'd be able to handle anything on the phone.

"My strength is greater than my struggle," I recited for what felt like the hundredth time since climbing into my car to drive here.

Affirmations and motivational quotes. They were my bread and butter. My fuel. The two things that kept me focused and assisted with redirecting any sudden distractions that might spring up in me, pushing me to self-doubt.

Self-doubt had no place in what I did. How far I've come. I never gave it a key in my vehicle toward success. I never even allowed self-doubt to be a passenger out of fear it might eventually take the wheel.

It was certainty or nothing, and idleness wasn't an option with all this breath God put in my body.

I unbuttoned my blazer and dropped it on my car's passenger seat before shutting the car's door. Dropped my phone into my pinstriped pants back pocket. I tucked the hem of my plain black tee into my pants' waistband as I took quick steps toward Dallas and Ayanna's front door.

It was pitch-black outside. Lights from neighboring towns glistened in the distance. Dallas made an excellent choice purchasing his property away from the busy life of Oakland. It was like his secret hideout. *Now* he and his fiancée, Ayanna's secret hideout.

Paparazzi could never find it, and I was grateful for that at that moment.

I blew air out my mouth as I approached their giant wooden door to ring the doorbell.

The door opened less than a second later. Standing on the other side was their housekeeper, Maribel. Behind her, all I could hear were Dallas and Ayanna.

Yelling. Loudly.

Maribel shut her eyes while shaking her head.

I asked, "Are they yelling at each other?"

"At other people on the phone," she replied, fixing her bag's strap over her shoulder. "Do you want for me to let them know you're here before I go?"

"No," I answered, my attention looking past her in search of them. All I could hear was their voices elevated, but I couldn't make out any words. "Where are they? The great room?"

"Upstairs," she replied. "Master bedroom. I go now."

"Okay," I acknowledged with a head bob. "You get home safely."

Maribel had stepped out, and I stepped inside, closing the door behind her.

Dallas and Ayanna's voices echoed around their property, sometimes at the same time, other times out of sync.

"Christ," I uttered, blowing air out of my mouth.

I swaggered toward their staircase that led to their bedroom, the bottoms of my suede moccasins echoing around me. Normally I'd remove my shoes, even when Dallas insisted I not, but tonight I couldn't bother with that.

I could hear them clearer by the time I got to their bedroom door. And when I pushed it opened, I could hear everything.

"Nigga, you 'bout to see me, believe that," Dallas yelled into his phone. "You done fucked up for real."

"You ain't never been a friend, Terri," Ayanna screamed on the other end of the room. "I should've known you'd do some dog ass shit like this."

"Oh, don't fucking worry, Dom," Dallas swore on the opposite end.

My head was on a swivel, attention moving from one end of their room to the other. They stood apart, shouting their fury into their devices.

I stood there for a few breaths, purposely taking in the chaos. I needed to ground myself in it to think us out of it.

"You gon' know *exactly* when I land in your city, nigga," Dallas spat into the phone before moving it off his ear to hold the phone's mic directly in front of his mouth then yelled, "Because I'm coming straight to you, you slimy motherfucker!"

"You are *so* damn trifling, I swear," Ayanna cried. "I put you in my wedding. I even bought your damn bridesmaid's dress. And you do this? Now I see why you refuse to come out here to get your fitting. Why it's felt like pulling teeth to get you to do the bare minimum. You are so foul. I can't believe you would do this to me. Oh my God!"

*Someone could record these phone calls*, was the thought that had me walking right up to Ayanna and gently taking the phone out of her hand.

"Hey!" she shouted.

I clicked the red button on her phone's screen as I approached Dallas. He was mid-argument when I took his phone out of his hand and ended his call, too.

"The fuck?" Dallas whipped his head in my direction. "Simeon?"

I dropped their phones into my pockets and held my hands up in front of me. "I need you two to calm down."

"Calm down?" Dallas challenged, his chest heaving like an impatient bull. "Did you hear what the hell this nigga Dom did?"

"I did." I nodded twice. "That's why I'm here."

My eyes on their own roamed around their room to see some of Dallas's clothing sprawled around the room, with a designer duffel bag opened on their bed.

"What's happening with all this stuff on the floor?"

"I'm flying down to Miami," Dallas answered. "Tonight."

"To do what?"

"I'm about to kill that nigga, that's what."

"Oh-kay." I ran my hand down my trimmed beard and turned to Ayanna.

She was sitting on the ottoman opposite her bed with her head in her hands and her fingers in her long curls.

"Ayanna," I said to her.

She lifted her head, and I noticed she had tears in her redlined eyes.

My shoulders sagged. "Dammit."

"Exactly," Dallas affirmed with a head tilt toward Ayanna. "I'm definitely killing that nigga."

"No one's killing anyone." I ran my hand down my fade and backed away to gather my thoughts.

"Terri, one of my bridesmaids and good friends from college, was the source who confirmed Dominick's allegations that he and I were together," Ayanna informed lowly, shaking her head. "I can barely get her ass on the phone or get her to fly out here to get fitted for the bridesmaids dress she made me buy for her because she claimed to be so broke and busy to buy it herself, but she can get on the phone with a gossip magazine for a check to tell all my fucking business."

I shut my eyes and held them tightly closed. I quickly released the tension on my eyelids and inhaled an encouraging breath.

"Okay, what do we know other than that?" I asked. "I was at dinner when I got the media alert and came straight here."

"Dominick has an album he announced he plans to release this summer," Dallas stated, taking a seat beside Ayanna. He draped an arm over her shoulder and guided her close to him, kissing the top of her head when she rested her head against his chest. "He's threatening to use a nude photo he has of Ayanna as his cover art and says he has a song on there that will be like a tell-all and will detail their relationship including how she cheated with me when they were still together."

I cringed.

Ayanna pulled away and was standing at her feet when Dallas grabbed her by the hand.

"Yaya," Dallas tried. "Baby, please."

But Ayanna pulled away again.

"I just need a second," she said with a shaky voice as she made her way to their en suite, closing the door the moment she was on the other side.

Dallas dropped his head to his chest and grunted. He nodded, then stood up again. "I'm chartering a jet for Miami tonight, man."

"Dallas, no—"

"Nah." He took large steps toward his and Ayanna's walk-in. "There's only one way for me to talk to Dominick. I know that fool like the back of my hand. He's only gonna get worse with this shit. That's what he does."

"And then what?" I quizzed, following him into his walk-in. "You go down there, you match his energy, then what?"

Dallas shook his head as he pulled down a box of sneakers.

"Young Prince," I tried this time, waiting for him to look my way before I continued. "You're getting married next month. You're launching your supplements line at the start of next year. Please, just stop *feeling* and *think* right now. Really use your head and think about what you're saying you're about to do, Dallas."

Dallas stopped moving and turned to lean his back against the table that divided his part of the closet from Ayanna's. He leaned his head back between his shoulders and took a breath. That was a good sign to me.

"You going down there will only add to the bad press and you don't want bad press."

"So, what's the other option?" He asked, leveling his head and focusing on me. "What's the plan? Because if we don't have a plan, I'm flying down there to put hands on him, Simeon. And I'm not letting up until he shuts the fuck up."

I arched both brows.

"I'm just keepin' it one-hundred with you, man."

"I'll handle it."

I did not know how I was going to do that. My head of PR left for her maternity leave a few weeks prior, notifying me she would not be returning. And the associates I had on the team now were mostly interns that I would never trust to handle a crisis as big as this one.

But I had to tell Dallas something, *anything* to keep him *here*, grounded in Oakland and not somewhere, adding to a fire that was showing all the potential of raging out of control.

"I know someone," I promised. "She works for a company that handles situations like this. She's very good at her job."

And who I haven't spoken to in over a decade and who won't answer any of the phone calls I've placed to her in the last two years since getting her contact information from her brother.

But again, I had to tell Dallas something.

He threw his hands up. "Does *she* have a name?"

"I'll share it with you soon," I exhaled. "Just..." I sighed next. "Let me contact her and see what we can have done. Trust me on this. You trust me, right?"

Dallas nodded, no hesitation. "One hundred percent."

"Okay." I smiled. "We'll get this all sorted out. I promise."

At least I hoped we would.

# THREE

**ERYN**

*What the hell was that?*

I'd heard something.

Or I thought I heard something.

That was the only reason my tired eyes peeled open.

I forgot to draw the curtains closed the night before. The harsh light of day streaming through my windows caused some light sensitivity, making me squint my eyes, which made them water in reaction.

I hadn't closed the curtains since the morning I returned home after getting fired from Opal Sands.

Only the thought of being fired made me pull my white duvet that was around my shoulders, up and over my head.

It had been five days since that day.

Five days of doing nothing but sleeping, drinking coffee, and eating —because I had to eat, right? Then going back to sleep only to repeat it all the next day. I'd wake up to light pouring through my window, my eyes watering, all because I was too lazy to draw the curtains closed each night.

The very little energy I had, I used it to wash my ass every night. I figured it was the least I could do.

But as far as cooking, cleaning, or giving a damn, I had done none of that.

Only ordered food from my phone app, barely making it to the door in time to accept it from the delivery person. I'd been collecting my food off my doorstep for the last five days, eating whatever I ordered and not caring to discard what I didn't finish into the trash.

"Oh my God," I heard from downstairs. "What the hell is that smell?"

That made me kick the covers off my head.

The deep voice sounded familiar, but I couldn't be too sure.

And a part of me... didn't care?

That part of me was hopeful it was someone breaking into my place. Here to make me the subject in a crime scene documentary taking me out of my misery because Lord knows I would probably do it myself if I had the balls or cared to do even that.

Because in that moment and for the past few days before it, I didn't feel like doing anything besides inhaling and exhaling.

And even that, breathing, was work I didn't want to do.

"Eryn?" I heard clearer. And when I did, I recognized the deep voice instantly.

I sat up immediately. "Ev?!"

The sound of my big brother climbing the stairs to my bedroom got louder outside my room's door, along with the audibly disgusted sounds he made all the way to me.

He appeared at the doorway, his face a mix of disgust and concern.

I blinked hard. "What are you doing here?"

Instead of answering my question, his eyes surveyed my room.

His attention fell on empty Chinese food paper takeout boxes, brown paperboard takeout containers, compostable clear drinking cups, and carryout paper bags strewn here, there, and everywhere.

Everett lifted his big hand to pinch his wide nose together and groaned. "What the fuck is that smell, baby sis?"

I sucked my teeth and fell back against my pillow, tossing the duvet over my head again. "What are you doing here? And how did you get in?"

"You never changed the locks from when we lived together, which I told you to do after I moved out of here. I still had the key. A part of me knew you wouldn't change them with your lazy ass." Everett took a seat on my bed beside me, his brawny weight weighing down the mattress a little. "I've been trying to get in contact with you since Saturday. You weren't answering. I got worried. I chartered a flight out here to see what was up."

"I've clearly been busy." I wrapped myself tighter under my covers like a strip of steak in a burrito.

He sighed. "I heard what happened."

I lowered the covers low enough to give my eyes a view of him.

"Brielle posted a photo of herself on social media at Opal Sands." He shook his head. "And tagged me."

I lowered the covers more.

"I thought nothing of it at first and ignored her." He shrugged. "I don't know why I didn't put two and two together. But then she messaged me privately, asking me how you were taking unemployment."

I let out a loud sound of annoyance and rolled my eyes. "I'm gonna hurt that woman something serious, I swear." I pushed myself up and into a seated position. "I really wish I didn't listen to you. I should've kept that sex tape of hers with those two models instead of breaking the CD in half."

"Eryn—"

"I could've had something to bribe the bitch with." I grunted. "I could've still had a job."

"Gahdamn!" Everett slapped his hand to his nose. "Yo, did you brush your teeth?!"

I pressed my hand to my mouth and leaned my back against my tufted headboard. "Shut up."

"And it smells worse in here." He peeked down beside his feet. "You got food molding in their containers in here. Look at this."

"Everett, please," I whined. "I'm going through some shit right now. Leave me alone."

He stood to his feet. "Come on, get up."

"No." I pushed myself back onto my pillow and was about to toss the covers over my head. "I just want to sleep right now."

"Nah, man." Everett pulled the covers completely off me, revealing my oversized tee and panties.

"Hey!"

"Get up," he ordered.

"I don't want to," I argued. "I don't want to do shit right now, but sleep and forget all the shit that happened last week."

He sighed.

"I gave that company everything." I turned to face him. "My heart, my soul. Everything! I sacrificed a lot and... and... shit, I did some things, Everett."

He turned to look at me. "Things?"

"Things."

"What things?"

I lowered my chin to my chest and stared at him under my long lashes. "*Things*, bro. Things you really don't want me to tell you about."

He held his stare with me and I watched his eyes get bigger and his brows go from wrinkled to arched.

"*Shh*," he pressed the side of his finger to his mouth. "Shut up. Don't say another damn word because I *don't* want to know."

"No, you don't," I added. "My point is, I've gone above and beyond for Opal Sands. It wasn't just a job for me. It wasn't only my career, either. It was... it was my life. My future."

"And it was never supposed to be all that to you, in the first place, Eryn," he said. "I've always told you that you gave too much to that company and it wasn't even yours. There was no actual career security working there. But you've been running from shit you won't let me know about, escaping through work by working all the time trying to just... I don't even know." He shook his head. "But what I know is you need to get up out of this bed, get in your bathroom, and do what you have to do to get yourself together."

I shook my head.

"Yes," he said to me, this time pulling the duvet off the bed and throwing it to the floor.

"Everett!"

"Get up!" He yelled back. "You can either get up on your own or I'm gonna get you up and throw you in the shower. You know I will."

I folded my arms over my chest.

"Go," he told me, pointing at my bathroom. "Now."

I glared at him and he softened his expression to one that was empathetic, softer. "Please, baby sis. It's killing me right now to see you like this."

The tears were right there in my eyes, welling and clouding my vision. And with anyone else, I would have wiped them away. But this was my big brother, my ace boom coon.

So, I let it rip.

And he was there, to wrap his strong arms around me and to pull me close, allowing me to get out all I'd been holding inside for the past five days.

# FOUR

**SIMEON**

I shook my wrist to twist the link on my yellow-gold chronograph so I could glance at the face. For the third time. The chronograph dial was in a different position, like the other two times I had checked, showing and validating what I was feeling...

I'd been sitting and waiting for way too long.

I inhaled a deep breath and let it out through my nose, running the tip of my tongue over the smooth surface of my top teeth. The time on my watch had clearly shown I'd been sitting in the conference room for longer than I should have been, but still, I checked my phone for good measure. Only for my device to confirm what my watch had already done the job of doing.

"This is so fucking unacceptable," I mumbled to myself. I'd said the one thing out loud that I'd been thinking... from ten minutes ago.

*Strike one.*

"Hello, good morning," the airy voice said as the owner of said voice entered the room. Her long blonde hair trailed behind her as she breezed into the room. "I am so sorry for the wait."

"Fifteen minutes," I voiced. "I've been waiting in this seat for fifteen minutes. Is that a normal wait time for OBM?"

Oakland's Best Marketing was an agency in, well, Oakland. And according to them, they were the best. Easy name, straight to the point. That was why I called them and booked the soonest appointment I could get to consider my PR options. I couldn't tell if they were the best yet, though.

I'd been going back and forth with myself on what direction to take with this whole Ayanna and Dallas scandal that Dallas's brother dropped on us. And one of those directions led me to OBM.

Waiting for fifteen fucking minutes.

"Not a normal wait time, no," she replied. "It's just been an extremely busy day for us."

She plopped herself into a seat across from me, only thinking to lean across the table with her hand extended after she was comfortable. "I'm Amber Palmetto. Your point of contact here at OBM."

I accepted her hand. "Pleasure to meet you, Amber."

"I see here that you are in search of PR for your client, Dallas, and his fiancée, Arianna."

"Ayanna," I corrected. "Her name is Ayanna."

"Oh." She giggled. "I'm sorry. Ayanna."

*Strike two.*

Not only is she late, but she can't even remember Ayanna's name?

Is she kidding me right now?

I inhaled another deep breath and let it out the same way.

*Let it go, Simeon.*

Because I'm desperate.

I told Dallas I would handle the drama concerning his older brother and his supposed album cover art featuring Ayanna's nude photo, and all the other bullshit that has come along with that drama. Out of all the times to be short of an in-house public relations representative, now was the worst time. I wasn't concerned when my head of public relations called while on maternity leave to inform me she wouldn't be returning.

My clients were minimal, only three, and they all were unproblematic black men. I thought I was good. Never expected this. It was like being thrown outside with no clothes on. But still I had to do something.

So, to start, I put my PR interns on the job of managing both Ayanna and Dallas's socials. The interns were under strict instructions not to disclose what was happening on Dallas and Ayanna's social media pages. I didn't want the interns sharing what comments were streaming in under Dallas and Ayanna's old posts. I especially didn't want to know what accounts were tagging the future Roques. And I didn't want the future Roques to know about any of what was happening outside of their home.

Ignorance was bliss in this situation. And it was important to me they didn't know what was happening on the web.

Since then, things have been okay. I was running out of time, though. Because I promised Dallas I had someone. And I did.

Eryn Peters.

My ex-girlfriend.

Who I haven't spoken to in over fifteen years and who wouldn't answer my phone calls when I tried to reach out to her two years ago when her brother gave me her new contact information.

It shocked me to learn she was right here in California and that she'd been living here for a while. In another city, yes. She was close, though.

I looked Eryn up the moment I got that information from her brother Everett. Learned she was a public relations manager at one of the top marketing agencies in the country.

I had even more incentive to get in contact with her back then because I was building my team at my company, KSM, and was short a PR rep.

But Eryn never answered or returned any of my phone calls.

It just seemed like a straightforward decision to reach out to her. Even though the way we left things was terrible.

However, every time I called her, she would either let the call ring out or would send my call to voicemail.

So, I stopped calling her. And I have been battling the thought of calling her now. When I needed her help.

"So," Amber continued, flipping open the powder blue folder she entered the conference room carrying. "It appears you are in search of crisis management for your client. What seems to be the crisis?"

"First," I straightened my back in my seat. "Can you share with me your experience with handling media crises? What is your process?"

"Well, we have a range of strategies that we execute to manage and mitigate media crises. Obviously, an immediate response would be necessary."

"Yes." I nodded.

"First, we'd do a rapid assessment, gathering facts about the situation. A press conference addressing whatever the crisis is would be our first order of business. Then, tackling media interviews with reputable entities would be our next step."

"So far, sounds good," I added.

"Great." Amber flashed a big smile. "So, what seems to be the crisis that your client, Dallas, and his fiancée, Arianna, have found themselves in?"

My eyes collapsed closed for only a moment before I reopened them. *Strike three.*

Dammit.

"Ayanna," I corrected for the second time. "It's Ayanna."

"Oh, God." She giggled once more, and that was the final straw. "I am so sorry, Mr. King."

"Yeah, I know, you said that," I replied. "And when you said it the first time, your one and only apology was one too many for me."

"It's just that we have a full roster of clients." She flipped her blonde hair over her shoulder. "One of our clients' names is Arianna, and—"

"She appears to be heavy on your mind." I smiled politely. "As she should be."

"No." Her eyes widened. "No, that's not it."

"I have been sitting and waiting for fifteen minutes, Amber." I licked my lips to maintain my reserve. "And the only reason I didn't walk out of here after the first five minutes elapsed is because I hate to waste effort. So now, fifteen minutes later, when you finally join me, you consistently get my client's fiancée's name wrong." I shook my head. "That doesn't help with my first impression of you or OBM, and it certainly doesn't reflect well on the company."

She sighed and shook her head. "It's our new client tactic. The wait. Between you and me, I don't agree with it, but it works. Appear a little too busy and juggling multiple clients, so new clients see our value and feel more obligated to work with us. It's—"

"A foolish strategy I'm not impressed with," I cut in. "In fact, it's counter effective for someone like myself who doesn't suffer from the fear of missing out. Because for me? It's the small things like remembering my client's fiancée's name that show a company's competence in delivering on their promises. Things like getting a name incorrect, give me all the insight I need regarding OBM's practices. The quality of your service, not the quantity of your clientele, measures your value. More to the point, if this is my first interaction with a strategy that is OBM approved, I don't have the confidence in the strategies you are going to suggest to me to help me with my problem."

"I—"

"Respectfully." I leaned forward in my seat to place my hand on the table. "I appreciate you taking this meeting at such short notice. As you mentioned, an immediate response is necessary, which is why I was adamant about booking a consult with you today. My advice? Focus the attention you planned to focus on my client on your client, *Arianna*, since she seems to have *all* your attention already."

"Mr. King, please—"

"As for me..." I pushed my seat back. "I must go. I've already wasted..." I glanced down at my watch. "Now... twenty minutes of time, I cannot get back. I made a promise to my client that I would have his situation handled and I keep my promises. My word is my life. And I can't in good faith present you to him when you were, *one*, late taking this meeting, *two*, executing a terrible strategy of making a future client wait, and *three* getting my client's fiancée's name wrong more than once which is more than enough for me."

She closed her eyes slowly and slumped her shoulders in her chair.

"Thanks again for your time and meeting with me," I said, sliding my designer shades over my eyes. "But I need to find a firm that doesn't play mind games and can at least get my client's future wife's name right —especially after being corrected. You have a great day."

With that, I exited the office, portraying the appearance of a man who was calm, cool, and had an abundance of options, but inside I was panicking in the worst way. Because it had been three days since the gossip website dropped the bomb about Dallas's brother and Ayanna's past relationship along with allegations of nudes he allegedly had in his possession, and I had no one to help extinguish the fire the bomb had created.

Only a few websites had reported on Dominick's news, but I knew it was only a matter of time before it all went viral. It would only take one reputable website to blow everything out of proportion.

"I trust myself. I have faith in myself. I believe in myself," I recited, pressing the elevator's call button. "Every challenge is a golden chance to grow. I got this."

Did I, though?

# FIVE

**ERYN**

I sat with my legs folded in the single armchair by my fireplace. The last of the cleaners my brother Everett hired to deep clean my condo were rolling out their equipment and tools through my front door.

"Thanks, guys," Everett told them as he closed the door behind the last person to leave.

My condo was looking like itself again. Too bad I wasn't.

At his insistence, more like the annoyance, I caved into my brother pushing me for another morning to get out of bed and go through my a.m. routine. He told me he'd hired cleaners to damn near fumigate my condo, so I'd have to look presentable when they arrived.

"I almost forgot how cute my place is," I joked, leaning back in my seat as he took a seat in the opposite armchair facing me.

"I'm just happy it smells like a home and not a back alley in Manhattan at the height of summer," he replied.

"Ha, ha," I mocked.

He smiled that handsome smile of his. "How you feeling today?"

I shrugged, not all that sure myself. "Like another day of nothing to do but sleep. Which I plan to do in the next few minutes."

"Or," Everett leaned forward in his seat, "you could switch up your days and fly back to New York with me."

"Ha!" I forced a laugh. "You're funny."

"I'm not joking."

"You *must* be because I know you *know* better."

"I actually don't." Everett's eyes scanned mine from his seat. "Because you won't tell me what your beef is with your hometown."

I kissed my teeth. "I am in no mood to get into this shit with you again today."

Everett inhaled a deep breath and let it out roughly. "You can't stay here, Eryn."

I held his stare with me.

"You literally cannot stay in this place, in this city, another day."

I swallowed hard next.

"When I got here," he started, "this place was a fucking mess. Ain't no other way to describe it. Shit was everywhere. It smelled like something died, and you looked like the dead yourself."

"Why, thank you."

"I'm serious, baby sis."

I closed my eyes and held my lids tight.

"It was looking a lot like how my place was looking after..." He sighed. "After all the shit that went down with Brielle."

"And coincidentally enough," I chimed in, "she's the same woman making my life a living hell. Would you look at that?"

"That's why I'm telling you to come back to New York with me."

I rolled my eyes away and shook my head.

New York wasn't home to me anymore. I disowned her ass the moment I decided I would move to California and live a different life. A life I felt in control of and that I could make significant enough to forget my old one. It was my luck my brother agreed to move with me. He too was looking for a change, but I think he came out here mostly because he didn't want me to be out here all alone.

Everett and New York were soulmates. He loved it so much he had our neighborhood of Bed-Stuy tatted on his forearm. He never made a home here in Cali. I was kind of happy he'd fallen in love with Brielle's ass because I knew that would make him forget New York. Finally. But the moment Brielle showed her true colors, Everett ran back to his first love. New York City. And life for him has been insurmountably better. He found someone new and was now engaged. And she was amazing. His perfect half. He had a business, a boxing gym in New York now. He was doing much better than he was doing in California.

I was not confident I could have the same outcome in dirty ass, grimy ass New York City.

"No." I shook my head a second time. "I can't. When I left that city, I *left* that *city*. And I promised myself I would never go back there."

"Why not?"

I closed my eyes and dropped my head.

"You never answer the question when I ask you it." He grunted. "You can be so damn secretive and closed off, but you're especially closed off whenever the subject is New York."

"I had dreams that just didn't come true there, Ev. No matter how much I worked to make them come true, my hard work always went in vain and my sugar always turned to shit. So..." I ran my hands through my hair. "Just please, I don't want to get into it."

"One week then," he reasoned with me. "I am begging you to fly out there and spend one week there. And if after one week you really don't want to stay, then come back."

"I *know* I won't want to stay there."

"Cool," he replied. "But you're not staying here after tonight. Because just like I told your ass when you wouldn't wash your ass, I would throw you in the shower? I will have no issue doing the same with getting you out of here for one week."

I scoffed a laugh.

"One week, sis." He held up a finger. "Give it one week. After that week, you can come back to L.A., and you won't hear anything from me about it again."

I twisted my lips to one side, thinking.

"What was it you said to me?" He asked. "You are not in the right city to be losing your shit like this? Remember that?"

"Yeah, but you were getting locked up over bride-to-be pussy. Remember that?"

"And you're locking yourself up in your bed over a job at a place that never deserved you."

He was right.

Everett shrugged. "I've been telling you, you need to take a vacation for years, anyway."

I scoffed. "If I needed a vacation, I most certainly wouldn't take one in New York, of all places."

"Let's start there." He winked. "Then you can fly out to wherever you want to. After one week. Deal?"

As much as I didn't love New York City, Los Angeles wasn't feeling like a place I wanted to be right now, either.

Maybe Mars or Venus were better options. Because earth was feeling like hell, having no place to escape to, to feel whole again.

But New York had my big brother, and having his company again for the past day and a half was nice.

So, I figured, if anything, I could cope with New York's bitch ass if he was there.

"One week," I agreed. "After that, I'm out."

———

What Everett didn't tell me was that I wouldn't be able to stay with him and his fiancée, Apryl, for that week. So, I had to call my mother.

"Eryn," she said as soon as she answered my call on the first ring. No hello. Not even pretending to see who was calling her. Just my name. And she said it so... lovingly. Which annoyed me, as always.

I hadn't spoken to her since Mother's Day earlier that month. I only called on her birthday and Mother's Day, and she never chastised me for it. She just always welcomed me with open arms whenever I called. And that just... *ugh*! My mother was so damn understanding and sweet. She was everything I wasn't.

"Hey, Ma, what's up?"

My mother and I had an interesting relationship. She was the sweetest woman you'd ever meet, and everyone loved her. She was perfect. Gave the greatest first impressions. Hence my problem with her.

"Everything right now," she giggled. "It's so good to hear your voice, my love. I feel lucky getting to talk to you twice this month. How are you?"

I bit back my smile, not wanting to give in.

My mother, Dr. Elizabeth "Liz" Peters, was everyone's savior. She was the woman everyone came to for answers. Their problems seemed to dissolve in her presence. To see her work was like watching magic happen. She made it look so easy. It's frustrating. To me, it's frustrating.

Here I was, her one and only daughter, sharing her physical features, including her smile and eyes, but the world felt like the most confusing place to me. She always seemed to have everything figured out, snapping her fingers, and everything fell into place like a perfect puzzle. I could struggle with something for ages, and she'd take one look, hear one thing, and it was like she pressed a button and it all went away.

It felt invalidating. Like my problems weren't as big as I made them out to be. Like my emotions were just figments of my imagination because there was always an easy fix. Her solutions made it feel like I didn't have to go through what I went through, which felt real when I was going through it. It invalidated me to my core. And that feeling made me invalidate my own feelings.

Do you see how conflicting and confusing that could be? Or am I bugging?

"I'll be in New York soon," I revealed. "Two days soon."

She gasped. "Oh my God, that's the best news I've heard all day."

I pressed my lips together.

"Your room is exactly the way you left it, so I hope you'll be staying here with me."

"Yup," I said, leaning back against my tufted headboard. "That's why I'm calling."

"Perfect!" she exclaimed, joy clear in her voice. "I'll make your favorite when you arrive. It's still shrimp fettuccine Alfredo, right?"

My stomach growled at the mention of it.

See, there wasn't anything my mother wasn't good at. She was a people person, an excellent cook, and the sweetest person you'd ever meet. She was everything I would never measure up to, and that frustrated me the most. Because I knew it must've taken a lot of work to be a woman like my mother. It took a lot of work to be the woman I was, and I was only half of what she was.

"Eryn, are you there?"

"Yeah, Ma, I'm here," I replied. "And yes, shrimp fettuccine Alfredo is still my favorite. At least *your* fettuccine is my favorite."

"Then I'll have it hot and ready when you arrive on Friday, okay, love?"

"Okay, Ma." I smiled, unable to hold it back. "I'll see you then."

# Six

**SIMEON**

"Oh, my God." I sighed. "What is this guy's problem?"

I stared at my computer screen through the gaps between my long fingers as I held my hands over each eye.

It was an early Thursday morning. I'd just sat at my desk, prepared to check emails, when one intern sent me the link to a podcast that Dominick was recently a guest on. A no-name podcast that was gaining recognition online because of his interview.

The podcast hosts were unknown. They were popular amongst a certain demographic. Single black jaded men. And while the podcast or their hosts weren't on a New York Times or Holidae Press media level, the public knew them well enough to cause some concern for me.

Dominick was on record, confirming that his new album cover art would indeed be one of Ayanna's nude photos he had in his possession. He also announced the album's release date.

June 23rd.

One day before Dallas and Ayanna's wedding. Which was in exactly one month.

*"I'm dropping my LP in one month on June 23rd,"* Dominick *announced with a smile in the video. "I got a song on there that's telling the truth. Everyone needs to hear about America's new favorite couple."*

*One podcaster laughed. "So, you're saying they frontin' for the people?"*

*"Major frontin' my dude." Dominick laughed. "They got y'all fooled. That ain't no black love what Dallas and Ayanna got. That's foul love. Ayanna was mine first. And she was in love with me."*

*"Word?" The other podcaster egged on.*

*"Word." Dominick chuckled. "She used to tell me that shit every chance she got."*

*"Females always claim to be in love, huh?" the other podcaster chimed in. "They be lying. Why females be lying all the time?"*

*"'Cause they're females," the second podcaster added. "The answer is right there in your question."*

*The first podcaster and Dominick both laughed hysterically.*

*"You're right," Dominick concurred. "You can't trust them."*

*"So why now?" the first podcaster inquired. "Why release this album and why use Ayanna's photo?"*

*"Because they're acting like I didn't play a part in their shit,"* Dominick *spat. "They're acting like their thing was destined and not that I was the reason. Them cheating behind my back, and now together living happily ever after? That shit's because of me. And I don't appreciate not being appreciated. Where's my recognition for bringing them together? Where's my mention?"*

I stopped the video, unable to take any more of it.

I rolled my leather office chair away from my wooden L-shape desk and dropped my head back between my shoulders, exhaling all the air out of my lungs.

Dominick had yet to prove he had the photos per se, but an article that the intern also sent me along with the podcast video, showed a blurred, pixelated version of the cover in the article and it appeared to be a woman photo'd from behind, with part of her backside in full view and a man's hand holding a bulk of her thick curly hair in his grip.

I tried my hardest not to let the situation get to my head, but it was truly a battle staying optimistic after seeing the article and listening to the podcast. Dominick was going for the jugular, and I couldn't understand why.

I was aware of Ayanna and Dominick's previous relationship. It was something Dallas disclosed to me the day I picked him up to fly out to Vegas with him to play in his first Summer League a few years ago. Dominick and Ayanna's past relationship was the one thing Dallas felt was keeping him and Ayanna from being together. Their story was unique, but the two of them were perfect for each other. To me, everything before them simply didn't matter. But image-wise, this was not looking good. For any of us.

I honestly never considered the possibility of Dallas's brother doing this. The first red flag should've been when Dominick revealed to the media that he was Dallas's brother in a past interview. This was when Dallas was gaining notoriety for playing for the Oakland Flames after the Flames' star player, Pryce Williams, left the team for the Bronx Ballers. But back when Dominick drew the link to his brother for the world to know, I didn't have any concerns. I didn't know the man could go this low.

I should've acted then.

I ran my hand down my trimmed beard and grunted.

The situation, this scandal, had all the makings of being impossible to overcome, but this wouldn't be the first hurdle I've had to work hard to defeat. When I wanted to go to an accredited university after being homeschooled my entire young life, I wrote dozens of writing samples to show my academic capabilities and to showcase my academic achievements. I got over fifty letters of recommendation from local farmers and city officials, took college courses at a local college in my Western New York town. And at the end of all that work, not only did I get into Langston U, I did so on a partial scholarship that was specifically for homeschooled students. Before starting college, I wanted to play basketball, or I *thought* I wanted to play basketball. So I stayed in shape, which wasn't hard to do, working on my parents' farm. But my workouts became rigorous to build strength, agility, and endurance, a habit I've maintained to this day. I also made sure I joined a local basketball league a few miles from my hometown, making it one of my extracurricular activities. I took part in showcases and tournaments around New York City – with a lot of resistance from my parents. I took part because I knew Langston University's coaches would be present and they would see me play and I could introduce myself. And that introduction was how the coach remembered me when I attended walk-on tryouts my first semester at LU and how I got selected to play point guard as a Blackbird. Eventually, my third semester, I decided playing ball wasn't my thing. My point is, I was used to pulling off the impossible.

In fact, I always strived to. It gave me a rush.

Dealing with this scandal and overcoming it should be nothing to me.

Then why was it feeling like it was becoming too much to handle?

My device buzzed with a call on my desk, pulling me out of the moment and immediately into a state of concern.

"Dallas," I said the moment I answered.

"Simeon, man." He grunted.

That alone let me know he'd gotten the news.

"I'm getting really tired over here sitting on my hands," he added. "Not with Dominick doing all this talking."

"I know. I've listened to Dominick's podcast interview."

"You told me you had it handled, Simeon."

"It's being handled."

"It's not being handled fast enough, though," he countered. "Because now this nigga is talking about releasing an album the day before my wedding?"

I squeezed my eyelids shut. "I am aware." I sighed next. "I don't know what his deal is—"

"He's pissed because he didn't get a wedding invite from me."

"What?"

"He feels slighted for not being invited to our wedding, which is wild because why the hell would I invite him to our wedding?"

"Some would say because he's your brother?"

"Man, fuck that," Dallas yelled. "He's my blood, but his intentions are that of an enemy. Dominick's always been jealous of me, even when I tried to show him we're equals. I'm done dealing with his petty shit.

Instead of working on himself, I have to tolerate his envy? Hell no, I wasn't inviting him to my wedding. For what? So, he could ruin it? I wouldn't have any peace if he were there, even if he behaved, which he obviously wouldn't. Look at what he's doing now!"

"I hear you."

Dallas exhaled into the phone. "I told you he was petty."

"Dallas I know, but—"

"And the only way I know how to deal with him is like I told you. With my hands, man."

"I don't want you to do that, Dallas."

He grunted. "But I may *need* to, Simeon."

"You have way too much to lose now. Way more than Dominick does, and that's why he's doing what he's doing. He wants attention."

"And he's about to get all of it from me," Dallas replied into the phone. "With these hands."

"Dallas—"

"Monday," he interjected.

"What?"

"You have until Monday to let me know what we're going to do," he explained. "That's four days. In four days, you'd have to have something for me, right?"

I scratched the back of my head. "Dallas."

"Simeon," Dallas said again. "Speaking as my friend right now, not my agent, let me ask you something."

I nodded. "Ask me anything."

"Is four days a reasonable amount of time for my agent to deliver me a solution he promised he'd have for me almost a week ago? A solution to a problem that has the potential to ruin my marriage before I can enjoy it?"

I closed my eyes and held my lids tightly closed over them.

"As a friend," I began, "I would say that's more than enough time for your agent to deliver on his promise. In fact, I would advise you to ensure he does it in a major way and if he can't, then he shouldn't be your agent. Because you're a superstar young Prince, only worthy of the best anyone offers. Nothing less. And don't you ever accept less than what you deserve."

"And *that's* why you're my agent, homey," Dallas replied. "And the best in the business, hands down." The sound of his voice was a sign he was smiling on the other end of my phone when he said that. "So, Monday. That's your deadline to deliver me a solution to all this. Aight?"

"Monday it is." I pinched the space between my eyes and quickly dipped my head, as if he could see me. "And no later."

# SEVEN

**ERYN**

I stood at the bottom of the stairs that led up to the front door of the brownstone I grew up in.

The neighborhood looked so different.

When my black car driver - that Everett and I shared from the private airport we flew into - pulled onto the block, I thought the driver brought me to the wrong place.

As agreed, I flew in with Everett on a chartered flight from Los Angeles, California to Bergen County, New Jersey's Teterboro Airport. The flight was a breeze. Honestly, it was the best part of my day.

Everett and I shared the black car, the first stop being his and Apryl's duplex in Manhattan. My ride to Brooklyn was an interesting one. All the dread I believed I'd feel, the discomfort I thought would be so overwhelming it would be unbearable after simply returning to New York, was not as bad as I assumed it would be.

But that was the thing about New York. She was a deceitful bitch. Stunning, fun, and a good time. But I knew all her secrets that people wouldn't believe she had.

New York was a lot like... me.

Everything everyone loved about her were the things I hated. The unforgiving summers and brutal winters. Hazy, humid air of the weeks leading from July to August. Disrespectful ass cold that brought with it unpredictable snowfalls that blanketed a city that never slept in white. New York had her ways, but even on her worst day, she was still the hottest bitch on the international stage.

I hated her performative ass deeply. Because she was one of the unofficial characters in one of the worst days of my life.

I took my time stepping up the steep stairs, making my way up to the front door. Considered knocking on its larger-than-life surface, but something told me to turn the knob instead.

And when I did, the door gave way to me. Immediately filling my sense of smell with the aroma of fresh evergreen and patchouli. I glanced knowingly at the bowl by the entrance, where, as always, a collection of dried flowers and leaves was piled atop one another.

"I can't believe she still uses this scent," I said to myself.

I was kind of happy about that. Because the first whiff of my childhood home brought with it a bunch of beautiful memories. Of me, running down the runner that extended from the entryway and down the hall where the living room appeared on the other side of the wall. The runner looked different, though. Less tattered, more of something from a high-end furniture store and less like my mother had picked it out at a furniture store in the nearby Fulton Street Mall, like the original one that was here when I was a kid.

I left my luggage at the front door and walked the path of the runner, soon entering the living room that offered the most perfect view of my Brooklyn block through beautiful bay windows.

I'd have friends call me to those bay windows to see if I could come outside and play with them. I snickered at the memory.

My childhood home looked as different as the block it resided, but still the same. The furniture was different; the mantel refinished and looking brand new. But the photos of Everett, me, my mother, and my father still crowded that mantel, positioned in the same way as I remembered.

My eyes fell on the coffee table that was carved out of African imported wood.

This was what home felt like. Effortless. Beholding so many memories between its walls like the lingering scent of a perfume you couldn't get enough of smelling.

New York was a jungle, but in this home, it was paradise.

"I'm glad you knew to just turn the knob and to walk right on in," I heard behind me.

I turned to find my mother standing behind me. Gorgeous as ever. Hair grayer, skin more radiant than when I left almost a decade ago.

She extended her arms and held them wide open, and I didn't hesitate to walk between them.

Her hug. Always the best.

Like I said, there wasn't a single thing my mother wasn't the best at.

I inhaled a deep breath and let it go at that thought.

When I drew in the air, the smell of melted Parmesan cheese, garlic, butter, and heavy cream filled my nose and went straight to my stomach, stirring up my appetite.

My mother stepped out of her hug and held me out at a distance.

"You look fantastic." Her dainty hands were in my long hair that I wore out. "And your hair. It's *so* long and straight."

"My good ol' blow-dryer and flatiron combo. The same since high school." I smiled. "One thing I've been doing right, I guess."

"You've been doing it all right."

I rolled my eyes while shaking my head and looking away.

"Well, dinner is ready," she informed. "Whenever you're ready for it."

"Thanks, Ma." I gestured behind me. "I left my carryon bag and rolling suitcase by the door so I'm gonna walk them up to my room, wash up, and will be back down to have some."

"I'll be waiting," she assured. "Take your time."

I nodded before walking off.

"Eryn," she said when I took steps out of the living room and stopped to look at her. "It's very good to have you home. It's been too long, my love."

I forced a smile and continued out of the living room.

Because honestly, it hadn't been long enough.

Being back home was a mixed bag of emotions.

In one way, I never wanted to return. I wanted to build a new life, clear across the country. I wanted to show I could create a life on my terms and by my rules. I wanted a life from my imagination, and I thought I was close to completing the picture but, clearly I was wrong and that fact was a little depressing.

The stairs creaked with each step, the familiar groan of wood that had seen better days. I could see the sliver of light under Everett's bedroom door, just like when we were kids. I used to peer through that gap to see if he was home. If he wasn't, I'd sneak into his room to steal his t-shirts or basketball shorts—he always had the coolest brands.

In front of my door, I didn't hesitate to push it open, immediately smiling at all that I saw. Pink was and always would be my favorite color, and my room reflected that. There wasn't a single thing in there that wasn't pink besides the windows. Pink bedding, pink metallic headboard, pink work desk with the matching furry pink office chair.

Baby, no one liked pink more than Eryn Peters loved pink growing up.

I giggled as I stepped into my room, closing my door once inside.

Photos of me and my friends from high school laid wedged between the wooden edge of my mirror and the mirror's glass itself. Stuffed vintage teddy bears I found at antique shops and garage sales still crowded my bed from one end of the queen-sized mattress to the other. The handmade furry light fixture I created sitting on the bed it hovered over was still there, making the room look like a scene out of Clueless, a movie that heavily influenced me growing up.

Everything seemed to still be the same.

Still.

All except me, I guess.

I stepped out of my taupe block heels and pulled off the baggy tee I wore tucked into my high-waist jeans. As I stepped out of my jeans last,

I approached my bed, pushing some bears to the side once I was in front of them so I could make room for me to climb in.

The mattress was still soft, cozy.

I know I told my mother I would be back down to eat, but sleep seemed way more appetizing to me in that instance.

And so I closed my eyes and did exactly that.

———

I wish I could say that catching a quick nap in my old teenage bed was just a one-time thing on that first afternoon. But here I was, day two in Brooklyn, and I'd barely left my room. Three times, tops—and two of those were just to grab coffee when I finally dragged myself out of bed.

And that's what I was doing at the moment.

Peeled my eyes open, sat up from my pillow, stretched my arms, and stepped off the bed, not once glancing at my en suite as I left the room to head down to the kitchen.

My mother had checked in on me at the same hour every day since I returned home. Always a few minutes after 5pm.

*"Eryn," she spoke on the other side of my bedroom door, hours after I'd arrived home. "Are you okay in there?"*

*I didn't make it back down to eat what she made. I fell asleep. And when I got up as the sky was transitioning from light blue to dark denim, I figured the day was pretty much over. So, I might as well go back to sleep.*

*"I'm fine," I answered, wrapping my covers snugger around me. "Just a little jet-lagged."*

*That part was partially true. I knew my mother wouldn't question that.*

*"Okay," she told me. "I brought you some water. I'll leave it here on your dresser. I also put your food away downstairs. Whenever you're ready, you can just pop it into the microwave to heat it up."*

By the next day, evening time, when I hadn't emerged from my room after waking and grabbing coffee in the a.m., she knocked on my door hours later with the same inquiry and I gave the same excuse.

It was now two days later, and I'd gotten up with my mind focused on one thing. Coffee.

I hadn't eaten since the day before. In the middle of the night, when I knew my mother would be asleep, I snuck down to the kitchen and warmed up the shrimp fettuccine Alfredo. It wasn't as creamy as I'm sure it was when she first made it, but even as the pasta and shrimp swam in a buttery pool of melted everything, the shrimp fettuccine was hitting every spot it could hit.

My mother was still amazing with a stove and spices.

The day prior when I left my bedroom, it was still bright and early. But today, when I got up, the sun was noticeably higher, which meant it was more so noon than the morning time.

I made my way down to the kitchen, stepping carefully to avoid the squeaky spots on the stairs.

Was I avoiding my mother? Hell yeah, I was.

I didn't want to face any of her questions that were always leading and always her way of non-intrusively intervening.

When I arrived in the kitchen, I went straight to the coffeemaker, opening the nearby cabinet to pull down a box of single-serve coffee containers.

It was empty.

No tiny coffee containers.

"Oh, come on."

My mother wasn't a coffee drinker. More of a tea lover. Though she kept coffee in the house and enjoyed having a cup every now and again - at least she did when I was younger - coffee wasn't really her thing.

And it showed, because the box of coffee containers was empty.

Remembering she had a coffeemaker down in the basement, where she received her clients for her practice, I opted to make my way down there.

I wasn't at all dressed to enter my mother's practice. But my need for coffee trumped any reservations I may have had as I stepped down the stairs and reached the bottom of those stairs arriving inside of her office.

My friends used to always think it was so cool that my mother worked from home. Her doctor's office looked nothing like a doctor's office. It was welcoming, a good vibe, it was beautiful. And it had gotten even more beautiful since I last saw it, clearly undergoing some changes only an interior designer could be responsible for.

No one was down there when I arrived. No one was visible.

My mother often had receptionists, but that was during the university school year and often the receptionists were interns looking to earn college credits working with a licensed psychologist who practiced psychotherapy.

I scanned the area in search of a coffeemaker, and my eyes landed on the coffeemaker that was identical to the one in our kitchen upstairs. I recognized the carousel of tiny coffee containers situated right beside it and went straight to it.

I considered only grabbing a single serve container and brewing my coffee upstairs but... I was already downstairs and thought nothing of just doing everything down there.

All was good as I plucked one of the tiny single-serve coffee containers from the tower and placed it inside of the coffeemaker. I pushed the brew button on the machine, checking over my shoulder, waiting for everything to finish.

It was quiet, with only the sound of the coffee brewing. Quiet until my mother's office door opened.

"I am *so* proud of you, Lauryn," I heard her say as she stepped out of her office. "Inspiring and helping your dad write his memoir is a *huge* step, not just for him, but for *you* as well. It's a way of healing, of understanding, and of letting go of the things that have weighed on your heart—"

I turned in time to see my mother's eyes ballooning as she stared at me before she fixed her expression.

My mother stood beside a fair-skinned black woman. Her hair was long like mine but jet black. She wore a smile as her eyes bounced between my mother and me.

"Eryn," my mother started, her eyes briefly giving me a once over, roaming from the top of my headscarf to the baggy tee I wore that covered the tiny shorts I sported underneath, and finally landing on my bare feet. "I wasn't expecting you down here."

"Eryn?" the woman asked beside her, turning to glance at my mother before focusing on me again. "*Your* daughter, Eryn?"

My mother smiled warmly at me while nodding. "Yes, my daughter Eryn."

"Oh, my God!" the woman exclaimed, pressing a hand to her chest and closing the space between us. "It's so nice to meet you. She's always talking about you."

"Well." I extended a hand to her, and she accepted. "It's nice to meet you too...?"

"Lauryn," she answered. "Lauryn James."

"Lauryn James." I smiled, shaking her hand and releasing it. "If what she spoke to you about me was good, then it's true. If it's bad? Then, girl, it's all lies. All of it."

Lauryn giggled and my mother snorted a laugh.

I lifted my mug to my lips to sip my coffee, my eyes falling to the floor and on Lauryn's sneakers. "Dope sneakers."

Lauryn peeked down at the pair of red and pink Nikes and smiled up at me. "Thank you."

"Lauryn," my mother said behind us. "I'll walk you out."

"Later," Lauryn said to me.

"Bye."

My back was to the door my mother escorted Lauryn out of. I was adding creamer to my coffee when my mother said, "I'm glad you left your room today."

I rolled my eyes to myself.

And so it begins.

My mother had a way of communicating with me and my brother.

She wasn't like most mothers. She was a psychotherapist. Which meant she knew exactly how to get into people's heads without them even realizing it. At least, that's what *she* did. And she did it so effortlessly. It was almost creepy how easily she could get someone to tell her anything.

"Only to get coffee," I said, adding a little sugar to the cup. "I'm about to head back upstairs."

"I was thinking." She walked up beside me. "Maybe... we could go shopping."

That made me rear my head back.

My mother was not a girly girl. At all. Not even a little. She barely wore makeup or carried a purse. I can't even remember if my mother ever wore heels on her feet. She shopped out of necessity, not for pleasure, and she knew it.

This was her way of trying to set up a therapy-like outing with me. She did it with Everett, taking him for hot cocoa, which he shared with me after the fact. And I knew she would try to do something like that with me.

Like always.

She always did that.

She knew I loved to shop and knew the only way to get me to talk was to have me out and about so she could casually question me and understand why I was feeling how I was visibly feeling, all so she could wave her magic wand and fix it.

Not today.

*Eryn, you're being so childish.*

And?

"You hate shopping, Ma."

"But you love it," she insisted. "And I would *love* to do whatever you want to do so we can spend a little time with each other out of the house."

I sighed, setting my mug down at the coffee bar.

"I haven't seen you in years and want to get to know my new Eryn."

"I'm the same ol' Eryn, Ma."

"The Eryn I know would never leave her room looking anything less like she belongs on the cover of a magazine."

"Why don't you come on out and say you don't want me in your office dressed like a bum?"

"Because I have no want or need to say that to you," she answered. "Besides, you're not dressed like a bum."

I shook my head. "I just came down here for coffee. There wasn't any in the kitchen upstairs, so I came down here to get it."

"That's fine," she said with a smile. "It's not a problem. You're always welcome."

"Cool." I nodded. "I'm gonna go back up to my room."

"Aren't you tired of sleeping, though?" She asked softly. "You've been sleeping since you got here."

"I got fired from my job," I blurted, throwing my hand up in the air.

"They fired me off some bullsh—" I cleared my throat. "Off some fool-ishness, and I've just been taking it a little hard. I'm fine."

"*Fine* is not sleeping all day, Eryn," she countered. "*Fine* is not you not leaving your bedroom without so much as washing your face first, my love."

"You know what?" I held my hand up in surrender. "Fuck the coffee."

She jerked her head back. "Eryn—"

"Clearly," I cut in, "me sleeping all day, as you put it, is causing some concern for you, so I'm going to see if I can sleep all day without judgment at Everett's."

"Eryn, no, I'm not judging you, love—"

"It's fine," I said, walking away. "At least, as I pack my stuff, I won't be upstairs sleeping all day, right?"

"Eryn, *please*—"

"Ma, I told you I'm fine."

"I was just trying to explain to you—"

"I'm fine, Ma!" I repeated, louder than the first time, as I climbed the stairs in twos in my effort to get away from her.

————

"What the hell are you doing here?" Everett asked the moment he saw me standing at his duplex's threshold.

"Your mother is mothering again," I told him as I adjusted the strap of my overnight bag over my shoulder. "I need to stay here."

"To hell you do," he said low.

"Eryn?!" Apryl shouted a few feet behind him. "Ah!"

He closed his eyes and held his lids tightly shut.

"Oh, my God!" Apryl wore the biggest smile on her face. "What are you doing here?" She gestured with her hands next. "Get on in here, come in."

"She can't," Everett insisted, stepping into my path and blocking the entrance to their duplex. "She was just on her way out."

I hissed in irritation and pushed past him. "You better move out of my way."

"*Ugh.*" He growled. "Come on!"

Apryl walked up to me and wrapped her arms around me. I reciprocated, giving her an even bigger hug.

Apryl was the first and only girlfriend of Everett's that I've ever liked. She differed from the others. Majorly. She had a brain that worked. Apryl was smart, funny, and an all-around girls', girl. She didn't see me as a problem or a threat. She was just so cool. Laidback, fun. She was great. Which was why she was Everett's fiancée now. And I so approved of his choice in a wife.

"Now *this* is the way I was expecting to be received at the door." I flipped my hair over my shoulder, peeking over my shoulder at Everett.

"How are you?" Apryl asked, as she looped her arm with mine and guided me toward their sitting area. "How are you feeling?"

"Better, now that I'm out of that damn brownstone."

Everett and Apryl's duplex was stunning. I'd only seen it via video calls. When Everett and I flew in from California, I didn't have time to come up.

In person, it was clear the video call could never have captured the beauty of their humble abode.

The penthouse/duplex had three bedrooms, a patio, and an incredibly high ceiling. The oversized windows offered the most perfect view of New York City's landmarks, like the Empire State Building and the Midtown skyline. It was black luxury at its finest. Sexy as hell. And already I was feeling relaxed and in my element again.

"You want to hang out in the living room or the patio?" Apryl asked.

"She wants to hang out in whatever mode of transportation she took to get here," Everett said behind us. "Because she's about to bounce."

"*Ew,* nigga," I whined as Apryl and I took a seat on the couch. "What the fuck is your deal?"

"Apryl and I were about to go lay down," Everett revealed.

I glanced outside, then dipped my hand into my jeans' back pocket to pull out my phone. I glanced at the screen and saw it was only after 9pm. "Why are y'all going to sleep so early?"

"I said *nothing* about sleeping," he clarified. "Now, did I?"

"Disgusting." I scrunched up my face and pointed at him. *"Really disgusting."*

"Apryl is in town for another twenty-four hours," he told me. "The day she flew into New York was the day I flew out to Cali to check on *you* when you weren't answering your phone."

I rolled my eyes.

"Me and my woman have kept missing each other. This is the *only* night I had free from the boxing gym *and* the rec center in Bed-Stuy to spend time with her and *here* you are, cockblocking, and getting in the way *again*."

I sucked my teeth. "I literally spent most of my day walking around funky ass Manhattan after leaving the brownstone earlier in the afternoon. I was purposeful in popping up here at night because I didn't want to interrupt anything."

"You're interrupting now," he argued.

"Look, it was *your* idea for me to fly back to this godforsaken city, and now you're acting like I'm freeloading, and I just got here."

He folded his brawny arms over his chest. "What happened at Ma's?"

I sucked my teeth again. "She tried that thing she *always* tries when she invites me to go out to my favorite place so she can have a way to talk to me."

"Oh, *wow*," he dragged out. "How awful. She's the worst, right?"

"Whatever," I spat. "You know *exactly* what I'm talking about when I say she's trying to do that *thing* she does, and you know how much I *hate* it when she does that shit."

"Well." He gestured with his hand. "That's why when I came back to New York, I got my place."

"I don't want to get a place because I don't plan to be here for more than a week." I snapped my neck with each word spoken. "Remember?"

He kissed his teeth, then shook his head.

"Why would I bother getting a rental if I don't plan on being here that long?"

"There are Airbnbs."

"That would take so much work to find a good enough place to stay, though."

"There you go, being lazy again," Everett mumbled.

"Whatever, Everett."

"And that's probably the real reason you don't want to stay in the Brooklyn Brownstone, because you know Ma will have you work through whatever headspace you're in and you don't want to do the work. Like always."

I turned to look at Apryl, who sat quietly watching as my brother and I went back and forth with each other.

"I don't know what you see in his stupid ass," I said to her.

She shoved me playfully while sputtering a laugh. "Don't call my man stupid."

"You know," I focused on Everett again. "Your crazy ex is the only reason I'm not in Cali right now, accepting a new promotion."

"She is something else," Apryl chimed in. "I've blocked her on all of my social media and it seems ever since I've done that, this sketchy ass faceless account has been leaving rude comments under my posts. She better be careful. I know where to find her since now I know where she works."

"I'd help you get past security," I promised. "'Cause she needs her ass beat, and I'd be more than happy to do it."

"Aight, enough," Everett said over us, eyes homed in on me. "You obviously are not trying to leave tonight, so stay in the guest bedroom down the hall."

"Thank you." I smiled.

"Oh, don't thank me yet." He scoffed. "Because when you hear Apryl hollering all night, you gonna wish you kept your ass in Brooklyn."

Apryl gasped, and I gagged.

"'Cause she's loud as hell the way I like her to be, and we're not keeping it down." He gestured at Apryl. "Baby, let's go to bed."

"Everett." Apryl peeked over at me. "Come on."

"Coming is *exactly* what I'm trying to do," he said under his breath.

"Oh, my God, Ev," I shrieked. "Shut the hell up!"

Apryl placed her hand on my shoulder. "We're just gonna go lay down and chill."

"Ha!" Everett hollered a laugh. "Don't lie to her."

She whipped her head in his direction. "Everett—"

"Apryl, baby, I'm hungry." He arched a brow at her. "Let's go."

"I don't know what the hell you mean by you being hungry, Ev." I pointed at him. "But it sounds nasty as fuck and I *really* wish you kept that to yourself."

"Goodnight, Eryn," he said, scooping Apryl up from her seat with one arm and tossing her over his shoulder like she weighed nothing. Her squeals traveled around me, and I couldn't help but laugh underneath my breath.

"Goodnight, girl," she shouted to me as she and my brother turned the corner, disappearing behind the wall.

"Goodnight," I said back.

I sighed as I stood to my feet and made my way around the duplex. I remembered the location of the guest bedroom from when they gave me a tour of their duplex via video call.

It seemed every room with oversized windows offered the perfect New York City skyline view.

I walked into the guest bedroom and nodded at the comfort. Like the other areas in the duplex, the guest bedroom offered a beautiful view of New York City's skyline.

"You sure are beautiful," I said to the view.

I understood the allure of New York City. The promise of being able to co-exist in a city that was so beautiful, it was inspiring. That inspiration was all lies, though, and a figment of the imagination. People were more in love with the idea of New York more than the city itself. I know I was.

After a stop in the guest bathroom to wash my hands and to tie my headscarf around my head, I returned to the bedroom and pulled down the bed's covers and climbed in.

I was two seconds away from drifting off when I heard the faint sound of a moan. I ignored it because in my sleepy daze state, I figured that couldn't be what it was.

But it was.

I turned over onto my side and took the pillow to press against my ear, but that only worked for the next half an hour because after that, it was unmistakable what the sound echoing from outside of the guest bedroom door was.

"Oh-kay," I said, kicking the covers off me. "Point made, Everett."

I was desperate to be out of the brownstone, but I wasn't that desperate to subject myself to listening to my brother and his fiancée have sex several rooms down from mine.

Just as easy as it was to peel off my clothes, I jumped back into them.

And the moment I got fully dressed and opened the guest room door, the faint moans became surround sound clear.

From them both.

"Oh, wow," I said to myself at the guest bedroom threshold. "They fucking, fucking."

And their sounds of pleasure were in sync, both leaving me impressed and with an upset stomach.

I took gigantic steps away from the noise and toward their front door, realizing that the brownstone might not be too bad to stay in.

Even if I had to endure a non-intrusive intervention when I returned.

# EIGHT

**SIMEON**

I sat on the armchair across from my bed with my phone in my hand. I tapped the pad of my thumb against the screen in rhythm with my heartbeat.

I was trying to gear myself up to reach out to Opal Sands Marketing Agency.

I'd put it off all morning. Finding different things to do. Desperate for a solution I could find to assure Dallas that I indeed had this complete debacle handled.

But I didn't have it handled.

After visiting a handful of marketing agencies, fielding calls from recommendations I got from the people closest to me who knew a person who knew a person who handled public relations, I was unsatisfied with the options.

It was now Monday, Dallas's deadline. Officially noon, and if I knew my client and friend the way I felt I did, he was waiting until 5pm to reach out, in search of an update.

He knew I closed KSM at that hour and would expect me to have something for him.

And I had nothing yet.

Hence my preparation to execute my last resort.

I inhaled a valiant breath, audibly grunting as I unlocked my phone and tapped into my contacts in search of Opal Sands' contact information.

Clicked on the number with the 213 area code and waited as the phone trilled.

"Opal Sands. This is Gina," the woman answered. "How may I direct your phone call?"

"Good afternoon, Gina," I spoke. "This is Simeon King from King Sports Management. How are you today?"

"I'm well. Thank you for asking," she replied.

"Good to hear." I cleared my throat. "I'm calling to speak with Eryn Peters." My tongue grew heavy in my mouth just saying her name. "Can you transfer my phone call to her, please?"

Gina sighed on the line, and that made me arch a brow.

"Unfortunately, Eryn Peters isn't with Opal Sands anymore."

I jumped to my feet. "I'm sorry?"

"Eryn is no longer working in PR at Opal Sands?"

"Since when?" I questioned, a little too loud and a little out of breath. My heart was picking up in pace. I pressed my hand to my chest to get a grip. "I apologize for my tone."

"No problem at all." She released a short, nervous giggle. "A lot of her clients have given the same reaction. We're all *not* thrilled she's not here anymore."

"Shit," I whispered. "Do you have any idea where she is now? Is she with another agency?"

"I don't have that information," Gina replied. "I'm sorry."

"Okay, no worries." I swallowed hard. "Thank you, Gina. You have a great day."

"You as well—"

I cut her farewell short after ending the call abruptly.

"Okay, this is *not* how I thought that would go."

Because there I was trying to get myself together so I could place that phone call. But at least I understood that if I called the agency she worked at, Eryn would know I was calling on business. She'd be more apt to answer my call on her business line. Because she hadn't been answering my phone calls to her personal phone.

"Oh, fuck." I dropped my head back between my shoulders. "Fuck, fuck, fuck, fuck..."

I held my hands up in front of me and forced myself to take two deep breaths.

"All right, calm the hell down, Simeon," I coached as I took a seat in my armchair again. "Calm down. You're fine. You're good. Just think. *Think.*"

I peeked down at my phone again, taking my time to navigate to my contacts again. Scrolled to my contacts with names that started with E and allowed my thumb to hover over her name.

I'd tried calling two years ago. Her brother gave me her phone number, and I tried calling her a few times but never got her to answer.

Taking that out of my mind, I clicked her name and listened as the phone trilled once before being sent to voicemail.

I shook my head and dropped my chin to my chest as I listened to the automated voicemail message, ending the call before it could get to the beep.

If this was back then, when I tried calling Eryn and always getting her voicemail, I would've hung up the phone and just went about my day, deciding I wouldn't try again.

But this was not back then.

If I could be so lucky.

I had time back then, and time was not of the essence right now.

So, I called her again. And this time, the call went straight to voicemail.

I straightened my back and waited for the beep. And when I heard it, I froze.

For two breaths I said nothing, and when I could finally peel my tongue off the roof of my mouth, I said, "Eryn, it's Simeon. I need your help with something extremely important. Business-related. Call me."

I ended the call and stood to my feet in the middle of my room for a moment, my mind racing with thoughts.

*What if she didn't call me back?*

*What if I'm on my own with this?*

I shook my head, trying to get the thoughts out of my head.

The thoughts of self-defeat.

This couldn't be it. I wouldn't allow it.

To accept defeat would be completely out of my character. Even though part of me felt so unsure, it was like I told Amber Palmetto at OBM. My word is my life. And I'd already given Dallas my word.

And I intended to keep my word with him by any means necessary.

My phone's screen was in front of me again. I tapped the arrow to exit Eryn's contact, ready to put my phone down and take a much-needed breath to figure out my next move. But the moment I clicked out of her contact and returned to the directory, my eyes landed on her brother's name, just a few spots down from hers in my contacts list.

I immediately clicked his name and then his phone number.

Everett and I bumped into each other at a gym in Manhattan when I was out there two years prior, looking to pitch one trainer at that gym, Apryl Wilde, to do some promo work for Dallas's nutritional brand, Pure Roque. Apryl agreed, and we've photographed her for a few campaigns after she signed on as a global brand ambassador. We had her out here in California a few months back to shoot for the supplements line Dallas planned to launch at the start of the next year. It was then, those few months back, that I learned that she and Everett were not only together but had gotten engaged, which made sense. The way he stared at her when he first saw her was clear she wasn't just someone beautiful to look at for him.

I've always liked Everett. When Eryn and I were in a relationship, he was never overbearing or unnecessarily protective of his little sister. Everett embraced me with open arms. We were always cool whenever he was around. Even when we bumped into each other at the gym. It was all love, despite me and his sister not being together anymore. So, I knew he would at least be willing to help me get in touch with her.

"Hey, Simeon," he greeted when he answered my call.

"Everett," I returned, smiling. "How's it going?"

"Great," he replied. "Aye, Apryl showed me the photos she took for Pure Roque, man. Beautiful."

"Thanks, man."

"No, thank you." He chuckled. "I always tell her she doesn't photograph well, which she never finds funny, but y'all captured the beauty she clearly is. I'm excited about this launch for real. Would love to get some of Pure Roque's products in my boxing gym when it's up for wholesale purchase."

"We can definitely talk about that." I nodded, holding up a hand as if he could see me. "And although I'm happy to talk business with you, I'm calling for something else."

"What's up?"

I sighed. "I need Eryn badly, man."

"What?!"

I laughed nervously. "That came out wrong."

"Sounded right to my ears."

I scoffed a laugh. "I've been trying to get in contact with her to handle a time-sensitive situation I'm dealing with that I'm sure she would know how to handle. I reached out to the agency you told me she worked at, Opal Sands? And they said she's no longer working there?"

"Yeah, man," he exhaled. "Some bullshit went down there involving my ex. It is such a long story, Simeon, I'm not even trying to get into it."

"I hear that. I don't have the time to get into it anyway, so no worries, but listen," I continued. "I *really* need to get in contact with Eryn, and she hasn't been answering my phone calls. Even when I called her when you gave me her number two years ago. She has never answered or returned my phone calls, even when I've left voicemails. Can I confirm her number with you?"

He chuckled. "It's the right phone number, Simeon. Eryn's just being stubborn. She knows you've been calling. She told me she's gotten your previous phone calls and message."

"I figured." I groaned.

"You know how she can be."

"And any other time, I'd let her be herself, but this isn't any other time," I explained. "I am *desperate* brother, like *really* desperate. I *must* get in contact with her. Do you think you can help me?"

"With Eryn? Nah," he answered. "She's impossible and is too much work to even bother with getting to do *anything* she doesn't want to do."

My shoulders sagged in defeat.

"But I can tell you this," he added.

"I'm listening," I told him. "Tell me whatever you can."

"She's out here in New York for another three days."

"Really?" I nodded. "Okay."

"She's staying at our mother's house in Brooklyn. You remember the brownstone in Bed-Stuy, right?"

"Yeah." I smiled. "It's hard to forget it."

He laughed. "Eryn would like to forget it if she could. She's developed this hate for New York that I can't understand. I had to beg her to come out here after everything went down at Opal Sands and even *that* was like pulling teeth. She's literally counting down the days to get out of this city, so look."

"Yeah?"

"If you want to give her no option but to talk to you, because, as you said, you're desperate?"

"*Very* desperate, Ev."

"Then you *gotta* come to New York. Getting her on the phone will never happen, Simeon. You gotta get face to face with her and give her no choice but to talk to you. That's what I do. That's how I deal with her."

I nodded.

"Coming out to Brooklyn is the only way you're gonna be able to talk to her. Forget calling."

"Say no more," I told him. "Can you text me your mother's address? I remember where it is, but I like to be sure, you know?"

"I definitely can," he replied. "I'm sending it now."

"Everett, thanks a lot, man. You do not know what you've done to help me, but you've done *a lot*."

"No problem at all," he told me. "And Simeon, good luck. You're gonna need it with her ass."

He wasn't lying about that.

But it's like one of my favorite quotes states, "Difficult does not mean impossible."

My next phone call was to my assistant, instructing her to book me on the next flight out of Oakland and to New York City. My phone call after that was to Dallas.

"I got somebody," I reported the moment he answered.

"Yeah?"

"Yes," I affirmed. It was a little premature of me to give him my word again, but I'd decided in that moment, I would not take no as an answer when I finally got Eryn face to face. "I'm flying out to New York in a few hours. I'll have an update for you by tomorrow night. Everything is being handled."

At least, I hoped it would be.

# NINE

**ERYN**

"*Eryn, it's Simeon. I need your help with something very important. Business-related. Call me.*"

I listened to the voicemail message for the third time, my question still the same.

"Why the hell is he calling me again?"

Clearly, he said it was business-related, but *what* business?

Simeon had tried reaching out to me a few times when my brother gave him my phone number two years ago, and each time he called, I sent his call to voicemail. I saw when his new call came in the two times it came in the day prior, but I was way too shocked and confused why his calls had started up again with me.

I had returned none of them when he started calling me two years ago and didn't plan to return the new ones he placed to me the day prior. He was in the past. So much so I filed his contact number under the name "The Past" because I wasn't looking to bring him into this future or any future after this one.

I had just woken up and was only checking my phone to see the time. Somehow, I'd missed the notification that he'd left a voicemail the day before, but there it was—the voicemail notification staring at me from my lock screen. Curious about what he had to say, I hit play.

His voice. *Ugh*. Still deep. Still unintentionally sensual. Still *so* Simeon fucking King.

I rolled my eyes and turned over on the bed.

I had two more days in New York and although I wasn't looking forward to returning to L.A. at all, I couldn't wait to bounce out of this brownstone.

I'd been avoiding my mother since returning to the brownstone from Everett's.

She was a creature of habit, so I knew when the kitchen was free to get coffee and to fill my stomach whenever needed.

Like right now, I knew she would have to have a client on her calendar. Like I said, it was after the noon hour, making it the perfect time to get out of bed.

For now.

Once I had my coffee, I would climb right back into my very pink bed that I hadn't made up since arriving the previous Friday.

For another day, I left my toothbrush and face wash untouched, deciding I'd bother with that once I returned upstairs, like always.

I padded out my bedroom door and walked my way to the top of the stairs.

The scent of coffee already in the air had me blinking a few times, but it wasn't too odd in that instance. It's like I also said, my mother wasn't a coffee drinker, more of a tea lover, but occasionally, I'd see her enjoy a cup of coffee.

But the coffee wasn't the only odd thing lingering in the air. There were voices. Hers and someone else's. My mother was talking to someone and had company. I only realized this when I was halfway down the staircase.

To get to the kitchen, I had to go through the living room. Luckily, the night before, I fell asleep in a tee and my brother's shorts I took from his room, so whomever she was meeting with should be fine with seeing some leg... I hoped.

I entered the living room, only expecting to greet her and whoever she was meeting with. But when I entered the living area, I nearly fell face first after tripping over my feet.

Because of *whom* I saw sitting on the antique upholstered sofa with my mother.

Our eyes locked and my jaw dropped.

*Am I sleepwalking right now?*

Simeon sat on my mother's sofa, staring right back at me.

And looking good as fuck.

*Gahdamn!*

Skin still that dark chocolate that always appeared to never have seen a blemish in its life. Lips as full and smooth as the days I used to find it hard to keep my mouth off them. Eyes still as penetrating. Jaw structure still pronounced. Posture still as authoritative. Body like a God if he ever walked the earth.

Oh my God! Why did he look *so* damn good?!

And there I was.

Standing before him, wearing a stretched-out tee that was no longer wearable outside so I wore it to sleep, matched with a pair of baggy ass basketball shorts I stole from my brother's room because I've been too lazy to throw my other sleep clothes, that were dirty, in the washing machine to clean.

Simeon and I stared at each other and said nothing for a few seconds. Soon, a smile appeared on his face. Not a fake one, but a genuinely beautiful one. The same smile I fell in love with the moment I first saw his Kodak grin, back when he was accepting cash at his parents' vendor table at the farmers' market—where I fell for him at first sight.

This motherfucker.

"I'm actually happy I don't have to lie and say I have a client, so I *have* to go, because..." My mother placed her mug on the coffee table in front of them. "I actually have a client, and I have to go."

Simeon pulled his eyes off me to focus on my mother. "Thank you so much for the hospitality, Mrs. Peters, as always."

"Please don't even mention it," she replied. "Oh, Simeon, it's *so* good to see you again. *Nothing* has changed with you." She smiled. "Still the very handsome gentleman of yesteryears."

I was too in shock, too frozen in place to come up with a snappy remark to challenge her comment. I had plenty. Years' worth of them, stored in my memory as stinging comebacks for arguments I had with him in my head. All created since we've broken up. Or ended things. Whatever happened to us that had me depressed for six whole years because he was suddenly no longer around.

My mother pressed a hand to the side of my face when she was close to me and smiled warmly right before she left the living room.

Leaving Simeon and me.

Alone.

I wanted to leave, too.

The feeling of storming out of the living room and stomping my way back to my room, closing and locking the door once I was inside. The urge to do all that was right there. But I couldn't move.

He was here, after only being in my ear seconds ago in the form of a voicemail.

"I called you," were his first words to me. "I've been calling you, and a close source told me you've been receiving those calls and avoiding me."

"So, you just pop up at my mother's house like some kind of CIA agent to...?"

He smiled again and my heart did leaps.

Dammit.

After all these years and my heart still didn't know how to act in direct view of that smile.

"I need to speak with you about something important, Eryn."

Without seeing him, I could tell his ass no. I'd been avoiding his phone calls like an expert escape artist. Face to face, he was melting the ice I swore I'd kept around my heart since I last saw him.

"I *must* be dreaming." I nodded my head and looked away. "Yes, that's it. I'm having one of those sleepwalking dreams. That's why I'm so lightheaded."

"You need coffee," he voiced. "You were always lightheaded in the mornings until you had a cup."

I turned to look at him again.

"I'll get it." He leaned forward a little to place his cup of coffee on the coffee table and stood to his feet a second later.

My eyes followed as he straightened his back, towering over me.

I wasn't very short, standing at five-foot-six, but Simeon was a cool six-foot-three, forcing me to lean my head back to keep my eyes in line with his. He ironed out the barely there wrinkles in his light brown polo shirt and brushed his big palms down his pressed cobalt blue trousers next.

With him close, I nearly melted at his scent that found its way up my nose when he moved the air when he stood out of his seat on the sofa.

His scent was warm, spicy. A blended aroma of vibrant pink pepper, warm rum, and sweet vanilla. Like the merriment of scents that wafted throughout a Brooklyn jazz cafe.

And like a jazz cafe, the brother was so fucking fly.

And I hated his ass for it.

"A little cream and a little sugar, right?" He asked. "You still like your coffee that way?"

"I can get my coffee," I told him as I turned toward the kitchen to walk that way.

He gently caught me by the arm, sending a wave of goosebumps that had a starting point at where he held me in a soft grip.

"It's not a bother for me to get it for you, Eryn, you know that," he reminded. "I still know my way around here. Plus, while I'm getting you coffee, you can go upstairs and freshen up."

Simeon had a way of tranquilizing people with sight alone. Making them immovable and stuck under his gaze. Or was that only me? Because to me, his eyes were unwavering, undefeated. When he locked eyes with me, he never broke eye contact first. And It wasn't an aggressive stare, or even a gaze fueled by ego. It was calm and mesmerizing, like the captivating focus of a snake charmer. He was effortlessly seductive, without even trying.

It was infuriating.

I slid my arm from his grip and instead of continuing toward the kitchen, I walked past him, heading towards the stairs.

I peeked behind me as I approached the steps and started climbing. I glanced that way to be sure I wasn't bugging.

My ex-boyfriend was *here*, in my mother's living room, about to get me coffee.

Just like the old days.

I ran my fingernails against my forehead as I climbed the last of the stairs.

And as soon as I entered my room, I went straight to my en suite. Switched on the lights and nearly screamed at the sight of me in the mirror.

I had rheum in both corners of my eyes. Yes, dried eye boogers had accumulated so much from all my sleeping, you couldn't miss them. And because that wasn't enough, I also had a tiny smear of dried saliva at the side of my mouth.

Yup, drool.

All from sleeping.

"Wow," I whispered, instantly getting a whiff of my morning breath. "Just great, Eryn."

I saw my ex for the first time in over a decade looking like shit with the breath to match.

One point for Simeon. No points for Eryn.

Just the idea of it though, that he was here, strangely brought a smile to my lips I tried with all my might to fight back but couldn't resist.

I was feeling a giddy feeling I hadn't felt in a long time. A feeling I'd been searching for ever since us. It washed over and through me slowly as I washed my face. I tried to fight it, but it was impossible.

Simeon was really here, and I wasn't too mad about that.

He knocked on my opened bedroom door as I was brushing my teeth. I poked my head out of the bathroom and gestured for him to come in.

Once I finished brushing and applying moisturizer to my face, I entered my bedroom to find him holding the coffee in one hand and one of the teddy bears he'd gotten for me for one of our many Valentine's Days in his other hand.

"Nothing has changed in here," he commented.

"Nothing but us," I replied.

His eyes fell on my clothes that were sprawled every which way around my room, the unmade bed, and the bevy of empty drinking glasses that were sitting everywhere there was a surface.

He cleared his throat as he returned the bear to my bed. And as messy as the room was and as embarrassed as the average woman would feel having her ex-man see her at her worst, seeing him bothered by the appearance of the environment brought some much-needed humor to the moment.

Reminded me of yesteryears. The only thing we would argue over. How messy I was and how clean and bothered he was because of my mess.

"You're still a neat freak, though," I said to him as I approached him. "That clearly has *not* changed." I accepted the mug he'd brought up to my room from the kitchen, and I inhaled the dancing white steam that swirled out the top like I always did. Brought the mug to my lips and took a sip.

I never understood how he could do it, but he could always make the perfect cup of coffee.

When I made mine, it always was a little too sweet or a little too bitter, always too hot to drink immediately, which I always wanted to do the moment I got it in my grip. But whenever Simeon made it, even in that moment, it was the perfect temperature for drinking and the perfect balance of sweet and bitter.

I couldn't help but to close my eyes and moan.

I opened my eyes to him staring at me and fighting back a smile.

"So, was this your plan?" I asked. "Pop up here looking like you stepped off a fashion billboard in Times Square and catch me looking crusty and dusty?"

"You just got up," he reasoned. "And I saw nothing I didn't see once upon a time. Many, many mornings."

"*Mm-hmm.*"

"You look good," he commented. "Even crusty and dusty."

The laugh that busted through me I couldn't contain. I rolled my eyes at myself.

"What are you doing here, Simeon?"

"I've been calling, and you haven't been answering, and I *really* need your help with a situation I'm assisting with."

"So, you show up at my mother's house, uninvited?"

He shrugged. "I've been calling, and you haven't been answering."

"How'd you even know I was here?"

"Everett."

"That nigga." I shook my head. "*Ugh.*"

"I wasn't expecting you to get such a late start in your day, though," he added. "I purposely stopped by at noon because I thought you'd be up and about."

"Surprise, surprise."

"Let's meet up later," Simeon suggested.

I scoffed. "You think it's that easy?"

He licked his lips, then ran his fingertips down the sides of his trimmed beard.

"You just pop up here after all these years and tell me 'let's meet up later?'" I mocked in a faux deep voice. I arched both brows next. "After everything, can we just meet up later?"

"We can if it's at Coney Island, right?"

I gasped. "You clever motherfucker."

He chuckled sexily, then held a sly smile on his lips.

I looked away to hide my smile and to get the warming of my cheeks under control.

"7pm," he proposed. "The sun will set, and I know how much you *love* Coney Island at sunset."

I stared at him.

"I can pick you up—"

"I'll meet you there."

He shook his head. "It's not a problem. I can pick you up, and we can drive there together."

"I'd much rather get there alone."

"How can I trust you'll actually meet me there?" He asked. "How do I know you're not telling me you'll meet me there to get me out of your room with no plans to actually show up?"

"Because it's Coney Island." I bit my lip, trying to hide a smile.

"You? I'd stand you up. Absolutely. But I'd *never* miss a date with Coney Island, and you know that."

"Well." He sighed. "I guess I can trust that, huh?"

"Hmph," I huffed. "I guess."

He pointed at my mug. "Enjoy your coffee. I'll see you tonight."

And just like that, he walked out of my room.

With a smooth ass stroll, and all.

Just like that, I was alone again, surrounded by pink, and feeling my heart do leaps.

Like old times.

For days, I have been in the dumps, and within a matter of minutes, Simeon had transformed that feeling into something else.

Something lighter.

Hopeful.

Exciting.

*Just* by being here.

"God, I hate when he does that." I took another sip of the coffee, closing my eyes and moaning at its perfection. "I love his coffees though. *Mmm.*"

# TEN

**SIMEON**

I switched the bag of pink and blue cotton candy from one hand to the other and twisted my wrist to turn my yellow-gold chronograph so I could check the face.

It was three minutes to seven. And although it wasn't the time I told Eryn to meet me at the amusement park, I couldn't help but to be concerned.

I had my contingency plan, though. I always had a contingency plan.

If she didn't show up like she said she would, I would travel back to her mother's house in Brooklyn and try again. This time, I would tell her exactly what I needed her for.

Doing things this way, having her meet me at one of her favorite places in the world, was for a reason besides reducing the awkwardness that's bound to be there between us. The one thing that will always remain clear to people is their wants. Not someone else's want, simply what's in it for them to care about anyone else's wants besides their own. What's In It For Me TV, or like I often called it - WIIFM. This was one of the first things I learned while I was getting my MBA in Miami. And ever since discovering that, I have used that knowledge to help with closing deals and attracting many clients as an agent at the sports agency I used to work. It came in excellent use when I branched out on my own, too.

I knew if we were in a place that she loved, she'd be more open. And me getting the yes I was desperate for would be easier to get.

So, I returned to my suite at a Manhattan hotel. A suite, my assistant booked for me right after booking me my flight. Changed out of my suit trousers and polo shirt and into something more casual - a textured fabric white short-sleeve button-up shirt, light beige slim-fitting trousers, and clean, white sneakers.

I told her the meeting was business, but I didn't have to look the part. Especially not out here in Brooklyn's famous playground.

The sun's brightness faded an hour prior, so the lights on rides and at neighboring attractions and restaurants were the city's flashlight. The weather out was unseasonal for late May. Even as the sun was setting, the weather had yet to dip below eighty degrees. Which, for me, did not differ from Oakland.

Coney Island was a sight to see at any time of the day, but in the evening hours and at night, it was breathtaking.

Coney Island and the Jersey Shore boardwalk were the two places Eryn and I would split our time when we were in college. She loved a good time. So, when she would slack with schoolwork, I'd promise a weekend day here, on me. Eryn was always excited to visit Coney Island. It helped us both get through those years at Langston U.

I checked the time again. It was exactly 7pm.

I peeked across the street at the train station in search of a familiar face.

Hers.

I didn't like her decision to come here alone. Me driving us out here would have given us time to catch up on the ride over. All so when I finally asked her to help me out with the whole Ayanna and Dallas scandal, our catching up would have her more open to saying yes and more open to care less about our past to get the job done.

But that was okay. I could adjust.

If there was one thing I knew how to do, it was to adjust to last-minute changes.

I often had no choice but to.

I was getting a little uneasy as I scanned the area for what felt like the millionth time until I glimpsed her emerging through the train station exit straight ahead.

I decided to wait for her in front of Nathan's, the famous hot dog stand. It was the most visible spot outside the amusement park and close to her favorite ride at Coney Island.

I bit back my smile when we locked eyes. I couldn't help licking my lips, though.

Because Eryn looked good.

She looked damn good.

Age had improved on something youth started in her. And that's saying a lot because she's always been a scene stealer.

Eryn has always been a five-foot something glamazon. Fine without trying and only breathing.

She attracted attention by only showing up.

All she wore was a fitted short sleeve cropped tee that showed her midriff just a little. The high-waisted, wide-leg olive green pleated pants she wore covered only a little above the waist.

It was a simple getup, matched with simple open-toe black sandals and a designer light brown crossbody bag, but she wore it like a model. Walked like one too. Switching her hips in her carefree stroll, those hips naturally swaying to a rhythm of their own. But even with as simple as her outfit was, she still turned the heads of a group of young men who were crossing in the opposite direction as she walked.

Their eyes all fell to her derriere that I'm sure swayed in those pleated olive green pants, beautifully.

Eryn's ass was everything. I couldn't keep my hands off it when we were together.

Her eyes met mine, and she tried to keep her pink-painted lips from curving into a smile. When she couldn't resist the pull of her smile, she simply looked away.

I chuckled to myself, assisting with closing the distance between us by taking steps toward her.

"Thank you for coming," I said to her when she was close.

Her perfume reached me before she did.

The key notes in her scent of citrus, apple, and something floral made my mouth water.

"I would never turn down a visit to Coney Island," she jested. "Despite whom extended the invitation."

My eyes roamed over to her hair. It was long. The ends stopping an inch below her elbows.

"I didn't realize your hair was so long," I couldn't help but to say. "You had it tied up in your headscarf, so I didn't get to see it earlier."

"You and my mother act like I was baldheaded when you two last saw me."

I chuckled.

"She can't get over the length either."

"You wore your hair in that cute, sharp-edged bob for as long as I could remember." I smiled. "I don't think you've ever worn your hair past your shoulders."

"Well, when I moved to Cali, I changed everything." She shrugged. "Including cutting my hair. I decided to grow it out instead."

"I like it," I added. "Like I said earlier, you look good."

"Good," she started. "'Cause I wasn't gonna let you catch me slipping twice today."

I snorted a laugh.

"Not when you popped up at my mother's house looking like new money." She licked her lips, her eyes scanning me. "You're looking like you got *a lot* of money, in fact. What's up with that?"

"I do well."

"It shows."

Her eyes found mine again, and they were smoldering, which was a natural Eryn look. She wore foreplay in her eyes, unintentionally. She was a tease, and I've always liked that about her. I tried to create a fist, my attempt at calming myself down when I felt my temperature rising having her focus all her attention on me. That's when I remembered the bag of pink and blue cotton candy I was holding. I lifted the clear bag in her view a second later.

"I got this for you."

Eryn quirked a perfectly arched brow. "Oh, he's trying to woo me for real."

I smiled and looked away.

"Coney Island just before sunset, pink and blue cotton candy," she listed. "What do you want?"

"For you to accompany me on the Wonder Wheel for now."

Her eyes grew like saucers, and she expelled a soft breath. "We're going on the Ferris wheel?"

"You still love them, right?"

She squinted her eyes at me, scanning my face.

"I already got our tickets." I gestured with my head. "Come on."

Luna Park was an hour away from closing. During the last days of May and the weeks before summer officially started, the park closed early.

I expected there to be a line to get on Deno's Wonder Wheel - Coney Island's oldest Ferris wheel. That's why I got the cotton candy. Plus, I figured waiting to get on the Ferris wheel would give Eryn and me the opportunity to talk before we shared a tiny space on the ride.

"I had a dream about you a few months ago," I revealed as we waited. There were only five people ahead of us, so I was sure we would get on the ride next.

At 150 feet, Coney Island's Wonder Wheel was the equivalent of a 15-story building. When the car reached the top of the wheel, you could see all of Brooklyn from high up.

It was breathtaking and made sense why Eryn loved it so much.

She turned to face me as she stuffed a pinch-full of the pink cotton candy into her mouth.

"We were somewhere unfamiliar," I continued. "Not in any city I knew. But there were many people around and yet I could still make you out in the crowd."

She blinked in response.

"You were too far away, though. And every time I opened my mouth to call your name, nothing would come out. I had no voice."

I ran my fingers down the sides of my beard.

"So, I figured, since I couldn't call you, I would run up and meet you up ahead."

"Did you?" She asked.

"The moment I took a step, I woke up from sleep." I nodded. "I knew from then that we would see each other soon. I didn't know when, or why, but I knew it would happen."

"Because of your dream?"

"Because of my dream."

She cracked a smile and pushed another pinch-full of cotton candy into her mouth. "Still letting your dreams be your crystal ball, huh?"

I lowered my head in agreement. "Oh, one hundred percent. They're my guide for sure. They help me make all my important decisions. I trust them with my life."

"Some people claim dreams are only dreams and are based on your moods, the events in the news, or sometimes because you ate too much."

"Some people also claimed the earth was flat, Eryn," I countered. "Should we really be trusting what some people say?"

Eryn smirked while turning forward, just in time for it to be our time to board the Ferris wheel. We got on the line for the stationary white cars. The Wonder Wheel had over twenty cars. Sixteen red and blue cars swung back and forth on a serpentine track and eight white cars remained stationary.

Eryn hated the swinging cars. Always had. I didn't mind it, but this visit to Coney Island wasn't about me.

Once we were in the car and the wheel was in motion, wheeling our car and the other twenty-three cars in a slow circle, I knew it was time for me to get to work and to give it my best. It was all or nothing.

Here goes everything.

*Make it good, Simeon.*

"I heard you aren't working at Opal Sands anymore."

She glanced over at me and held her stare with me.

"I'd called there in search of your services, and they said you were no longer with the company."

"Because of some bullshit," she spat, folding her arms and facing forward. "I really don't want to get into it."

"And I don't want you to feel you have to," I agreed. "It's their loss, anyway. Firing you was a foolish decision."

She looked over at me again.

"When your brother told me you were working there when I ran into him at a gym in Manhattan, I looked you up."

"You looked me up."

"I did." I smiled. "And I learned you single-handedly carried Opal Sands on your back. Especially in media crises. And there were *many*. Every product recall, every scandal involving key figures at corporations, data breaches, even social media missteps by your celebrity clientele, Eryn Peters was on the job handling media crises like they were nothing."

"I busted my ass working for them." She shook her head slowly. "I made some bad and questionable decisions; I will admit that. But all with the purpose of moving up in the company." Eryn kissed her teeth. "I was literally this close..." She held her index finger and thumb fingers in a visible pinch. "This close to getting promoted. And then boom, just like that, it all ended."

"It all ended for the better. I'm positive about it. Your future is bright, Eryn. Never doubt that."

She stared at me for a couple of beats before she said, "Simeon, don't smooth talk me, nigga."

I snorted a laugh, and that made her crack a smile.

Straight shooter. Like always.

She did not know how much out of all the things I missed about her; I missed *that* the very most.

Her slick ass mouth that had no filter whatsoever and that central Brooklyn accent of hers. She always put up such a tough exterior, but I knew exactly how to melt her, how to make her go soft just for me.

"You pop up where I'm at, giving me no choice but to talk to you," she rattled off. "Invite me here. Try to sweeten me up with cotton candy, the Wonder Wheel, and now this pour-into-me quote of the night.

Simeon, what do you want from me? Huh? Because I know you want something."

"I want your expertise," I made known. "I *need* it. Badly."

She said nothing in response. But she was listening.

I inhaled a deep breath and turned in my seat to stare out in front of us, glimpsing at the sky, turning a sorbet blue and pink.

"Do you know Dallas Roque?"

"Who in Cali doesn't?"

"Do you know I represent him?"

"Everett told me."

"He's involved in some shit. Have you heard about it?"

She shrugged. "I have heard little of anything these past few days. I haven't taken my dismissal from Opal Sands very well. Why? What's up?"

"He's getting married next month... to his brother's ex-girlfriend."

Her brows shot up over her eyes.

"A fact that only became common knowledge last week," I explained. "Not the getting married part. That his fiancée was with his brother first."

Eryn whistled in response. "Damn."

"That's not the worse part," I exhaled. "Dallas's brother has some nude photos of Dallas's fiancée, and his brother is threatening to use one of them as his album art. An album he's planning to release the day before Dallas and his fiancée's wedding."

"Diabolical," she uttered.

"In the worst way." I pinched the corners of my eyes. "Legally, we're good. A gag order is already in the works with plans to go out by tomorrow. The album will never see the light of day because Dallas's brother photographed his fiancée nude without her consent or knowledge. So, I'm not worried about that. It's the threat to Dallas's image that's got me sweating in my sleep at night."

She nodded.

"Legally, we can stop all this mess from going down," I continued. "But public image wise? The public has a very long memory. And the man is getting married next month, his basketball career is taking off, and he's planning to launch a major product in his nutritional products line at the start of next year. And none of what his brother has been orchestrating will help Dallas's image in the long run."

"Not in the least."

"But I know with your help," I added, turning to face her. "His image can survive this. In my heart of hearts, I know you'd be able to spin this in our favor."

She shook her head. "Simeon."

"You are the best in the business."

"*Was* the best in the business. Yes." She sighed. "But now... I don't even know if I can ever get back into the PR rat race. I gave my life to Opal Sands. I sacrificed *a lot* to climb that corporate ladder. Sleeping with my boss..."

I reared my head back, suddenly finding it difficult to swallow.

"Burning the candle on both ends most days," she continued without pause. "Twenty-four-seven of constant working only for it to all go away because the company I would've given a limb to gets bought out and instantly forgot my value to it." She shook her head. "No. I don't think I have it in me to continue with a public relations career if I'm keeping it real with you."

Her revelation, the sleeping with her boss thing, I can't even lie. It took me aback. But I refused to let it knock me off my block. I didn't come all that way, only to come all that way and to let what she told me to stop me.

"Eryn, I flew out here to New York specifically for you," I revealed.

"You wasted your time," she said to the view of Brooklyn.

"Did I?"

"Yes." She turned to look at me. "I won't be of any use to you. I'm back in my lazy girl era, Simeon, and honestly, I don't know when I'm leaving. As much as I love Coney Island right now, I cannot wait to get back to the brownstone to sleep until my flight on Friday. Which I'm not looking forward to because though I hate NYC, L.A. ain't looking so sexy to me right now with no job to return to."

"So come to Oakland."

The Wonder Wheel was going for its final spin around.

"You know I have *never* been a begging man, Eryn," I told her. "And that has not changed, but right now? I am *begging* you."

Eryn only stared at me.

"You were my first choice when I was thinking about putting together a PR team and right now, you are my last resort. I have tapped out *all* my options, all of my resources, and have no one else to tackle this."

She rubbed her lips together.

"Now I know we have our history and I'm sure it's playing a major part in you wanting to tell me no right now." I pressed my hands together into prayer hands. "But beyond Dallas being my client, he's a good friend. An *excellent* friend. And his fiancée, Ayanna, and he are the most beautiful couple you will ever meet. I can't have this scandal ruin what they have before it even starts. I just can't. And I know with your help, we can spin this mess into something phenomenal. I know it in my heart of hearts, Eryn. Please."

Eryn was parting her lips to say something when I added, "I know how much your annual salary was at Opal Sands. One hundred thousand, before taxes, correct?"

She jerked her head back. "How do you know that?"

"I'm willing to double it, just for your work on Dallas's scandal."

"Double?"

"Double," I confirmed.

"*Only* for this Dallas situation?"

"*Only* for Dallas," I affirmed. "And I'm good for it. You have my word on that."

Eryn sat back in her seat and focused ahead of us.

"You'll have a reason to leave New York and to not return to L.A. right now. And you'll make bank," I pitched. "Also, Dallas will be your first independently gained client, and he's about to be a household name by next year, for sure. Trust me on that. Off just him and handling this situation, Eryn, honestly? You may never have to submit your resume to another PR agency. You could work for yourself. Start your own agency. Be your own boss."

She was quiet for a moment. Visibly thinking.

The Wonder Wheel was turning periodically, letting down people, one car at a time. Our section was the last to let off.

"Simeon King scores again." She shook her head slowly. "If there's one thing you've mastered, it's persuasion. In fact, I think you might have gotten even better at it since college." She smirked. "You're a lethal weapon now. Wow."

"So...?" I asked. "Is that a, yes?"

She nodded. "Sure. I'll help."

I dropped my head back against the seat and exhaled all the air I'd been holding in. "Thank you, God."

"But we have to keep it business," she explained, holding up a finger. "I'm not sleeping with the head nigga in charge *ever* again in this lifetime. Plus, we've got our fractured ass past that I have no interest in picking apart or addressing while working with you. You feel me?"

"Understood." I acknowledged with the tilt of my head. "Strictly business."

She wouldn't get any argument from me. Not after the decision she made that inevitably caused us to break up. And like her, I wasn't looking to rehash or discuss anything either. Especially when what she did was done and she could never undo it. I didn't trust Eryn, but I trusted her with this - her capabilities with helping me with Dallas's situation, and that had to matter for something.

"As soon as I settle everything in Oakland," she added. "I'm leaving for L.A. Okay?"

"Okay," I concurred.

"Okay," she affirmed with finality.

The worker unhooked the gate to our car, allowing us to step off.

I checked my chronograph as I stepped out behind Eryn. We still had half an hour before Luna Park closed.

"We still have a little time before the park closes," I announced. "Want to check out the Cyclone?"

Eryn's face lit up, and my heart melted at the sight.

"Hell yeah I do!" She nodded. "A Ferris wheel ride *and* a roller-coaster at my favorite place in the world? You do not have to ask me twice, okay?" She winked. "Let's go."

# Eleven

## ERYN

“Oh yeah.” I nodded. “This is the one.” I pulled open the linen white kitchen cabinets, checking to hear any squeaks in the hinges.

“There is a terrace that you can access from the living room,” the real estate agent, Manuel, detailed. “Perfect for watching sunsets. And the apartment comes with private parking at the lower level.”

I peeked over at Simeon, who was busy typing something on his phone. For someone who insisted he come with me, apartment hunting in Oakland, he sure wasn’t present in the least.

“I love it so far,” I said to Manuel. “Show me the master bedroom, please. I hope it has an en suite.”

“It does,” he answered, leading the way. Simeon followed us as we left the kitchen. Eyes still down on his phone. I was in Oakland and feeling a wee-bit more optimistic than I did a few days prior.

Simeon got me to fly out with him the next day after our Coney Island visit. For the last three days, I have called a hotel room in downtown Oakland home. The very next day, after landing, I reached out to a real estate agent's office and put them on the job of finding me a place. Because we weren't sure how long I'd be in Oakland, I specifically asked to tour places that offered six-month leases. A condo would have been my first pick, but I wasn't looking to spend much cash. Even if Simeon was doubling the salary I earned at Opal Sands.

Manuel pushed open the double doors at the far end of the hall, revealing a beautifully staged bedroom. "This is the master bedroom."

"*Mm-hmm.*" I smiled as I walked past him and entered the room. It was big enough to satisfy my want of space. The room had oversized windows that offered a stunning view of Oakland, like the other areas in the apartment. I checked over my shoulder to see Simeon scanning the surrounding space, then returning his attention to his phone again. He wasn't lying when he said he'd keep it all business.

I knew Simeon as the smart stylish farm boy. Responsible, diligent, neat, and orderly. Even when we were only in college, he spoke in terms of the future. He lived in the future. Still, he was my boyfriend back then. Every and anything I wanted to do, he'd do it, even if it was out of his comfort zone. He laughed more back then, was a little more of a daredevil for my sake. Simeon was more in the moment back then, too. Now Simeon behaved like a boss. Observed more than spoke. Like now. He was clearly present, but he was handling business and speaking very little. Told me he wanted to accompany me on my apartment search and hadn't contributed a single word to the conversation I was having with Manuel.

I'd looked at five apartments since arriving in Oakland three days ago. Six, including this one. And while I'd only been in a hotel room for only three days, it was three days too many. There's a certain vibe a hotel room gives off. I called it the stench of temporary. The bed didn't feel like mine. The bathroom was lifeless, lacking any kind of color. I was ready to get my place and make my home, and this one was looking like it would be a great place to catch my *ZZ's* for the next six months or so.

"I really love the location," I expressed to Manuel. I made my way to the en suite and pulled back the shower curtain to see inside of the tub.

It was a good size. Smaller than the tub in my bathroom in L.A., but it would do. After meeting with Ayanna and Dallas, I didn't expect I would have to work too hard on this image Simeon was adamant about protecting. They were absolutely beautiful.

*I sat at their kitchen table, watching them as they moved around the space. It was my second day in Oakland when Simeon told me that Ayanna and Dallas had invited us over for dinner. They were cooking it, and I guess they got caught up doing other things because when we arrived at 7pm as instructed, dinner wasn't ready.*

*"I'm so sorry we're making you wait," Ayanna apologized. "It's Dallas's fault." I moved my eyes over to Dallas to see him folding his lips into his mouth to keep from laughing. Ayanna approached a boiling pot of hot water to drop a fist full of pasta into the pot. "He has a hard time knowing how to wait for things."*

*Dallas walked up to her and whispered something into her ear, and she giggled while bumping him away. When we arrived and Ayanna greeted me, I noticed the trail of hickeys on her neck. If I was a blushing woman with skin visible enough to see me blushing, I would have. I think I know exactly what the things were that she was talking about, that Dallas had a hard time waiting for.*

*I'd said very little between the time we arrived and until the two of them plated Simeon and my food. Every so often, I'd glance over at Simeon to see him looking my way, trying to get a good read on what I thought about them. Much like me getting to know Simeon as the businessman, he had to get to know me as a crisis management expert. I did this with all my new clients. Whether they were movie stars or CEOs. I'd go to wherever they felt the most comfortable, and I'd watch them. People reveal so much about themselves once their guards are down, and they are simply being themselves. Scandals get blown out of proportion, and gossipmongers can be ruthless the most towards people they didn't feel were real people with real feelings, just like them. So, I watched my clients, looking for that one relatable thing that made them human, flesh and blood, and most of all, authentic. Because we would use that one relatable thing to build trust. Once you had trust, you had people who would root for you, and if they rooted for you, they fought for you in your absence. And I made that the focus when implementing crisis management. Not all crises were the same. So, I never handled them the same way. I enjoyed implementing unorthodox strategies because they always worked out in my clients' favor.*

*For Ayanna and Dallas, after watching them joke and play around with each other in the kitchen as they prepared their meal, forgetting that Simeon and I were there at some moments, I knew exactly how we were going to help them regain the trust Simeon feared they lost because of the scandal and that could jeopardize Dallas's image. "I adore them," I whispered to Simeon once dinner was over and Ayanna and Dallas collected our plates, busying themselves in the kitchen again. "We're gonna lean on that adoration, 'cause I know I'm not the only one to be enamored by them." I winked. "And I won't be the last."*

I was still putting together a plan. Before stepping out to satisfy the real estate agent's appointment, I'd completed my research and coverage tracking - monitoring the little but still relevant media coverage of Ayanna and Dallas from the announcement of their relationship to the scandal that arose a few weeks prior. I still had some details to organize regarding our strategy, but I was very confident about my plan for them. For now, I wanted this apartment we were looking at. It would be the perfect place for me to call home as I continued to work on their crisis.

"I'll take it," I said to Manuel. "What's our next step?"

"Perfect!" Manuel smiled big and clapped once. "The apartment needs a few repairs and quick renovations. But it will be ready for you to move in three weeks from now."

I blinked hard. "Three weeks?"

Manuel frowned. "Is that not good?"

"It's not good, Manuel." I sighed, my eyes roaming around the space again. "It's not good at all. For me at least."

We hadn't spent many days searching for a place for me, but I really wasn't looking to look anymore. And I wanted out of the hotel.

"Manuel," Simeon voiced behind us. "Can you give Eryn and me one moment, please?"

"Yes. Of course." Manuel nodded with a smile. "Take all the time you need. I'll be out in the living room when you're ready for me."

"Thank you," Simeon replied.

"Oh, he speaks," I snarked, rolling my eyes. "I didn't know you were present with your eyes glued to your phone's screen the whole time you've been here. Busy much?"

"I was completing something," Simeon replied, dropping his phone into the back pocket of his white shorts. The man was killing me softly with his style. He could dress it up or dress it down and he wore it so damn well. It was the weekend, so he was in his casual mood. Light linen top, the buttons from his neck to the top of his chest undone. On his feet, he wore dark brown sandals with a contoured cork for footbeds. Toes looked great, which was a priority for me with men. Simeon really was fine from head to toe.

"You can stay with me until the apartment is ready." That snapped me out of my lustful daze. Simeon had brought me to Ayanna and Dallas and had taken me out to dinner since that night. But he has not once invited me to his home. Which wasn't too out of the norm. Even when we were in college, he never invited me to his dorm room. Not to sleep, at least. To study, to pick up some clothes so he could spend the night in *my* dorm, yes. But to stay in a space that belonged to Simeon King for more than a few hours? Never. So, imagine the shock I wore on my face hearing those words come out of his mouth.

"Did I just hear what I just heard?" I asked.

He scoffed a laugh and dropped his head briefly.

"Are you inviting me to your palace, Mr. King?" I joked. "Am I that worthy?"

He folded his brawny arms over his chest. "I need you in a clear head space. You've expressed more than once how much you're tired of staying in your hotel. And I need you as comfortable as possible working on this Ayanna and Dallas situation. So..." He shrugged, releasing his arms from their fold. "If offering you a place to stay in the interim of them getting the apartment that you love ready, I can cope with three weeks."

"Cope?"

"I used the correct word," he threw back. "Considering how messy you can be and how frustrating it is to me, coping is *exactly* what I'll need to do."

I made a shrugging expression with the sides of my lips. "Aw, touché."

"Dallas and Ayanna's wedding in New York is in three weeks, and by the time we get back from it, your place will be ready. It'll be perfect timing."

"We?" I blinked twice. "I'm going to the wedding? I didn't realize I was attending their wedding."

He nodded. "We're going to need you at their wedding."

"I hope I'm not impeding on your date." I didn't really care, but then again, I did? Simeon hadn't disclosed if he was seeing anybody. I didn't either. But a part of me was curious if he was seeing anyone.

*I shouldn't have been curious, though, right?*

"I'm a groomsman, so no, you will not be impeding on my date," he informed. "I have no date." He shook his head next. "But let's get back on topic. What do you say? You stay with me until the apartment is ready, and you move in after we return from the wedding in New York. Does this work for you?"

Living with Simeon for three entire weeks. Seeing him every day when only a week ago, I wouldn't take his phone call. If nothing else, the experience would be interesting. Hopefully, we could survive it.

"It works," I confirmed. "Let's do that, roomie."

# TWELVE

## SIMEON

I heard Eryn stepping up the stairs that led to the private guest bedroom she would stay in for the next few weeks. After viewing the sixth apartment in her search for a place to live temporarily in Oakland, and receiving the news that the apartment she liked would be ready for her to move in, in three weeks, Eryn and I agreed she could stay with me during that time until the apartment was ready. That was the day prior. We had dinner after parting with the real estate agent, and she returned to her hotel for one last night. And tonight was her first night here at my place.

My condo had two bedrooms. When I first moved in, I considered turning the second bedroom into an office but decided against it, opting to turn my sun-lit bonus loft space upstairs into my home office.

"What scent is blowing through my room downstairs?"

*Her room.* I should've cringed at her laying stake to the space, but something about her claiming it as hers made me smile to myself. I kind of liked the sound of that coming from her. *I shouldn't like the sound of that coming from her.*

"Sandalwood, vanilla, and amber," I replied.

"*Mmm*," she moaned. That simple, innocent expression made me firm a little in my black shorts. "It smells amazing. This *place* is amazing."

"Thank you."

"The city skyline view," she said, approaching the door to the patio. My eyes instinctively fell to her round ass, swaying as she moved in her cream lounge dress. "These oversized windows. This is the three-level loft-like condo I would've loved to move into in L.A. when Everett and I first arrived there."

I dragged my gaze away from her and forced myself to concentrate on the salad bowl in front of me, scattering chopped tomatoes over the spring lettuce.

We'd been going out for dinner these past few nights since Eryn flew in with me from New York, but tonight I wanted to make something. I knew she loved pasta, so I made a simple red sauce and linguine meal with garlic bread and tossed salad as sides. It was easy enough for me to prepare without burning it.

"Textured tile floors. Clean as fuck, of course," she added, walking up to the island that divided the dining area from the kitchen. "This is a real bachelor's palace, Mr. King. It's *so* you."

I threw a glance over my shoulder. "I hope that's a good thing."

"Wouldn't you like to know?"

I barked a laugh, and she giggled.

She said, "Your clients must be paying you top dollar to afford a place like this on the busier side of Oakland."

I moved to the sauce in the pot to turn off the burner under it. "I don't only make my money off my clients," I revealed. "Too much of a risk. It only takes one injury or a health problem to arise for their careers to stall or worse end. I don't like putting that kind of pressure on them either. Greed clouds good judgment."

"Okay..."

"I'm a silent partner in a few enterprises," I revealed. "I have many outside investments. They help and make up most of my income."

"Outside investments?" Eryn took a seat on one of the island stools. Visibly interested. "Such as?"

"Well." I turned to face her. "I have an investment in my parents' farm, of course. I broker deals with supermarkets in the city to supply those markets with the fruits and vegetables grown on our soil. We supply milk, a variety of cheeses, and other artisan dairy products that have become in high demand, especially because it's organic and our cows are grass-fed. Then there's my investment in Dallas's nutritional products brand, which I know is going to blow up, so I absolutely wanted in on that."

"*Mm-hmm...*" She nodded.

"I also have an investment in a black-owned diaper company." I smiled at that one. "Pretty proud of that one because I know their reusable and disposable diapers will always be in demand. People are *always* having babies, right?"

Our eyes locked across the island for a moment before she blinked her eyes, breaking eye contact. She swallowed hard, then ran her fingers through her long hair and looked away for a moment. "That's what I hear."

I stared for a moment longer before I cleared my throat. My attempt at trying to rid the awkward energy between us. "But... there's a business I'm a silent partner in that's far more lucrative than the diaper company, if you can believe that."

"And that one is?"

"A sex toy brand."

That got her attention. "Come again?"

I smirked. "Pun intended?"

She hollered a laugh, and I was grateful to see her mood get back in order. "A sex toy company?" She leaned forward to rest her elbows on the island. "Your most lucrative investment is in a sex toy company?"

I nodded. "Good-Vibes. It's black-owned. They specialize in velvety soft, brown and black skin tone vibrators."

"Vibrators?"

I turned to one of my kitchen drawers and pulled out a tiny, slim matte black box. I placed the box on the island and slid it over to her. Eryn didn't hesitate to open the box. That's what I've always admired about her. Her curiosity, her openness to whatever. She never hesitated to do things out of her norm. And that was both a good and bad thing. Unfortunately, I got to know the bad side of that lack of hesitation to execute.

"Oh, wow," she expressed, pulling out the onyx black vibrator that fit into her palm. She twisted the tiny cylindrical, slightly tapered form unit between her fingers to get a better look at it. "It's so soft and weightless."

"It's a patented silicone-encasement. Unlike any other. An ergonomic design that's eco-friendly and body-safe, very California."

She glanced up at me and then back down at the box. "It even comes with its own satin bag and everything. Okay! This is classy. I see you."

I chuckled.

"So, you just have sex toys lying around your kitchen like some kind of 90s pornstar?" she asked.

I laughed this time. "I got it from a launch party a few months ago. I left it in the drawer because it was the closest thing to me when I got back from the event."

"Hmph." Eryn returned the toy to its box and was closing the lid when she asked, "Used this on anyone yet?"

She and I shared a look.

"No." I shook my head. "This one is brand new and untouched."

"Why?" Eryn asked next.

"Why is it untouched?"

"No, sorry." She giggled. "Why would you invest in a sex toy brand of all things?"

"Simply because it's a smart investment, Eryn."

She wrinkled her brows.

"The market for high-end adult toys is booming, and Good-Vibes is at the forefront of innovation and quality." I shrugged. "Plus, it's about more than just money. These products promote sexual health and well-being, which is important. And let's be real, normalizing conversations around pleasure and removing the stigma is something I believe in.

Diversifying my portfolio with a reputable and forward-thinking company just made sense."

"Okay." Eryn made a shrugging motion with the corners of her mouth. "Points were made."

"They say sex sells, but it's the promise of pleasure that's really the appeal," I added. "We all look for some form of pleasure. It's a feeling that never gets old and that we seek out in good and bad times. It'll always be in demand, which is another reason I jumped at the first chance I got to be a silent partner in Good-Vibes."

She arched a brow then slid the closed box back to me.

I told her, "Keep it."

"Huh?"

"Keep it," I repeated, turning to my cabinets to pull down a couple of plates so we could start eating. "Consider it my welcome to Oakland gift to you."

"My fingers work fine, thank you."

"I guarantee if you played with that toy, you'd disagree."

"How would you know?" She asked as I plated the food. "Tried it on yourself?"

I turned to look at her over my shoulder. "The reviews speak for themselves, and there are a lot of happy Good-Vibes customers."

She pursed her lips to keep from smiling.

———

It was an hour after dinner, and I'd retired to my bedroom. It was still relatively early, 9:30pm, but I was having the hardest time going to sleep. I'd powered on my remote-controlled tower scent dispenser. Scents of oud wood, sandalwood, and leather fragranced the room. Normally, just me lying in bed with my room smelling cozy, and my sound machine playing the sounds of crashing ocean waves, I'd drift off to sleep. I had to be at the office bright and early the next day, but sleep was escaping me. I could feel her energy. Even though Eryn was in the private guest bedroom downstairs on the lower level of my condo, I could still sense her. And only the thought she was here, in my home, in my space, only two staircases between us, was making my dick hard.

"Dammit," I said, sitting up in bed. I could've jerked off, but that would only serve as a prelude to me wanting more than that. So, I got out of bed, pulled on a simple blue tee, black trousers, and canvas sneakers and stepped out, sending a text on my way to my BMW.

Even as I drove on the road, my mind was on Eryn. I wondered if I should have told her I was leaving the condo for a couple of hours. Wondered if she was okay down there on her first night. I shook my head, trying to shake those thoughts loose because I shouldn't have been thinking any of that. Not even about her. That's why I was driving to Hazel's house a few miles from me. When I texted her, asking if she would be interested in having some company over, she immediately replied with yes. This was our hour anyway. When we liked to link up. Like I said, we'd been seeing each other for over a year and had only gone out once. Twice, if you include the dinner, we had three weeks ago, the one I had to prematurely leave.

So, I knew when I texted her, asking if I could stop by, she'd welcome me with open arms. And open arms, she did. As soon as I parked my car in her driveway and approached her front door, she was there to greet me in a short silk white robe that showed off her beautiful dark brown legs. I forced a smile, realizing in that moment I probably should have been clear about why I was stopping by. She wrapped her arms around me the moment I stepped inside, hands rubbing my chest next as she balanced herself on the arches of her feet to kiss me. And before returning to Oakland, before reuniting with Eryn, this would have been par for the course. We wasted no time. Got right to it the moment I stepped through her door. But I didn't come to her place that night for any of that. I should've told her that before arriving.

I gently wrapped my hands around her forearms, encouraging her to let go. "Can we... *uh*... just... talk tonight?" I asked as I placed her arms down at her sides.

"Excuse me?" She wore her hair up in a high bun, face clear of makeup. This was Hazel's usual look for nights like this whenever I stopped by.

"I actually didn't ask to come here for that," I admitted. "I really just wanted to stop by, enjoy your company, and just talk."

"Just... *talk*?" She arched a brow. "You want to talk?"

"Yeah."

"Yeah, no," she countered.

I tilted my head to one side, and she scoffed a laugh. "Wh-what?"

"Let me get this straight." She folded her arms over her chest. "I haven't heard from you since you up and left the restaurant after getting the alert about Dallas and Ayanna. The next time I hear from you, it's when you text me asking to come over, not for sex, but to talk?"

I blinked in response.

"And in this talk we're about to have, are you going to give me a comment regarding Dallas and Ayanna's growing scandal, or...?"

"Hazel, you know I will not give you any comment about that."

"Then I *know* you're about to get the hell up out of my house."

"Huh?"

"*Huh*, nothing. You must be kidding me." Hazel poked me in the chest. "I'm going to have *the* fine-ass Simeon King in *my* home, and he's not just here to deny me his dick—*especially* when he's so damn well-endowed, I have to add..."

*A dick she never could take all of, and runs from every time I get her in my grip. But I admired her tenacity with always trying to.*

"...but," she continued, "he's *also* not going to give me the one thing that would get me promoted at my job which is an exclusive comment from a source close to the couple everyone won't shut the hell up about?"

"I mean... when you put it like that..."

"Oh, *uh-uh*." Hazel was turning me with force towards her front door and pushing me out of it a cool second later. "I know when I'm being friend-zoned."

"Friend? No," I insisted. "I'm not friend-zoning you."

"Yeah, okay, look, call me when you're ready to give me either dick or a comment. Got it?"

"Damn!" I exclaimed. "Hazel—"

"No." She shook her head, folding her arms over her chest. "First, it's *'I just want to talk'*. Then it will be you just wanting to hang out and I'm not falling for that okey-doke. Dinner the other night was fine. It showed that we were heading in a good direction. But you come here at damn near ten at night only to *talk*? No. I don't just talk to men, Simeon." She pointed at me. "I fuck them. You got that? Goodnight."

She slammed her door a second later, making me step back to keep from getting hit upside the head. And instead of upsetting me, our whole interaction tonight only made me snort a laugh. "Wow." I chuckled as I turned to step away from her front door and to walk to my car. "Tell me how you really feel." I was not expecting that.

But like I said, Hazel was bold and audacious, and I was drawn to women like that. One of them was in my home right now. Eryn was also why I didn't go straight home after leaving Hazel's. I spent most of the night driving around Oakland until my eyes got so heavy that all I could think about was getting to bed—and not getting into Eryn's.

As the cool Oakland night air blew in through my open car windows, I questioned, with as heavy as Eryn was on my mind, could I keep it strictly business after all, like I promised her I would? Seeing her in my environment was not as bad as I initially expected it to be. Granted, it was only the first night, but seeing Eryn in my setting, making herself comfortable, satisfied a forgotten wish in me.

I ran my hand down my face and shook my head. Because I really needed to keep things, including my relationship or lack thereof, out of my head and my mind centered on Dallas and Ayanna and their situation. And nothing else.

"Absolutely nothing else," I added out loud.

Because I can't do that with her ever again, anyway. Not even a little.

# THIRTEEN

## ERYN

I heard the click of Simeon's front door as he closed it while leaving. This was my second night in his beautiful loft-like condo, and another night of him leaving me alone in it. The night before, my first night, he didn't let me know he was stepping out. Not that it made a difference since I had no intentions of speaking with him past us having dinner. But it surprised me to hear the front door close. When I reached the main floor, I arrived just in time to see him in the driver's seat of his blue BMW, pulling out of the parking lot.

Tonight, though, he let me know he was leaving his condo for the evening and if I needed anything, that I could call him. Which I wouldn't. When he left the night before, I figured he was going to see a woman. It was late. Very few things stayed open at that hour besides bars and women's legs, as my elderly next-door neighbor in Bed-Stuy used to say when I was younger amongst her friends, when she thought I wasn't listening.

Wherever he went, he didn't stay there overnight. Because he was back home in time to place a cup of perfectly hot and sweetened coffee on my night table, waiting for me when I got up. Simeon used to get me coffee every morning when we were in college. Whether we spent the night together in my dorm room or apart with me in mine and him in his, he was always either at my door or placing a paper cup of coffee on my night table.

Always coffee on my night table brought to me by Simeon. Only this time it was *his* night table… for the next three weeks at least. Simeon's guest bedroom appeared untouched and never slept in. The colors in the bedroom were neutral, with large windows to enjoy the view, even as a guest. The room's scent was honestly one of its best features, and that's saying a lot because the room was beautiful. My sleep last night was amazing, and I was anticipating getting a repeat of that snooze, when sleep arrived tonight.

I wasn't tired, though. I don't know if it was because I was in a new city or because I had some new fire to put out, but I was feeling energized by the plans I couldn't wait to execute in this whole Dallas and Ayanna scandal. Simeon informed me he had a few of his interns managing both Dallas and Ayanna's socials. I had a plan that would have them back in control of their social media without their boundaries being tested by gossipmongers. My plan would have us using those people who loved to spread gossip to do most of the work.

To get a good handle of Dallas and Ayanna's social media presence through the voices of the people who were watching them, I logged onto social media to do a quick search. I was all business for the first fifteen minutes of research. But then my nosy ass wanted to see what Opal Sands was up to. The team I managed also took care of Opal Sands' social media presence. I had the interns at the firm walk around the office, snapping random pictures of the faces behind the scenes. And when I tapped into Opal Sands' page, I saw a lot of those familiar photos. All except one. This one was new. And it was of Richard and Brielle. I clenched my teeth, tightening my jaw. The post was announcing Brielle as Opal Sands' new COO.

That wicked bitch was smiling so damn big I could see her back molars from the front. But regardless of how big she smiled; Richard smiled bigger. "I don't remember him ever smiling that damn big with me," I mumbled. Why did I even care? I didn't. But I cared enough to tap on Brielle's handle that was tagged in the post. The moment I arrived on her page, I saw another photo of her and Richard as her latest upload. This one was not in an office setting. It was of them out to eat, dressed casually, and holding hands. The caption - "When you were only starting your new day at your new company, but life had other new plans for you."

"These motherfuckers," I sneered. I really shouldn't have given a shit, but a minor part of me did. I never saw a future with Richard. Like I said, he was simply a pawn in my strategy to get to the top at Opal Sands. But we had *something*. And after over four years of only fucking, some feelings would have had to surface between us, right? At least they did with me. Which was why it hurt a little that he didn't let me know Opal Sands' plans to enter buying agreements beforehand. Looking at things now, I wouldn't have been able to stop anything. But I would have liked to be prepared for what inevitably happened.

Seeing that, seeing them - Richard and Brielle - made it all the clearer to me why I would have to keep things business between Simeon and I. It seems even with our past, there was still something there between us that gave me butterflies every time we were in the same room.

"Nope." I shook my head. "Uh-uh, stop it right now, Eryn." Because one thing I was not about to do was to fall for Simeon again. Not after everything. Nothing good would come out of the two of us, making it anything but business between us. Especially if we haven't had the talk, addressing the enormous elephant in the room. Our breakup and the reason behind it. And how much he probably blames me for ruining our relationship.

———

"Hey, guys," I said over my smartphone. "I wanted to have a quick phone call with you two. Do you have a moment?" Simeon stood only feet away, leaning his back against his kitchen's wall. I'd just dialed up

Ayanna's phone and asked her if Dallas was nearby. After completing my rapid assessment the night before and detailing in a twenty-page strategy outline I planned to share with Simeon's PR team at King Sports Management, I wanted to let the future Roques know what I wanted to work on with them. Their social media management. Where the people who we needed talking spent most of their time.

"Yeah, we definitely have a moment," Ayanna confirmed first. "Dallas just walked in."

"What's up, Eryn?" Dallas said from afar.

"Hey, Dallas," I greeted. "Okay, cool, this will be super quick," I started. "So, I've completed a strategy outline that I hope I can share with you soon face-to-face. For now, though, I think we should start with your social media management strategy, since that seems to be where most of the conversation is being held."

"Got it," Ayanna said. "I'll do anything. Please know that."

"Perfect," I stated. "And I'm happy you said that, Ayanna, because I'm gonna need you to be the *most* present online. More than you've ever been. Starting tomorrow."

"Okay..." she replied.

"Simeon told me he put his interns on the job of managing your social accounts. I reached out to them and asked them to go through all your posts and to turn your comments off. They will keep your comments off until we can get a better handle over everything."

Simeon nodded across from me.

"From now and until at least two days before your wedding, I think it would be a great idea for you to be transparent with your wedding plans and bliss." I smiled. "I'm talking post photos of your nails on your left hand so they can get a view of that gorgeous engagement ring. Post a photo of your wedding shoes. Show what flowers you guys are considering. You smiling and in a caption saying you're excited about your impending wedding day. Ooey, gooey, sugary bride-to-be excitement through and through, but in your voice and your style. Authentically, okay?"

"Oooh, okay!" She gushed. "I'm with it."

"Anything wedding, anything that shows you and Dallas working as a team, living your best lives as if this whole thing with Dallas's brother never happened is our angle." I nodded. "You two are beautiful individually, but together? You are the envy of the town, especially right now. Show that unity you two are still maintaining. You're getting married, and you're thrilled about it, despite the bullshit, which you don't see because you're so high on cloud nine, it's beneath you. What's happening outside of you two does not exist. Show them how above this shit you are."

Simeon made a shrugging motion with the side of his lips.

"Between us four..." I glanced up at Simeon, "I don't think you need to sell your relationship to anyone. You two are in love, and it shows. Even I'm a new fan of it, and couple stuff annoys me."

Ayanna and Dallas laughed.

"But since they want to talk, let's bombard them with happy moments of you simply living your best life... with the comments off. Let's let them enjoy the highlight reel online, without giving them access to give any feedback. I'll continue to enforce with the team to keep your comments off and to remove any negative comments because we don't need none of that."

"At all," Ayanna echoed with a giggle.

"Let's start there, and whenever we meet up again," I explained, "We can discuss the next steps. I'm still ironing out the details, but I think we have a solid bounce back in the works, you two."

"You're a godsend, for real," Dallas commented. "Simeon was so right about you."

I looked up at Simeon again to see him smiling at me.

"He gets it right sometimes, I guess." I smirked.

"Don't play my big homey like that." Dallas laughed. "Simeon gets it right *all* the time. Aight?"

"I like you, Dallas, so I won't argue with you, okay?"

Ayanna and Dallas's humor echoed through the phone. I even got a chuckle out of Simeon.

"That's it for now, y'all," I said. "We'll talk soon."

As soon as I ended the call, Simeon began to applaud, clapping his hands.

"Just like I knew it," he started. "You gave us something to work with."

"It's a little somethin', somethin' but *something* to start with. They're stunning." I started gathering the loose typed pages I had sprawled all over Simeon's island. "And the public knows it too. That's why they fell in love with them to begin with. They've just forgotten that very important fact because of Dallas's brother and his ill attempt to tarnish their love's image. We'll have that nipped in the bud before Ayanna and Dallas's name in ink has the chance to dry on their marriage license."

"Like music to my ears," Simeon commented on an exhale. "Anyway, I'm about to head out for a bit."

For a third night in a row, Simeon was planning to leave his own home. I had said nothing about it, but tonight I couldn't keep quiet anymore.

"Running off to go chill with your boo, again?"

He couldn't hide his sly grin if he tried.

"That's where you're running off to for the third night in a row, right?"

"If my boo is my client who insists I listen to some of the rap songs, he's recorded at a studio a few miles from here, then sure." He smirked. "I'm running off to see my boo."

I blinked in response.

"He thinks he's the next Rakim." He threw his hands up in front of him. "I've heard some of his material, and I don't see it, but I'm going to go anyway to show support. He's having a little listening party, and I'm his agent and his guiding light. So, I must be there."

"And the other two nights? You were spending them at the studio too?"

I bit my tongue the moment the questions rolled off it. I knew better. *What the hell was even that, Eryn?*

"Goodnight, Eryn." Simeon bit his bottom lip and smiled as he backed away. "See you in the morning."

I sucked my teeth at myself as I watched him walk out, all sexy-like, and close the door behind him.

*Girl, why do you even care where that man is putting his dick?*

Because it's a big dick.

"*Ugh!*" I stood to my feet and made my way to the guest bedroom with the typed papers cradled in my arms and that question on repeat in my mental space. The question was on my mind as I showered. Even heavier on my mind when I brushed my teeth and climbed into bed after I was done.

The thought of Simeon with another woman went from kind of annoying and menacing to encouraging my imagination to fill in the blanks. Whoever she was, she was the luckiest woman in this galaxy. Because sex with Simeon wasn't just sex. It was an outer space voyage. An all-night soiree at the next planet over. Sometimes I think I was in such a depressive slump after we broke up when he left, because I wasn't only mourning the death of our relationship.

I was lamenting the loss of his touch, his intimacy.

Translation: that dick.

The moment my thoughts wandered to the allure of his body, a vivid memory surged, igniting a tingling ache that sent my hand sneaking beneath the covers to relieve. I could execute the move, but I really didn't feel like doing the work. So, my eyes moved before I did to the box that stored the vibrator. The one he gave to me my first night in his condo.

Without a second thought, I was out of the bed with the vibrator in my open hand, walking the tiny black toy to the en suite so I could wash it with a little soap and water. With it cleaned to my heart's content and dried off, I laid in bed on my back and pushed one of the two soft buttons at the center of the vibrator which activated the toy instantly. It buzzed in my hand, making me bite my lip at the pulsing it was doing.

I've owned a sex toy or two. I'd order one when the nights felt a little too lonely and I needed a quick fix. But they never quite compared to the feeling of a real oral touch down there. Still, they made for a decent substitute. I slid the device under the covers, placed the smooth, rounded tip between my lower lips, and gasped at the sensation. It didn't take long for me to find my rhythm. I closed my eyes, and without much effort, Simeon's face came to mind—specifically, the way he looked when we made love. And when I say made love, I mean it with every fiber of my being. Because what we had was real, created from scratch, and nothing could ever compare or substitute for it.

My body trembled when the silicone tip of the toy buzzed against my bundle of nerves. Simeon was every bit of a gentleman on the bed as much as he was off it. He took his time, never in a rush. Not the type to bang a headboard against a wall. Not with that monster between his two long legs. Simeon was an Usher Raymond song in human form, always taking things nice and slow without fail. And as a woman who swore she liked it rough, Simeon's brand of nice and slow always gave me multiple orgasms that took over my entire body. In slow, undulating successions, the sensations sent me to the brink of insanity—or at least that's how they felt. They gave my proud ass no choice but to surrender to his power over me.

Simeon had a big dick. And when I say big, I mean extra-large. No exaggeration. And while a lot of women's mouths water at the thought of having a big dick, it was truly an acquired taste.

I pushed the crown of my head into my pillow and folded my lips into my mouth to suppress my moaning. The way he'd slowly drive himself into me with such patience and care every single time. It was decadent torture. Because Simeon didn't fuck. He identified his target and drilled, slowly, never letting up off it, not even for a second to catch a breath, only stopping when I was a shaking, mumbling, and sweating ass mess.

And he had a knack for talking me through my orgasms.

*God.*

Whispering encouragements when he wasn't moaning, moaning when he wasn't whispering. Body to body was his preference. If the sex position didn't have us close enough that air couldn't pass between us, we weren't making love. It was as if he wanted no chance for us to disconnect below the waist. He wanted us joined between our thighs until I erupted. And that dick always felt too much to take, but I'd never show it. I'd take it. Every width and length of it. Because my ego would never allow me to cower in front of him and from experience I knew the pain mixed with pleasure would morph into only pleasure if I withstood the pressure long enough. But not just any pleasure. Indulgent pleasure that made my whole body vibrate, and my mind transport me to another mental plane. It felt like we were soaring through the cosmos in a spaceship built for two, just us, adrift in the infinite, wrapped in the electric quiet of the universe.

Every. Single. Time.

I hollered a moan into the room, slapping my hand over my mouth to muffle the noise. My chest rose and fell as I slid the vibrator off my clit and allowed it and my arms to fall at my sides.

The release was decent, but nothing—absolutely nothing—could ever compare to Simeon.

# FOURTEEN

**SIMEON**

I stopped in front of Eryn's door and knocked. It was a few minutes after 7am, and my plans were to be at KSM's office in an hour. Since staying with me in Oakland, Eryn seemed to have kicked her late sleeping habit. This gave me an opportunity to know when she would be awake so I could leave a cup of coffee on the guest bedroom's night table so it would be ready for her to drink.

Ask me why I assigned myself the role of being her personal barista, and I wouldn't know how to answer it. Only that I genuinely enjoyed getting her coffee. I knocked again but didn't get an answer. It was our second semester in college when I figured out how the barista at our school cafe at Langston U could make the perfect cup of coffee, as said by Eryn. Every day when we'd stop there, and Eryn would order her usual black coffee with a little cream and a little sugar, the barista would hand the paper cup to Eryn and Eryn would always moan when she took a sip.

And that moan… *shit*.

If someone told me Eryn's moan was at the top of the steepest, most dangerous hill, and the only way to hear it again was to climb it, I'd scale that hill barefoot without hesitation—just to hear it one more time.

So, one morning, when I told Eryn I'd get her a cup, I asked the barista what she did to get the coffee to be the perfect temperature. And she shared she made it extra hot, then dropped two ice cubes in it to cool it down quickly but to still maintain most of its heat.

I locked that into memory and never forgot it, making sure to duplicate the process so I could hear that moan she always made after she took her first sip. Privately.

When I hadn't gotten an answer after the second knock, I turned the doorknob and nuzzled the door open.

First, I spotted the empty unmade bed and then I heard the flow of shower water in the guest bedroom's en suite. So, I entered the room, deciding to leave the mug of coffee on her table before leaving for the office.

In Eryn fashion, she left the guest room disorganized. There were loose papers sprawled along the surface of the mirrored dresser, empty drink glasses, and like I said, the bed messy and unmade.

I lifted my wrist and shook it a little to turn my chronograph to check the time. I enjoyed being the first one in at KSM on the days I came into work. It was nice to check up on how things were running when my team didn't know I'd be there. KSM opened in half an hour. At least that was when my first team member on my legal team arrived. And I should've got going after dropping off the coffee, but her damn bed.

It looked messy, the bedding extremely wrinkled, and not a big deal if I knew Eryn would make it when she finished showering. But I knew she wouldn't. She hadn't made the bed not once since she's arrived. I glanced down at myself. Fully dressed in a light-colored button-down shirt, slightly unbuttoned, and tucked into a pair of dark trousers. I was ready to go. Brown leather loafers were already on my feet and everything. But it's like Eryn said. I'm a neat freak and I couldn't take another day seeing that damn bed unmade.

I placed the mug down on the night table and grabbed at one end of the summer down comforter that covered the mattress. The moment I shook the covers out, a tiny black object went flying across the mattress. I peeked over the bedding to see the onyx black Good-Vibes vibrator lying near the edge of the bed.

I scoffed a laugh when I glimpsed the toy. My eyes, on their own, moved to where the shower water made cascading sounds on the other side of the en suite's door.

I stretched my arm across the mattress lifted and relocated the toy on her night table and continued to make the bed. And when I finished making the bed, my ass should've left, right? I was already in her room, as she called it, longer than I had planned.

But... curiosity got the best of me.

I picked up the vibrator and stared at it for a moment.

Imagining for a second what she looked like using it. Positive she looked damn good.

Remembering in that instance the beautiful sex faces and sounds Eryn used to make whenever I was inside of her.

When I say Eryn was perfect for me, I mean that in every sense of the word. She had a personality that was interesting and exciting. *So* exciting. Eryn was every bit of the city girl, I always found myself fascinated by living on a farm in Western New York. But the thing I loved as much was her ability to take all of me boldly and like it was nothing to do it.

See, in my experience, sex was never a priority because it always came with work I didn't want to do.

Work ethic was important to me and tackling impossible tasks is my forte and something I don't shy away from. But with sex, while I will do the work, resorting to giving only a little of myself because I know a woman can't truly take all of me, is, well, unfulfilling and makes me not want to do it at all.

What I mean is that since my first time with a woman, I realized my dick was bigger than average.

And while that might do a lot for the male ego, actually working with what *I* got can be daunting, depending on who I'm working with it on.

Women would always get excited when I'd tell them I might be too much for them. After getting disappointed one too many times, I'd stopped telling them that and took my time with moving my relationship with them to the next level. Toward anything, something physical.

Because every time I'd tell them, and they'd get excited, when it came time to show them what I meant, they'd realize I wasn't lying about my size. But them wanting that? A big dick? That was the lie.

A lot of the women I'd bed would cringe or repeatedly exhale sounds of discomfort no matter how slow I went.

And I moved slowly for that reason, never in a rush, never relying on a quick pace to please a woman. The work I did with what I had was more than enough.

But few could really handle it.

Even with Hazel, who swore my dick was the thing she loved. Considering her reaction the day I stopped by to talk, you'd think she liked to take control in bed, but she didn't. Often, she cowered at the dick I served her. Holding her hand against my stomach or asking me to wait or give her a moment to adjust to my girth, which she never could do. And honestly, I empathized and was sensitive to her feelings; I wholeheartedly understood. But unfortunately, it ruined the moment. It distracted me and had sex feeling like a chore and something to simply finish with, and be relieved of the task. That meant me focusing on only my nut, which took the excitement out of sex for me. But that's what I'd resort to because I just wanted to get it over with whenever women like Hazel grew visibly uncomfortable. The stretch was too much to bear because the idea of being with a big dick is more appealing than actually being with a big dick.

Never Eryn, though.

She took it like a champ, mostly because of her ego and her refusal to show me I was way too much for her. And honestly? Even her rebelling against admitting defeat, her persistence in conquering me, was a major turn on for me.

I took pleasure in watching her surrender. There was a profound strength in her letting go, in her handing over control to me.

If my size was ever something that was too much, she rarely showed it. And when she stuck with the act long enough, the results of the time and effort invested showed in her face and in her eyes, treating us both to one of the most amazing sights, if not *the* most amazing sights I've ever beheld.

Eryn has been the *only* woman I've ever been able to lose myself with in the act. I missed that terribly. I missed both sex with her and losing myself inside of her. I missed it a lot.

So much so, I lifted the vibrator to place on the made-up bed and instead of doing only that; I brought the cylindrical toy to my nose and took a whiff of her scent on it.

It was light, barely there, but I could pick up the traces of her pussy's sweet essence from anywhere, blindfolded.

I inhaled it again when I heard the shower water in her bathroom shut off. Licked my lips and palmed my erection as I placed the vibrator at the center of her made-up bed and swaggered out of the room before she could see me.

Being a fucking creep. I know.

I snickered to myself as I made my way up the stairs to leave my condo.

God, I missed her scent. It pleased me to know it hadn't changed.

I was even more pleased she used the vibrator I gave her... and I really shouldn't have allowed that thought to linger.

But it did.

And it found a corner in my mind to get comfortable in.

I was fucked from that very moment.

Because it was then things stopped being only business for me.

# Fifteen

**ERYN**

I pulled open the bathroom door to get some of the steam from my shower out. It was day four, and I was feeling really proud of myself for getting out of bed at the same early time as the day prior.

I hated to admit it, but coming to Oakland as insisted by Simeon might have been one of the best things I could have done.

I was feeling a little more like myself, working on a strategy to tackle the Ayanna and Dallas situation, and I was very confident that what I came up with would work.

After brushing my teeth and washing my face, I redid and folded down the towel I wrapped around myself when I left the shower and stepped out of the bathroom.

I smelled the coffee before I saw it.

And I couldn't help my face from warming up.

I could get used to this.

In a crazy way, I could get used to whatever this was that Simeon and I had going on.

Even though his nightly disappearances in Oakland annoyed me a little, his thoughtfulness in always leaving a mug of coffee on my nightstand for when I woke up was a love language I had forgotten we shared.

When I saw the coffee, I also saw the made-up bed, and that made me laugh, because I knew his ass would crack.

It surprised me when he hadn't made the bed my first morning in his home. Simeon was the most orderly man I'd ever met, and I'd met plenty since him. None of them compared to how tidy that man was, though.

Him waiting so long to make the bed wasn't the only thing to surprise me that morning.

The sight of the onyx vibrator he gave me on my first night here nearly floored me. There it was, resting on the neatly made bed, blatantly in view.

"Oh, no." I closed my eyes and tucked my lips into my mouth to swallow back my laugh.

I snatched up the toy and dropped it into the side table drawer. I don't even know why I had that reaction.

Because I didn't want him knowing I used it, that's why. And him having that knowledge had me feeling a little embarrassed...

And a little turned on?

I smiled slyly as I imagined what his face must've looked like when he found it. The gentleman he was, he probably wouldn't say anything about it when we saw each other later.

Simeon had told me, if I wanted to, I could work from an office at KSM, but I declined. His patio had two seating areas. One under a pergola that offered shading from the sun, and the other, lounge couches right beneath the sun to catch a golden tan. Oakland had nice weather. Warmer than L.A. but nice this time of year. So, I preferred to work out there during the day.

I really liked his place.

I didn't like that he'd found my toy, though. Or the toy he gave me. Whatever.

As I sipped the coffee he left for me on the night table, then got dressed for the day, preparing to sit out on the patio to continue working on the strategy I mentioned to Ayanna and Dallas, I couldn't wait to see the expression on Simeon's face when I asked him about finding the vibrator.

———

It was the smell of lasagna wafting through the air and that made its way down to the private bedroom where I laid, that got me up. It smelled so good, the food's aroma got me out of bed and had me following its smell up the stairs to join Simeon in the kitchen.

For the fourth night, he was cooking again. It seems he knew his way around a kitchen, and that fascinated me. I hadn't gotten into the habit of making food often. Between working night and day at Opal Sands with a focus on being promoted and running around with clients putting out media fires, I barely had time to do simple things like cook. It seems that wasn't the case with Simeon.

He was so damn perfect it was frustrating.

"Smells good in here," I commented as I entered the kitchen.

I saw him sliding a glass casserole dish into his oven that was filled with what I thought I smelled - cheese, sauce, and pasta.

"And I hope it tastes good." He closed the oven door and thumbed in numbers on his stove to set a timer. "I got the recipe from one of my employees at the office. I told her you liked pasta, and she shared a recipe with me she knew you'd love."

I smiled while taking a seat at his kitchen's island. "That was thoughtful of her and you."

He bowed his head and turned to face his sink to rinse his hands.

"It was also very thoughtful of you to make a bed you didn't sleep in this morning."

He paused while reaching for a paper towel to dry his hands but recovered, clearly wearing a smile I could see from behind him.

"Found anything while making my bed, Simeon?"

He turned to face me and pressed his hands on the counter behind him. "I did."

"*Mmm-hmm.*" I was fighting like hell to keep my smile to myself.

"And what did your thoughtful ass do when you found that thing you found?"

"I placed it on your bed, as I'm sure you saw."

"What did you do *before* you placed it on the bed?"

He scoffed a laugh, then pressed the tip of his tongue to the inside of his cheek.

"Did you just pick it up then place it down?"

"I may have…" He gestured with his hands. "Inspected it."

"Inspected it," I repeated. "With your eyes, or…"

He licked his lips. "Why are you asking?"

"Oh, you know, just asking out of curiosity." I smirked. "You know how I do."

He balled his lips together then released them long enough to reveal, "I smelled it, okay?"

"You smelled it?" I feigned shock, pressing my hand to my chest. "Simeon. *Wow*. Why would you do that?"

I wasn't shocked at all. When we were together, Simeon had a little of an obsession with my scent. Before we'd make love, he'd remove my panties just to bring them to his nose to inhale deeply, groaning the deepest groans every time. He's even admitted to refusing to wash his hands and inhaling my scent for hours after having his hands between my thighs. The man was a gentleman, but he was filthy, too.

And I loved that shit.

Missed it a lot too.

"I did." He shrugged. "I smelled it."

I hollered a laugh that made him chuckle lowly.

"You just couldn't help yourself, huh?"

He shook his head at himself. "Eryn, please."

"Nasty ass," I uttered low, biting my bottom lip after. "*Mmm-hmm.*"

He licked his lips and shrugged again. "Did you enjoy it?"

"Knowing you smelled it?"

"Using the vibrator."

"It was…" I moved my freshly flat ironed hair off my shoulder. "It was okay."

Simeon arched both brows. "*Just*, okay?"

I half shrugged. "I told you that my fingers do just fine. So..."

I was lying like a dog. That vibrator was the most powerful I'd ever experienced. The intense speed paired with the soft texture had me using it more than once last night.

I wouldn't give him the pleasure of knowing that, though.

"World-class engineers and industrial designers," he began, "those are the minds behind that vibrator. They used state-of-the-art tools to craft that tiny device you just called *only okay.*"

"Oh-kay," I teased.

He scoffed. "Okay?"

"I mean, it's a toy, right?" I tried. "It did what it was supposed to do, but I won't be recording a testimonial for Good-Vibes on a late-night infomercial."

"So..." He folded his arms over his chest. "Are you telling me the vibrator didn't impress?"

"Simeon, like I said." I smiled maniacally. "It was *oh-kay.*"

He stared at me for a moment, squinting his eyes, reading me.

I rolled my eyes. "What? Why are you staring and saying nothing?"

He held up a finger and told me, "Wait right here. I'll be right back."

He left the kitchen before I could ask him where he was going and he returned shortly after.

In his hand, he carried a similar box to the one he had slid over to me my first night in his home. When he was close, Simeon positioned the box in front of me.

I peeked down at the lid that had the logo Good-Vibes etched on the top in foil gold.

"I want you to try this one."

"What?" I laughed. "So, you really have sex toys just lying around your house for real, huh?"

"I already told you that as a silent partner, I attend their product launch parties and as such they have gift bags that include the toys."

I opened the box and peeked inside of it.

The device was flesh tone brown, almost similar to my dark brown complexion. While the toy he gave me my first night in his home was small and slender, the toy he presented me with tonight was wider and had more of a pronounced c-curve to it. I plucked the toy out of the box to get a better look at it.

"It's a panty vibrator."

I glanced up at him.

"The vibes are powerful with this one." He leaned over the counter to gesture with his long finger at the area on the toy that protruded out just a little. "This part goes on your clit, and the back part of the device rests easily in the seat of any panty you wear, including a G-string."

"I just love how comfortable you are about explaining to me what these sex toys do. Like we're talking about car models are something."

"It's that good of a toy." He nodded. "Sophisticated and, as you called it, classy."

"*Mm-hmm.*"

"Ayanna and Dallas have invited us out to dinner tomorrow night to discuss the strategy you mentioned during your phone call with them."

I nodded. "Okay."

"They implemented your social media plan and have been getting excellent results. According to the interns who have been tracking coverage and engagement as per your instructions, the response and engagement have been positive too. So, Ayanna and Dallas want to know what else you want for them to do. They're ready to do whatever you tell them." He smiled. "They trust you."

"Good." My face lit up. "Good to hear."

He gestured at the toy in my hand. "I want you to wear the vibrator tomorrow night when we go out."

I arched both brows. "Excuse me?"

He smirked. "You heard me."

"Why on earth would I wear this to what sounds like a business meeting?"

"Because wearing the vibrator is business for me."

I tsked softly.

"I'm serious."

"Simeon whatever." I placed the toy back in the box. "We agreed to keep this shit here." I gestured between us. "Strictly business."

"And it *is* strictly business, Eryn."

"Oh, yeah?" I challenged. "How?"

"I've spent a lot of money investing in this company based on the support Good-Vibes has gotten and the hordes of positive reviews their products have received. Admittedly, I've had no one to test the products out on to give me an honest assessment. I've only gone based on what I've been told and now I'm second-guessing things after your comment."

I stared at him.

"Dinner tomorrow night would be the perfect setting to test the toy's capabilities." He was fighting so hard to maintain a serious expression, pointing at the toy. "The engineers designed this vibrator to be used out in public."

I sucked my teeth.

"It's whisper quiet, so no one will hear its vibes. Well." He shrugged. "They're not supposed to."

I pursed my lips together next.

"You said the one I gave you was just *oh-kay*, right?"

I bit down on my lips to keep from smiling. He was calling my bluff, just like old times, and I wasn't about to cave—never could back then, either, whenever he tried to call me out on my shit. I wouldn't give him the satisfaction of knowing I enjoyed anything he gave me, or let him hear me admit that I was bullshitting when I said the toy was only okay.

"Yeah," I answered. "I said that."

"So, help me see if I made a terrible investment so I can back out of it if that's the case." He licked his lips slowly and leaned in. "I'd *really* appreciate your help on this one too, Eryn."

"Nigga, don't play with me."

He tossed his head back in a laugh and dropped his head to his chest after.

"You're playing with me right now," I said through my teeth. "I *know* you're messing with me."

Simeon lifted his head and looked at me with smoldering eyes. "No games. I'm so serious."

Having him only a few inches away from me, wearing those eyes and looking as good as he wanted to look, was making me squeeze my thighs together under his kitchen's island.

At that moment, he was lucky there was an island between us.

"This is absolute bullshit, but you know I'm crazy enough to play along, and that's why you're trying me right now."

"So... you'll wear it?"

"I'll wear it."

He winked. "Cool." He was upright again when he told me, "After dinner tonight, I have to head out for a few."

"Late meeting again?"

He smirked as he turned to pull down plates from his cabinet.

I wanted to roll my eyes but stopped myself. I told myself I wouldn't care, and I shouldn't, and it was important that I kept that energy.

I couldn't help wondering, though.

*Who is this woman he keeps leaving me in the house to go see? And how serious are they?*

# Sixteen

**SIMEON**

I closed out my phone after downloading the Good-Vibes app to the device and tossed the phone into my pocket. Grabbing the tiny palm-sized white remote that lay on my dresser in front of me, I dropped it in my other pocket. I checked my wrist to see the time, then glanced up in the mirror to get another look at my reflection.

I couldn't help but feel excited for the night—a feeling I hadn't experienced in a long time. Besides the thrill of combining my two worlds—something old, Eryn, with something new, Ayanna and Dallas —Eryn agreeing to wear the panty vibrator definitely did something for me.

The thrill of persuading her to try something I knew she'd enjoy even more than me took me back to those moments when she was upset with me, and I'd pull out all the stops, challenging her anger, determined to sway her mood.

*"Don't touch me," Eryn said as we lay in her bed in her dorm room one night. She shared the space with a roommate, but that roommate had a boyfriend too and Eryn's roommate spent most of her time in her boyfriend's dorm room on campus. Which was the basis of Eryn's and my argument that night. Well... her argument with me.*

*"Beloved," I voiced behind her.*

*"Don't even try that shit right now."*

*I smirked in the dark.*

*"Every time you want to sweet-talk me, you call me that," she spat. "You can keep that shit to yourself."*

*Eryn lay with her back to me, arms folded as she reclined. She was upset because she wanted to spend the night in my dorm room, and I wouldn't allow it. My space was sacred. My home away from my home on my parents' farm. Growing up on a farm and being homeschooled from grade school age to high school age, I didn't cohabitate with anyone other than my parents. By the time I was seventeen, I wanted my space, deciding to build a tiny house with the help of my father, only a few feet away from our farmhouse. My parents never had more children. My mother's pregnancy with me was a difficult one, so after she had me, she decided she didn't want any more. So, it was just me, and I was used to having my own everything. It was a bit of a shock having to share a room when I arrived on campus at Langston U. But I lucked out, getting paired with a roommate who was a lot like me. We had no problems.*

*Whenever Eryn visited my dorm room, though, even if it were for only a short time, she left a mess behind. It was like a mess trailed her. And while I loved her a lot, it was hard to love that.*

*"I don't like when you're mad at me." I draped an arm over her waist from behind. "What can I do to fix it?"*

*She turned her head to look at me through the side of her eyes. "Let me spend the night in your room."*

*"Oh-kay." I puffed my cheeks with air. "What else can I do to fix it?"*

*She bumped me with her ass, and I couldn't help but chuckle. I would never tell her the reason I didn't want her to spend the night in my dorm room was because I knew if she spent the night even just once, that wouldn't be enough because she'd want to spend the night again. And then she'd want to spend all her time there and soon, the mess would arrive.*

*Her room when we arrived that night was a mess. I refused to go to sleep until I helped her straighten up. She was my girl, though. My one and only beloved, and I loved her so much, I was willing to look past that one and only flaw of hers... if it stayed here. In her dorm room. Contained.*

*I kissed the back of her neck, but she shrugged me off. I slid my hand between her thighs, and she clamped them together, trapping my wrist. I kissed her again, catching that little moan of hers, which made me moan back.*

*"You better shut up," she whispered.*

*I snickered a little.*

*"Whatever. I don't even care." She loosened the tension on her thighs around my wrist. "I'm not gonna get into it anyway, so waste your time."*

*"Oh, yeah?" I whispered into her ear. "Is that a challenge? Are you challenging me, knowing how much I love when you do that?"*

*I slid my fingers even further between her thighs, only stopping when my fingertips dipped between her two lower lips. Wetness slicked my fingers, and soon I found her swollen pink pearl between those wet lips. She released a long exhale when I began circling my finger over the smooth surface slowly. The longer I stroked it, the heavier her exhales got.*

*"Are you sure you will not get into it, beloved?"*

*"Nope," she whispered.*

*"No?" I pressed my finger firmer against her ball. Scooted in a little closer to her to draw in her earlobe with my tongue. "How about now, beloved?"*

*She let a whimper escape, and that brought a smile to my face. "Good girl."*

*"Shut up." Eryn turned in my arms to face me and pinched my chest. "Asshole."*

*I chuckled, pulling her closer to me.*

*"You love it." I pecked her on the lips.*

*"I love you, you jackass," she said on my lips before pulling me closer and into a kiss.*

I adjusted the collar of my slim-fit white linen shirt then stepped back to tuck the hem deeper into the waistband of my tailored vertical white pinstripe patterned trousers.

Tonight was dinner with Ayanna and Dallas. After returning to my condo from KSM earlier, I let Eryn know I would be in my room freshening up and getting dressed, and she promised she would do the same. I didn't bother reminding her to put on the panty vibrator. I'd find out if she was wearing it soon enough.

I chuckled to myself at just the thought.

Satisfied with everything, I stepped out of my room and made my way down to the kitchen to grab a glass of water. I could smell her perfume before seeing her, and when I saw her, I had to blink twice at the sight.

Dressed in a white halter-neck dress with a fitted bodice, she looked damn good and unintentionally matched me. She looked like a black Marilyn Monroe wearing a dress with a voluminous bottom half skirt that fell mid-calf length. Eryn's dress was like the dress the actress wore in the iconic movie shot of her standing over subway grates as the rush of air beneath her billowed her dress up.

Eryn's dress had a deep V-neckline that stressed her décolletage, but she wasn't showing too much cleavage. Tasteful. Always tasteful.

She wore her hair slicked back and in a low ponytail, the long ends of her full ponytail feathering the air when she glanced over at me when I entered the space.

"Showstopper," I commented, throwing a glance at the bright red high-heeled shoes on her feet. "Like always."

She looked me up and down and said, "Ditto," wearing a grin.

I grabbed a drinking glass from my kitchen's cabinet and walked it to the water dispenser on my French door fridge. "Did you remember to wear what I asked you to wear underneath that beautiful dress?"

"Maybe," she replied. "Maybe not."

I turned with my glass of water to face her and brought the rim to my lips at the same time as I dipped my hand into my pocket. I palmed the small remote I dropped in there earlier and pushed the only button on it. I watched as her body jerked forward, breasts bouncing because of her sudden move. I smirked at the small scream that left her lips.

Her wide eyes slammed into mine next.

"Yup." I smiled over the rim of my glass. "You're wearing it."

"What the hell?!" She pressed one hand to her chest and the other over her crotch. "What was that?"

"The vibrator."

"How, though?" She glanced around, then down at herself. "What just happened? How did that go off?"

I held up the small remote in my hand and pressed the button again and left it on for a little longer, watching and hearing her release a sharp gasp this time. She forced in a deep breath after I pressed the button again to shut the vibrator off.

"Did I forget to tell you this vibrator is remote-controlled?"

"Simeon, you sneaky motherfuc—"

"Time to go." I said, smiling and walking past her, swaggering toward the door. "We don't want to be late."

# SEVENTEEN

**ERYN**

"I can't hold it in anymore, I'm sorry," Ayanna expressed beside me. "You and Simeon are so beautiful together. Has anyone ever told you two that?"

I peeked across the table at Simeon, who simply chuckled to himself. We all met at a small Italian restaurant and wine bar in downtown Oakland. The spot was quaint, with the cutest vintage navy-blue awning outside. Inside, the space was cozy and simple. Booths that shared tables with individual brown chairs. Plain wooden tables with the walls decorated with family pictures. The centerpiece of the restaurant was the massive wine bar. It was there I'd ordered red wine, Ayanna white wine, our dates—if you could call Simeon that to me—having the wines we had.

I was about two seconds away from sucker-punching Simeon. From the time we arrived, he had been toying with the remote for the vibrator, making me squeeze my thighs together and needing to suppress my gasps so I wouldn't draw any attention towards me.

"The first time I noticed it was when he brought you to Dallas and my house for our first meeting," Ayanna said with a smile. "I didn't want to make it awkward saying it then, though."

I lifted my wineglass to take a sip of my chianti. "So, you chose awkward now, huh?"

Dallas and Ayanna snickered at that. Just then, the vibrator buzzed between my thighs, making me gasp, then clear my throat.

Ayanna asked, "You okay?"

"*Mmm*, I'm fine." I sighed, taking another sip of my wine. "This wine is something else."

"Is it *that* good?" Ayanna asked, frowning. She pointed at Dallas. "I knew I should've gotten red."

I shot Simeon a look from across the table.

"You and Simeon started dating in high school, right?" Dallas asked, sipping the last of his white wine. "I remember him mentioning that at least once."

"Well," Simeon spoke. "Eryn was in high school, and my high school was in the form of homeschool, but yeah." He nodded. "We started dating when we were both seventeen."

"Wait, how did I not know you were homeschooled?" Ayanna asked.

"Wait until he tells you he grew up on a farm in Western New York."

Ayanna's jaw dropped. "You're a farmer, Simeon?"

Simeon chuckled. "My parents are, yes."

Ayanna smiled big. "I would not have guessed that, Mr. GQ."

"I know, right?" I giggled at that. "Shocked me too. We actually met at his parents' vendor table at a farmers' market in Brooklyn near my high school. I was in the Senior Year Committee and had to go to meetings on the weekends in the weeks leading up to senior year. And every time I saw him, he was always the only one styling and profiling behind his parents' register." I smiled at the memory. "Everyone else working the farmers' market always looked so granola, but not Simeon. Big ol' out-of-place, fancy pants ass."

The buzz of the vibrator went off again, and I squeezed my thighs together while tucking my lips into my mouth. That buzz did something this time, making me grip the side of the table and clench my teeth together to suppress my moan. I shifted in my seat at the rolling sensation. That's because Simeon left the shit on longer than any other time. The moment he let go of that button, I kicked his shin underneath the table, and he snorted a laugh in reaction.

"*Aww*," Ayanna cooed. "You two still have your own inside jokes. 'Cause I don't even know what that was about."

"What it's about is I'm about to kick your fiancée's agent's ass up and down this restaurant," I said, fighting back a laugh. "And he'll know *exactly* why I did."

Simeon chuckled.

"But seriously, before the food gets here." I moved my wine glass out of the way. "I'd like to talk to you guys about our next move."

I shot a glance over at Simeon and asked through my teeth, "Can I talk about that now, Simeon? With *no* surprises while I'm talking about it?" I arched both brows.

"Please." He gestured with his hand, grinning. "Be my guest. Floor's all yours."

I playfully rolled my eyes away from him.

"I did a little research on you two," I said, bouncing my eyes from Ayanna and then to Dallas before returning my attention to Ayanna. "You two have never spoken about your relationship to any entertainment publications other than For The Culture Magazine. In fact, Dallas." I focused on him. "You barely agree to interviews outside of your post-game press conferences and have only spoken to a handful of publications. But even in those publications, the quotes they get from you are not even a paragraph long. Your longest interview was for For The Culture and coincidentally enough." I turned to look at Ayanna. "*You* were the journalist who conducted that interview."

Ayanna blushed. "He was saving his first published interview for me."

That made me smile. "Oh my God. My heart is about to burst."

Everyone laughed.

"I want you two to go back to For The Culture, then."

Ayanna arched both brows.

"And I want you to tell them everything."

"Everything?" Ayanna questioned.

"Every single thing." I sat up. "We're going to lay out the timeline of you and Dallas's relationship like a Marvel universe cheat sheet dating from your relationship's inception—you two meeting in college—to you using Dallas for your lick back against his brother. You're gonna briefly detail how Dominick cheated on you. Not too much on that, because this story ain't about him, but it will satisfy the gossip he started and show it's not what he's making it out to be. And then, you're going to tell all about how you and Dallas went from being friends to getting engaged. Every tiny detail from you having hesitations at first because you dated his brother, like you told me, to you deciding at the last minute to move out here with him after interviewing him for For The Culture. Him saving the interview for you since college. All that. Everything."

"Everything?" Ayanna questioned again, worry lines wrinkling her forehead.

"Yes, girl." I winked. "Trust me on this. We can trust For The Culture. They are the ones who broke the story about your relationship when you two made things official. We'll give them the *only* access, including a seat at the wedding for the journalist who will conduct the interview. You already have rapport with the magazine, having worked there for a short while, and you will not share this story or do any other interview about you and Dallas after that. FTC will get the scoop and you will not only regain the trust of those who are fans of your relationship, you'll also clear the air once and for all and set a clear boundary. Laying everything out from start to finish would make anyone who dares to ask for more unreasonable. Then after that, you will never have to talk about it ever again. No comment from here on out. Done. Anything else after that, anything anyone else has to say, will only be fodder and not taken seriously. I promise."

"That's genius," Simeon commented across from me. "I like it. Clear the air, put it all out there instead of running from it while controlling the optics." He nodded next. "I like it a lot."

"I love it," Dallas added.

"I think I love you, Eryn," Ayanna said last, and that made me giggle.

Our food arrived, and we eagerly dug in, steering the conversation away from my reflections on how much New York had changed, with Ayanna and Dallas nodding in agreement. The topic changed again to their wedding plans and how it wasn't even a question where they'd get married since most of their family were on the East Coast.

"You're wearing the hairstyle I want my girls to wear at my wedding," Ayanna revealed.

I moved the food I chewed in my mouth around with my tongue. "Oh, yeah?"

"*Mm-hmm.*" She nodded. "Which leads me to my next question."

I turned my head to focus on her. "What's up?"

"This is gonna sound like a weird request, but I hope you'll say yes."

"*Uh-oh.*" I glanced over at Dallas with a smirk. "Should your man be worried? Are we about to pull a plot twist and run off together, girl?"

She burst into laughter. "You are so crazy. No." Ayanna waved her hand in the air. "Okay, I'm just gonna come right out and ask. Will you be a bridesmaid in my wedding?"

My eyes ballooned. "Say what now?"

She laughed. "I know we just met, and that's a pretty serious question to ask, but I'm short a bridesmaid after my friend Terri betrayed me and went telling my business to the media for a check."

"Okay..."

"And since you're already wearing your hair like how I want my girls to wear their hair, giving me a pretty good picture of how you'd look, it would really mean the world to me if you said yes."

"Wow."

"I have the dress and you and Terri are about the same size. She's never had the dress fitted with her trifling ass since she's never picked it up after making me buy it. Talking about she can't afford the price the dress cost." She waved her hand in the air. "Anyway, she's never worn the dress. It just needs to be tailored a little at the hips since you're more of a Coca-Cola bottle shape than her, but other than that, it's ready to go."

"*Aww,* Ayanna." I smiled.

"You'd be Simeon's date since she was supposed to walk with him during the ceremony, which means my wedding pictures are gonna be popping because you two are super fine together. So..."

I peeked over at Simeon to see him smiling back at the two of us.

"All I need you to say is yes."

"Damn." I snorted. "I definitely was *not* expecting you to ask me *that* when you asked if you could ask me a question."

"Please say yes," she begged. "I literally have no one else and my wedding is only in two weeks, as you know. It would mean the world if you—"

"I'll do it." I gave a quick nod. "Don't worry about it. This won't be the first time I go above and beyond for a client or my job. This will be light work for me. I promise."

"Really?" she squealed.

I nodded once more. "Really. I got you."

She clapped her hands, then threw her arms around me, pulling back after her hug. "Damn, you smell good, Eryn. What you got on?"

———

"Oh, before I forget," I said the moment Simeon and I returned to his condo. "Let me get that remote, please, Mr. trigger fingers."

Dinner with Ayanna and Dallas went well. They loved my idea to have them tell all to For The Culture and they looked visibly more confident in the handling of their situation. Overall, I was feeling great about everything. My decision to come to Oakland. My decision to work with them. Everything was feeling... good. Even the panty vibrator Simeon kept toying with throughout the night. He didn't take it too far, like I knew he wouldn't. But him having so much power, and me allowing it, was a reminder of how he could get me to be a softie for him and only him. And I was ready for him to relinquish his power. So, I thought.

He chuckled as he slid his hand into one of his pinstriped trousers' pockets and pulled out the tiny white remote. Though he didn't take things far, he was a menace holding that thing. His simple tap on the button would send a wave of sensations around my core that went from alarming to soothing. One of those clicks of the button lasted longer than the others and made me circle my hips and forget where I was for a few breaths. He placed the remote into my palm when he was close, and I forced a smile.

"Thank you," I told him, closing my fingers around the tiny remote and turning to walk away. Little did he know, I was about to have a little fun with this tiny remote tonight.

I was only a few feet away from him when I felt a brief buzz down below again. I peeked down at the remote, thinking I'd accidentally pressed the button, but while I was staring at the thing in my palm, my fingers nowhere near the button, the vibrator went off again. I twisted on my red heels to look Simeon's way. He smiled and turned his phone's screen to face in my direction. The screen lit up with the same Good-Vibes logo appearing above what seemed to be digital buttons.

"Did I forget to mention the vibrator you're wearing has an app that operates the unit, too?"

I dropped my jaw at the sight of the app on his phone.

"See, that's why I like Good-Vibes," he added. "They're so innovative. An app controlled vibrator. Just brilliant, right?"

He pressed one prompt on the screen and the panty vibrator buzzed again. I gasped, then giggled while pointing at him. "I promise I'm about to hurt you."

"Cool, but, first..." He smirked. "Let's really see what that little thing you got on can do. You know, for research purposes."

"Simeon—"

He pressed something on the screen that made the vibrator vibrate on low instantly shutting me up. As instructed before leaving for the night, I placed the vibrator in my panty, impressed by how comfortable it fit because of the unit's shape. Just as he told me to do, I placed the area on the unit that protruded against my clit. So that thing was nestled real good between my lips and laying flush against my pink pearl. So, I could feel every bit of the buzz intensely. Even now with it on low. But of course, I wouldn't show that.

"Now from what I understand," he said as he approached with his phone in his hand. "The vibrator you're wearing has about seven vibrational modes."

I swallowed hard and took a breath.

"There's this one." He selected a mode, and the unit vibrated like a heartbeat. "Then there's this one." The next selection vibrated in a wavelike pattern, interrupting my breathing only a little.

Simeon smiled menacingly at that. "But the vibration that happy customers can't stop talking about is *this* one."

My exhale became stuttered when he selected a mode that pulsed. Now that one? I couldn't help closing my eyes and licking my lips to. It was *the* one. I've had vibrators, like I've said. And they would do what they were supposed to do. But never did it for me. This one, though? It was doing *it*. I licked my lips again and shifted on my heels.

"That's the one, huh?" He asked low, now standing in front of me. "Good to know. But this vibe's on low, though. Let's not be shy about it."

I inhaled and exhaled through my lips.

"We must test its full capabilities." He grinned. "It's important for us to be thorough here, so I'm bringing it all the way up. Cool?"

The rumbly vibrations gradually increased, going from a feathery soft vibe to a blood-boosting sensation. A moan escaped my lips and my knees buckled a second later. Simeon caught me and gently pushed me back until my back kissed his kitchen's wall. I tried to shake it off, resist the delicate friction the vibrator was causing, but after a few seconds of trying, I realized it was a futile mission.

There was no use in pretending anymore. Because Simeon was in front of me now. His warm, spicy scent, paired with his warm touch against my abdomen as he held me up against the wall, was breaking me down quicker than a sandcastle in water. I had no choice but to give in. I mean, I *had* a choice. He gave me the remote. I could have switched off the vibrator at any time if I wanted to. But I didn't. Not after he dropped the phone into his back pocket, the vibrator still going, so he could run his finger down my bottom lip. I closed my eyes to his touch, moaning even louder as I felt myself inching closer and closer to a release.

"Damn," he whispered. "Good girl, beloved."

*"Hold on one second, beloved."*

*I jerked my head back and sat up slowly in bed. It was 9pm on a school night, and I was on the phone with Simeon. We'd been on the phone since*

*5pm that day, so I just knew my mother would be at my door any minute now asking me to return the house's cordless phone to its base before it lost charge. Just as our call was winding down, Simeon had to step away from his phone, referring to me with a name I'd never heard him call me before that day.*

*"Yeah, I'm back," he said the moment he returned to the line. "I'm sorry about that."*

*"What did you just call me?"*

*There was silence for a moment before he asked, "Beloved?"*

*The smile that appeared on my lips the first time he said it reappeared, instantly aching my cheeks from how hard it pulled at the corners of my mouth.*

*"Is that a problem?" he asked when I had said nothing. "Because, if you don't like it—"*

*"I love it," I whispered. "A lot."*

*"Good." He chuckled nervously. "Great."*

*"What does it mean, though?" I folded my legs, pressing the phone closer to my ear. "I've heard it before. There's a book and a movie with the same name, you know?"*

*Simeon laughed lowly.*

*"But what does it mean... when you call me beloved?"*

*Simeon and I had been officially dating for three months, and I was still getting to know the boy I'd met at a farmers' market just a week before my senior year began—the boy who lived six hours away. Aside from the weekends he drove up to the city with his parents to help them run their farmers' market stand in either Brooklyn or Manhattan, and I'd steal him from them near the tail end of their visit in the city, Simeon and I spent most of our relationship on the phone before we started college together. But what we'd cultivated on our phone lines was feeling like something more than just two teenagers getting to know each other in their long-distance relationship.*

*"It means..." He scoffed a laugh and then he inhaled a deep breath next. "It means dearly loved and I call you that because... you're dearly loved. By me."*

I leveled my head the moment I heard his pet name for me. He'd only speak it when he wanted to cast me under his spell. When he first called me beloved, it was innocent and his way of telling me he loved me. Later in our relationship and the older we got, he'd call me beloved whenever we'd get into arguments. He'd say it so softly in my ear to calm me down when I was red hot pissed with him over something. Eventually, he used *beloved* when we were intimate and eventually *good girl* when he wanted me to melt into a puddle of everything with him inside of me. He'd bury himself so deep, my walls would quiver around his girth, and he'd stroke past the resistance as he fucked me into nirvana, whispering "beloved" and "good girl" in my ear through his moans.

Every.

Time.

My release hit me like a sweet wave, warming the soles of my feet in my heels. Like always, when we'd make love, I kept my eyes on his and he kept his on me. Simeon sucked his bottom lip into his mouth and kept his lip in place with the bite of his teeth. His eyes fell to my chest, which was heaving as the peak of my climax rippled through me in sync with the rumbling happening in my panties. I fisted his shirt near the tail end of that release. And he let me. I used my grip to pull him closer to me. And he let me do that, too. He was close enough to press his lips against mine, and I swore I could taste them already.

But instead of his lips landing on mine, he bypassed them completely, choosing my ear instead.

"Goodnight, Eryn," he whispered before slowly stepping back, retrieving his phone from his back pocket, and switching off the vibrator before walking away. Leaving me panting against the fucking wall. Alone.

"This nigga," I said to myself with the little breath I had. What a way to end the night, though, huh?

# EIGHTEEN

**SIMEON**

"Yes, that's correct," I spoke into my cell phone, talking to my assistant, Grace. "I'm working from home today, so please send all my office calls to my cell when they come in."

"Will do, Mr. King," Grace replied. "Let me know if you need anything else."

Last night did not go as planned. Dinner with Ayanna and Dallas was a success, which I knew it would be with Eryn on the job. But what happened after, when we returned to my condo, was *not* what I intended to happen.

"Thank you," I said to Grace. "Talk soon."

It was a Friday, the end of the week. And although Eryn and I returned to my home after dinner with Ayanna and Dallas at a decent hour, after I went a little too far with the vibrator she wore, I spent the entire night jerking off to the point of my wrist aching the next morning.

I ran my hand down my face and leaned back in the armchair across from my bed. I had to talk myself out of asking Eryn to join me last night in that bed. The amount of self-discipline and restraint I had to practice not to have that woman sleep with me last night had reached monk level. My diligence impressed me, keeping my dick in my pants. Because getting reacquainted with her come face was not on my bingo card for that night.

My plan was to mess with her. Turn the vibrator on, then off to tease her, knock her off her block a little. Really, I wanted her ass to retract her comment because I knew she was bullshitting me by saying the vibrator was only okay. No, I'd never used it. But it was a top-selling vibrator that had minimal advertising on and off the web. They were flying off Good-Vibes' shelves based on word of mouth alone. Do you know how powerful a product would have to be when people are buying it based on what other people are saying about it?

So, yeah, I wanted to call her bluff a little. Get a good laugh out of shaking her up because Eryn was a tough woman to shake up. I never intended to make her come in front of me like that. But then I saw her knees buckle, and I saw that look in her eyes when she was feeling good. That tamed look that was always my goal post in bed with her when we were once something. An innocence she didn't show others. And that willingness to yield she wore in her eyes last night was like a drug I thought I'd kicked but realized I was still a fiend for. And I just had to see more, forgetting my promise to myself. My promise to her. To keep things strictly business.

I toed the line by asking her to wear the vibrator, to begin with. I know that. But I crossed that line when I made her come on it. I shook my head, trying to get her face off my mind. Her face was the last thing I thought about before going to sleep and the first thing I thought about when I got up.

I still got her coffee, knowing the hour she got up.

*I brought the mug to her room just as she was pushing herself up and into a seat on her bed.*

*"Good morning," I said, the moment I stepped in after knocking and*

*her telling me to come in. She was just getting up for the day, so she was stretching her arms above her head the moment she sat up in bed.*

*"How'd you sleep?" I asked as I placed her mug of coffee on the night table beside her.*

*"Like a baby," she answered with little humor.*

*I nodded while turning to walk away.*

*"That's it?" she asked.*

*I turned to glance at her over my shoulder.*

*"You just walk in here with coffee like what happened last night didn't happen?"*

*I pressed the tip of my tongue against the inside of my cheek to keep from smiling.*

*"I'm working from home today," I said, instead of answering her question. "If you need anything, I'll be in my room..." I gestured over my head. "Or I'll be in the office in the loft space above."*

*She sucked her teeth as I turned to leave her room.*

I wasn't playing any games. I promise I wasn't. I was making sure I protected my heart, doing what I had to do to avoid disappointment. Doing everything I could to avoid the disappointment and heartbreak I experienced with her that had me walking away from our once beautiful relationship together.

I swapped the armchair for a spot on my bed, flipping open my laptop and accessing my email app. As I pulled up an email from earlier in the week, I grabbed my phone and dialed one of my contacts. After two rings, a familiar voice came through, instantly bringing a smile to my face.

"Oh, now I know it's a good day when my baby is calling me bright and early."

I smiled even wider. "Hey, Mama."

"Hey, baby, how's it going?" She asked. "Why am I so lucky hearing from you this early?"

"Yeah," my father echoed in the background. "Usually, when we hear from you, it's always in the afternoon."

"I had a late night." I shook my head at myself, put the phone on speaker, and set it on the bed beside me. "So, I'm working from home today. My work-from-home load is always light because I don't like to work too hard in the same place I go to sleep."

They chuckled.

"I'm calling because I got an email earlier this week," I explained. "A proposition which is going to be *huge* for the farm."

Kings Farm was a farm that was passed down to my father by his father. It was a farm my father was ready to pass down to me too, but I'd decided the farm life wasn't the life for me the day my parents brought me to the city when I was fourteen to help them run their stand at a Manhattan farmers' market.

Our farm was one of the most illustrious farms in New York, though. In Dewittville, NY, our farm was six hours from the city and was truly amazing. I could see how amazing it was after moving off it and growing up. But when I called the farm home, I took it for granted. Thankfully, I made sure not to do that in my adulthood.

As soon as I earned my MBA and realized Miami wouldn't be my home much longer, I used what I'd learned to help my parents increase profits on the farm, grow their business, and secure grants. They'd already done well by selling the fresh fruits and vegetables we grew on the farm to local markets. They had more than a few arrangements with local butchers who bought the animals we raised and bred as well. Seasonally, they'd open the farm for apple picking in the autumn and strawberry picking in the summer. As far as getting by and never needing for anything, my parents had managed the farm and the profits from them wonderfully. But I always saw more for them. And more seemed to have arrived as this email I was calling them to discuss.

"Do you two know Bryant Greene? The multi-billionaire who owns just about any and everything around New York City?"

"Can't say I have," my mother spoke first.

"Yeah, I'd have to echo your mother's comment," my father chimed in next.

"Well, his latest investment is in a small village he's financing and building. It's called Greene Gardens. Everything is in motion now. He has this plan to have this community of black businesses and black residents living and thriving in this village. It really is an amazing plan I've been researching since his team reached out to us."

Like I told Eryn, I had my hands in a few businesses as a silent part-ner. One of those businesses was my family's farm business and as such, I managed all communication with my assistant.

"They want for us to supply their one and only village supermarket. They're almost finished building and are interested in our fruits, vegeta-bles, and dairy offerings."

"Really?!" my mother shrieked.

"Wow," my father seconded.

"This is the big one, guys." I beamed, affirming with a slight nod. "This deal is life-changing and very permanent. And it's going to set up a foundation to build on for our family for many generations to come."

"Well, I *love* the sound of the building of generations," my mother started. "Because my one and only son is almost 40 years old and I haven't had a single grandchild to rock to sleep yet."

I chuckled nervously, dropping my head to scratch the back of it. My door swinging open and Eryn stomping her way into my bedroom had me lifting my head again to focus her way.

"Here are your *things*, you jerk." She hurled the two vibrators I gave her at my chest.

I looked up at her in shock and humor. I pressed my finger to my lips next, trying to signal her to be quiet.

"No," she said low, slapping my hand from my mouth. "I'm so sick of your shit, Simeon."

"Wait a minute," my mother said, her sweet voice streaming out of my phone's speaker. "Is that who I think it is?"

"*Uh...*" I stared up at Eryn, wide-eyed.

"Is that Eryn?" My mother asked this time. "That can't be Eryn."

Eryn gasped, then slapped her hand to her mouth to cover it.

"Is it?" My mother asked louder. "Eryn Peters? Is that her?"

I snorted a laugh. "Yeah, Mama. That's fireball Eryn."

"Oh, my word!" My mother exclaimed, and laughed gleefully. "Eryn, it's *so* good to hear your voice. How are you?"

Eryn squeezed her eyes closed. "I'm good. How are you?"

"We're great," my mother replied. "I'm here with Simeon's Pa."

"Hey there, Eryn," my father greeted.

"Oh wow, the whole family is on the line." Eryn face-palmed her forehead. "Hey y'all."

I couldn't help but laugh at that.

"You sound mad, girl," my father commented with a chuckle. "What did he do to you?"

"Oh, nothing." Eryn lifted her head out of her hand. "I'm only playing with him. You know how I do."

"*Mm-hmm,*" my mother replied. "I'm gonna pretend like I didn't hear you cussing at my baby because I'm sincerely so happy to hear your voice. I swear I could pick out your Brooklyn accent from a lineup, honey! What a blast from the past you are!"

"We're only working together, you guys," I clarified.

Eryn reared her head back.

"Eryn's helping me with a client's situation, so..." I cleared my throat. "*That's* why she's here."

Eryn stood over me, staring down at me with narrowed eyes, the tip of her tongue massaging the inside of her cheek. She nodded slowly, giving me the look of death.

"Oh, well, that's good," my mother added. "I'mma pray for a little old-time spark, though." She chuckled next.

"Us both," my father added.

"Anyway, *uhh...*" I picked up the phone off my bed and took it off speaker. I turned a little from Eryn, and said, "I'll be in New York in two weeks for a client's wedding. I want to stop by and bring you guys the paperwork for us to look at this deal Bryant and his team are proposing. Is that all right with y'all?"

"It's more than okay," my mother replied. "And when you come up here, maybe you can bring Eryn with you. I'd really *love* to see her, Simeon. It's been way too long."

"*Uhh...*" I turned in the direction I left Eryn standing to see her no longer in the room. My attention behind me made me lower my eyes to my bed to see the toys she threw at me gone, too.

"Maybe Mama," I said into the phone, leaning back a little in my seat on the bed to peer through my opened bedroom door, searching for any trace of Eryn, but finding nothing. "We'll see."

# Nineteen

**ERYN**

I took careful steps up the staircase, doing my best to avoid any possible creaking sounds on Simeon's see-through stairs. This was my second time taking these stairs to his bedroom. Before earlier today, when I stomped up his staircase to confront him in his room and to return the toys he so graciously gave me, I hadn't set foot up the stairs that led to his room.

I'd been in his condo for almost a week, and not once did I have a reason to take the stairs to his bedroom. Until now. I was done with his shit on so many levels earlier. The last straw was him leaving me sexually frustrated the night prior. And he was about to pay for that.

I was close to the top of his stairs when I noticed the lights on in his bedroom. The hour was close to 10pm. From what I remembered him telling me, he didn't work weekends often, but sometimes he made the exception. His decision to stay home and not go into his office earlier was surprising. It was as if the man hardly spent time in his home, if I were to judge. Because every morning, he would leave his condo after leaving my mug of coffee by my bed as I was waking up, or he was leaving his condo after making us dinner.

Tonight, we ordered in, and he ate his meal out on the patio, leaving me to eat mine at his kitchen's island alone. Honestly, I think that was what gave me the final incentive to do what I had been considering doing when I took the vibrators back.

I had every intention of giving them back to him earlier. Simeon had a mischievous side to him that few, if anyone other than me, knew about. He was a bit of a troublemaker. Simeon used his knack for persuasion positively, yes, but he was so good at it, his knack bordered on manipulation. He knew how to toe the line between saint and sinner with the best of them. Simeon was who he was by choice, which made him a little diabolical. He was intentional about every damn thing he did. If he wanted to, he could be sinister. Trust me. But he isn't because it doesn't fit his vision of perfection. That's why he likes to walk the thin line between naughty and nice, like a skilled tightrope walker.

So, I knew he was fucking with me when he gave me the first vibrator, on my first night at his condo. But when he gave me the second one, I knew he was being the mischievous boy I knew in yesteryears that no one close to him knew he could be.

I was in front of his door when I turned the doorknob and noticed it giving way. Good. He left the door unlocked. This allowed me to twist the knob all the way and to push the door open next, to find a shirtless Simeon doing pushups on the floor.

His body lifted and lowered with the help of his brawny arms and hands as he forced air out through his mouth with each exhale. Every muscle in his body flexed and contracted with his actions. Except for the pair of lounge pants Simeon wore, that was slung low at his waist, he had nothing else on. Not even on his feet.

Between his armchair and the foot of his bed, I counted seven pushups before he looked up from the floor to find me standing at the threshold of his door. He immediately pushed up off the floor, using the assistance of his feet to stand long enough to take a seat in his armchair. He panted as he held a stare with me before he ran his hand down his face to clear it of sweat. With his face obstructed, I moved my eyes to his chest. Hard, squared, and glazed with sweat.

Simeon has had a body to worship since I met him as a teenager. When I asked him how often he worked out, he'd say often because of the work he would do on his parents' farm. He'd always say he couldn't wait to leave the feeling of sweat-stiff clothing from lifting and moving farm machinery. Would often complain about the jarring feeling of swinging an axe hard enough to have it bite into a chopping block. But it seemed all that labor helped chisel his muscles naturally. Because Simeon has always and probably would forever stay stacked from his shoulders to his wrists.

"Did I miss the knock?" He exhaled, eyes back on me as he caught his breath in his seat.

"Nope," I answered, entering the room and closing the door. "I didn't bother knocking."

"Oh." He chuckled to himself. "I see."

"I was just too excited to share my new findings with the vibrator you gave me on my first night here. You know for research purposes."

Simeon shut his eyes and exhaled. "Eryn—"

Holding the onyx black vibrator for him to see, I said, "I think I understand why this vibrator didn't have the effect that your brand's customers have been raving about."

"Is that so?"

"*Mm-hmm.*" I stopped inches in front of him. "I discovered the thing that was missing when I used it... was you."

"Eryn—"

"As made clear by last night, right? So..." I turned to approach the foot of his bed. "Since I want to make good on my promise to help you out, you know..." I turned to face him. "For business purposes, right?"

He scoffed a laugh.

"I'm going to play with the toy again, up here and on *your* bed," I told him as I took a seat on the bed. "With you watching me."

His jaw slacked and he tried to form words with his mouth before giving up and simply shaking his head. "Eryn, you don't have to do that."

"Oh, I *really* want to." I placed the vibrator on the bed.

"Okay, look." He held his hands up in surrender as he scooted to the edge of his seat. "I went too far last night. I apologize."

"Apology rejected." I pulled at the hem of my lounge dress until it was up over my hips. "Don't punk out on me."

"Oh fuck," came out as a whisper from Simeon when he realized I wasn't wearing any panties. "Eryn, please."

"No begging." I smirked. "You don't beg, remember?"

Exposed, I could feel the air in the room against my pussy that was already wet from watching him work out.

I sat on his bed and leaned back a little, propping myself up on one elbow. I spread my legs wide and wasted no time using my free hand to press the vibrator against my clit. I watched Simeon push air out through his mouth as I switched on the vibrator, and I trembled a little from the buzz of the vibes.

I allowed my moan to emanate out of me with ease, closing my eyes only a little to get into it. But that wouldn't take too much work because of the setup alone. Simeon was sitting only inches away, attention entirely on me, the scent of sandalwood and oud dispensing from one of his tower dispensers somewhere in his room I didn't care to search for. Pair all of that with the pulsing buzz of the vibrator on one of the most sensitive spots on my body. Everything had me turned on to the max.

"Let's talk," I whispered, gyrating my hips against the vibrator's round tip, slowly sailing the toy's cylindrical, slightly tapered form up and down my wet clit.

"Shit, Eryn." He groaned, dropping his head. "This is *not* a good idea."

"It's a great idea," I countered through a moan. "Now lock in on me."

He lifted his head slowly. Simeon inhaled and exhaled through his mouth, then licked his lips so slowly even that made me hotter.

I dropped my head a little and closed my eyes, feeling my imminent release. I purposely started the vibrator on low. I didn't want to get to my end too quickly. For once, I wanted to take my time.

"Are you seeing anyone, Simeon?" I bit my bottom lip. "Because if you are, then that will be the *only* reason I stop."

"You kept the tattoo," he murmured, eyes fixed on my inner thigh.

"Are you seeing anyone?"

"No," he replied in a huskier voice.

"Then why do you keep leaving me here in your house all by myself every single night?"

The vibrator landed on a sensitive nerve that made my lower half shiver. My walls contracted, and I bit my lip at the feeling.

"I tried to see a woman your first night here, but she kicked me out because I wouldn't sleep with her."

I lifted my head and focused on him. His lids were low, chest rising and falling at a steady pace. My eyes journeyed past his chest and his abs to see his dick tenting his lounge pants. I dropped my jaw and exhaled through my mouth at the sight of one of my favorite things enticing me from a distance.

"And I'm not seeing anyone else, nor am I planning to be with anyone when I leave you here on your own." he revealed. "I drive around Oakland for hours every night, just burning through gas, only returning home when I'm too exhausted to think about how badly I want to be inside of you, Eryn."

I moaned, throwing my head back as my walls contracted again and again, the sensation guiding me closer to the release that was just out of reach. Mid-breath, Simeon snatched the vibrator from my hand, tossed it against the wall, and grabbed my thighs, pulling me to the edge of the bed. In one swift move, he replaced the buzzing with the warm, wet touch of his tongue.

I gasped and grabbed the back of his head with both hands and arched my back off his mattress, circling my hips in rhythm with his tongue. I lowered my attention as he lifted his gaze to watch me as he licked me through my climax.

"Ooooh!" I yelled, my voice echoing around us.

And he didn't stop. He kept going. Holding my wrists down now on each side of me when I tried to push his head away because of sensitivity. He rolled his tongue and circled my clit slower, delivering soft kisses against the ball between tongue kisses until my body relaxed again. When I stopped trying to push him away, he resumed spiraling his tongue, flicking the tip from left to right in a practiced pattern. I couldn't help but snatch my wrist free, grabbing his head to pull him closer, riding his mouth until the sensitivity transformed into a new wave of yearning—a desperate need to come.

"Right there," I whispered. "*Mm-hmm*, right there."

And he kept doing it just like that and right there until my body came alive again with another orgasm, this more intense and breathtaking, elevating high and then bottoming out way too quickly for me. It was still strong enough to make me fall back onto his mattress to catch my breath.

Simeon kissed his lips off my lips and balanced himself on his arms and hands, moving his way up until he hovered over me. His lips and beard glistened, his eyes smoldered, making his pupils appear dark like black diamonds.

I lifted from my flatback position on his bed to crash my mouth into his and he kissed me back with so much force, my toes curled.

Our lips parted, our tongues met, and we both exhaled into each other's mouths as if we'd been holding our breath, waiting to release it. I know I had been. Waiting for another man to make me feel every emotion I could feel with only a kiss. Just from touching me. And I'd come up short so often, I just stopped looking and started waiting. Waiting to feel something, *anything*, close to this.

I slid one hand between us and into his lounge pants in search of his dick. And when I found it, I wrapped my fingers around its thick column. I salivated at the veins I felt against my palm, the heat, me only holding it in a grip, produced. When I tried to pull it out, Simeon broke our kiss and shook his head.

I grabbed his face and pulled him to me again, but he pulled away. I was ready to jump him right then and there, but instead, I watched as he walked over to his nightstand and slid open the drawer. He pulled out a sealed box of condoms, tearing it open, and I didn't know what pleased me more—that he had them on hand or that the box was still unopened. But I barely had time to dwell on that or even consider waiting, as I crawled toward him on his bed. He stepped out of his lounge pants and sheathed his erection, and I couldn't help but smile, almost forgetting just how big he was.

He met me halfway, positioning me beneath him with one strong arm. His mouth found mine again, his chest pressing against mine as he guided the head of his erection to my wetness. There was resistance as he tried to glide in, and it instantly brought back memories. With Simeon, it always took some adjusting—always. Just like before, he lifted his chest off mine, balancing on his knees to find a better angle. He was big, and it always made me feel impossibly tight. The journey from the initial ache to pure pleasure was a familiar one. Watching him struggle to keep control as he worked his way inside was a sight I hadn't seen in too long.

I didn't know if my pussy was reacting like an earring hole that hadn't been used in years, but as he eased his way in, the sweet ache of the past had me pressing my hands against his abs to brace myself—something I'd never done before. He glanced down between us, then smirked at me, still working himself deeper between my walls.

"What's this, *hmm*?" he challenged, gently taking me by the wrist. Simeon lifted my arm and pinned it above my head. He did the same with the other, keeping both wrists pinned down as he slid in and out. The restraint made me wetter, helping him glide even smoother.

"When have you ever done that with me?"

"Never," I whispered back.

"So why are you doing it now?" he asked, gazing down at me with soft eyes. "You're not my good girl anymore?"

"I am."

"Are you telling me you can't handle all of me then, beloved? Has it been that long?"

I held his gaze, feeling my walls stretch to accommodate his girth, the friction between us turning into pure, white-hot heat.

"Am I too much for you, Eryn?" His tone was firmer now. Serious, too. "Do you want me to stop?"

I shook my head.

He licked his lips. "Are you able?"

I shuddered beneath him as he pushed a little harder past the resistance. Simeon was a lot, just like always, but I managed to tell him, "I'm more than able."

He let out a deep, guttural grunt, his face contorting in pleasure at my response. "Are you still mine?"

"I never stopped being yours."

He nodded, his voice rough. "Show me."

I widened my legs even more, slowly gyrating back and forth, fucking him back, and he groaned with each stroke he delivered.

"Good girl, beloved," he murmured, biting his bottom lip as a shudder ran through him with each thrust. "*Fuck*."

With every thrust from him, I countered with one of my own. Our bodies collided, causing his arms to tremble and his head to drop forward as he sucked in air through his teeth.

"*Mmm*." He grunted, then lifted his head to lock eyes with me. "Your pussy is still so perfect," he groaned.

All I could do was nod. The friction was so intense that the sweet ache that nearly had me running a few strokes ago had morphed into a sensual numbness. It made it hard to focus on anything but the pulsing change from nothing to everything.

"I'm... close," I whispered, barely able to get those two words out.

"I know, I feel it. I've got you," Simeon exhaled above me, his grip tightening around my wrists. "Take your time, ease into it for me. No rushing, okay?" The slick sounds between us grew louder, and so did I. "Just like that—keep gripping me tight *just* like that"

It had been so long since a man had fucked me properly. I almost forgot how to receive something so intense, so consuming. It had me shaking uncontrollably every time he eased in and out.

"*Mm-hmm*." He gave a slow, deliberate nod. "Yeah, you're still mine all right."

He stroked, and I shook as he drilled past the pressure building to an agonizing crescendo inside me. Simeon moved to a rhythm only he could hear, consistent and satisfying, targeting that delicate spot deep inside me. Most men only knew the mechanics—in and out with no plan or direction. Simeon wasn't most men. He searched diligently with his strokes, and when he found my trigger, he refused to let up until I detonated, leaving me boneless beneath him. That hadn't changed—not tonight, at least.

I lifted my head high enough to witness what he was doing to me, watching in awe as he buried every inch of himself between my tender walls with methodical thrusts. And just when I thought I couldn't take any more, when I thought I would burst, an explosion erupted inside me, pulsing through my body so slowly, leaving behind a wave of goosebumps that pimpled my skin, even under his grip around my wrists.

"Now *you* lock in on *me*," he ordered. "Focus here, beautiful."

I locked eyes with him, staring up at him in disbelief, shocked that he could still get me here after so long.

"Sim... Simeon," I stuttered in a whisper. "I... I love you... I miss... *oooh*, baby I've missed you so fucking much—"

"*Shh*, easy," he breathed. "I know, beloved. I know. I love you, and I've missed you so much, too."

The gentle whisper of his breath against my face deepened the trance, silencing my need to speak. I closed my eyes, letting my head fall back against his mattress, relinquishing control and completely losing myself in the moment.

He panted, driving into me. "God, Eryn, I wish you could see how beautiful you are right now."

I couldn't have replied even if I wanted to. I was overwhelmed with gratitude, reunited with a feeling I had convinced myself was lost forever after he left. All I could feel was that sensation—it was like standing at the gates of heaven, being ushered in by a blaze of emotions that lifted me into a euphoric high. A high I never wanted to end.

Simeon released one of my wrists to grab my jaw, pressing his lips to mine, grounding me back to earth. I felt like he'd hollowed me out and filled me with electricity, the way I was pulsing and vibrating all over. I was gone—out of my mind and so damn gone. I wanted this feeling to live inside me forever. Fuck everything else I said. Let's just pretend I didn't say any of it. Because *this*? Right here? Being up under a man like Simeon, who could make my body do *that* with just the slow thrust of his pelvis and his gentle grip around my wrists? Yeah. This was everything. *He* was everything. And when I said I was over him, that was a damn lie.

# TWENTY

## SIMEON

"See, now?" Dallas shouted as we fell into our seats in his rented luxury SUV. "Right now? It's official."

The sun had set in the Flatbush section of Brooklyn, casting an orange glow over the neighborhood and painting the sky in peach-colored clouds.

We were back in New York City, and it was the eve of Dallas and Ayanna's wedding.

People gathered on the block where Dallas parked his car, taking pictures of Dallas through his SUV's windows with their smartphones.

He thought he could just swing by Brooklyn, returning to the neighborhood he once called home during his final years at Langston University, to get a haircut at a barbershop called Kuts Kings. But the fanfare said otherwise.

And although all the attention had me a little on edge, since we traveled to Brooklyn with no security for Dallas, the man himself was unaffected.

He was on cloud nine.

"Now that I got a fresh cut at my favorite barbershop in the world." He smiled big. "I'm ready to get married."

He started up his SUV and waved at the people who were still gathering on the block where he parked.

Dallas even lowered his window to give an autograph to a kid who ran up the block just as he was pulling off, signing the boy's basketball with a smile.

"Aight, kid," Dallas said to the boy. "I gotta go now, 'cause I gotta go get married."

I laughed to myself.

For the past week, he's been saying the same line.

And without dread.

Excited and with so much enthusiasm, it was a little infectious.

"Man," he exhaled as we stopped at the first red light up the block we'd left. "Ain't nothing like being in New York."

That I could agree with.

It was a Friday night, and the streets were bustling with energy. Reggae music played from a jerk chicken spot and echoed around the neighborhood as people made their ways up and down the busy blocks.

When Dallas said he was going to Brooklyn to check out the venue for the wedding, which was also in Brooklyn, and would get a haircut at a nearby barbershop he used to frequent, I volunteered to tag along. Decided to get a shape-up myself, which the barber and shop owner, Manny, at Kuts Kings did a good job with. And that's saying a lot with my picky standards.

With that done, we were on our way to Dallas's bachelor party that was being held in a cigar lounge in Manhattan.

He and Ayanna promised each other they wouldn't do the stereotypical thing of having strippers at their gatherings, so it would simply be a laid-back night with their wedding parties.

With that thought about their wedding parties, it called to mind Eryn, as she was now a part of Ayanna's wedding party.

Eryn and I had not been keeping things strictly business since hooking up two weeks prior.

Her decision to play with her toy in my bedroom in front of me, sort of say, was the catalyst to neither one of us sleeping alone since that night.

*"Send me your proposal and I'll have my legal team review it," I said into the phone to a prospective vendor who was looking to supply Dallas's Pure Roque brand with eco-friendly packaging.*

*I was just wrapping up work and was making my way down from the loft-space on the top floor of my condo.*

*It was the day after Eryn and I hooked up. I was out of my bed before her and didn't bother waking her since I kept her up all night the night before and I needed to get my head straight after everything.*

*I rarely worked on the weekends, but after what happened the prior night, I needed a distraction. And I did good at keeping myself distracted throughout the day. This kept me busy, which also kept Eryn and me apart.*

*Believing that would be a good thing, all that changed when I caught her from my peripheral making her way down to her private guest bedroom in the lower level of my condo.*

*"Hold on, Monte," I said into the phone, putting the call on mute. "Hey, you," I said to Eryn.*

*She stopped in the middle of the stairs to glance my way. Her hair was up in a messy ponytail, the hem of her white lounge dress in her hand, my guess so she wouldn't trip on it as she descended the stairs.*

*"Hey." She tried but failed to hide the smirk on her lips.*

*And I couldn't help smiling back.*

*"What's down there?" I asked, closing the distance between us a little.*

*"My bed, duh." Eryn pressed her back to the wall beside the staircase. "I'm going to turn in early. I'm still tired from yesterday."*

*I licked my lips, my smile pulling even harder at the corners of my mouth. "You want to sleep in your bed after last night?"*

*"Last night is exactly why I want to sleep in my bed, sir, yes." She giggled. "The coffee you brought me this morning did very little with getting the sleep out of my eyes. I've been tired all day."*

*"Well, I'd love it if you got your rest in my bed tonight... again."*

*She arched both brows.*

*"You know." I shrugged. "Only if you wanted to."*

*"Will you let me sleep?"*

*"I don't know." I bit my bottom lip. "Maybe not?"*

*She shook her head while smiling.*

*"I'll see you up there," I told her, taking my call off mute. "I'll be up there in a few."*

And since that night, Eryn and I have been sleeping together.

Literally having sex every night since.

It was as if I'd been starving and didn't even know it. And now I was concerned I was overeating.

It was her tattoo that really did it. Her using the vibrator in front of me was insanely sexy, yes, but her tattoo had me standing up from my seat and dropping to my knees in front of her opened legs.

It was a tattoo I would've thought she'd have removed after everything happened between us. My name on her thigh, in my handwriting, that she only showed me *after* she'd gotten it.

*She burst through my dorm room door, all excited and eager to show me this thing she swore I'd love. But when she finally showed it to me, I was floored.*

*"What the fuck?" I exclaimed, moving in closer to see it. "Eryn, what the...? Why would you...?"*

*"You don't like it?"*

Simeon's. *It said Simeon's. My name inked on her skin.*

*Written in my handwriting and tattooed on the curve of her right inner thigh.*

*It was the evening of my twenty-first birthday, and our third year at Langston U, when she showed me her gift.*

*"Is this what you made me write on that piece of paper you gave me yesterday?"*

*She stopped by my dorm room early in the morning, right before I had to go to class.*

*Spring break was the following week. Eryn and I were flying out to Cancun then, after she bought tickets and told me that's where we would spend our spring break from LU. Her buying the tickets was yet another thing she did, that we never discussed, and only told me about it after she did it. So when she gave me the piece of paper and told me to write "Simeon's" on it, I did it quickly. I found it odd she was asking me to write that, but like I said, I was running late for class, and I figured I'd ask her about it later.*

*"Yeah." She shrugged. "I thought it was a cute idea and would be a good birthday present."*

*I ran my hand down my face. "You had your legs opened for a guy to tattoo this on you, Eryn?"*

*"Of course not." She smiled. "A woman did it."*

*"Well." I sighed. "At least a woman did it, right?"*

*Eryn took a seat on my lap and wrapped her arms around the back of my neck. "I'm yours. I just wanted to show you how much I'm yours."*

And when she wasn't anymore, I thought for sure she'd have the tattoo removed. So, years later, when she barged into my room, sat at the edge of my bed with her legs spread wide, and I saw the tattoo—still there, still present—I lost control and broke the damn promise I made to myself.

To us.

*"You kept the tattoo," I said behind her.*

*"I did," she replied.*

*We were in bed, the night after the night of our hookup.*

*She was lying in my bed on her side, her back to me, smelling amazing as always and making me bide my time before I was all over her without restraint.*

*The tattoo had been on my mind since I got up and out of bed.*

*"I'm surprised you kept it," I whispered into the dark. "After everything... I can't believe you didn't have it removed."*

*"When I got it, I never planned on getting it removed," Eryn said, turning to face me. Her hand slid down my bare chest as we locked eyes. "Believe it or not... after everything, my feelings for you were as permanent as the ink."*

"Hey Dallas," I beckoned as we approached another red light.

The Brooklyn Bridge was right in front of us, the necklace lights on its cables bright as the sky that was transitioning into a true-blue hue.

"What's up?" He asked, glancing at me.

"You're young, black, rich, and in high demand," I started. "Your stock is all the way up, as some would say."

"Hold up." He volleyed his attention between me and the windshield in front of him as we drove toward the bridge's entrance. "Are you buttering me up to hit me with some bad news?"

"No." I chuckled while shaking my head. "This whole thing is for selfish reasons, if you can believe that."

"A selfish Simeon?" He chuckled. "I can't believe that, but I'm curious, so please, go on."

"Why get married?"

He glanced at me and cracked a smile.

"Most men, the night before their wedding, would be in a state of contemplation. Let's be honest here, marriage is really for women."

"True." He nodded. "True."

"But you're happy," I added. "Genuinely excited. I haven't seen you question your decision to go through with marrying Ayanna." I held up a hand. "Who is a wonderful woman, so I'm not aiming my question at her. I just..." I chuckled. "With signing with the Flames and moving to Oakland, I noticed your hesitation. With signing on the dotted line to purchase your home on the hills and to sign the lease for Pure Roque's headquarters, I saw you hesitate with those, too. But with every step of the way of planning this wedding, not once have you hesitated with that."

"Ain't nothing to hesitate on," he said.

I focused on him.

"I'm marrying my best friend, Simeon." He grinned. "A woman who makes me want to do this thing called life with every damn day. And I'm not stupid enough to think it'll be easy. Life never is, so I would imagine marriage has its challenges too. But I'm excited to do all that shit with her, man. Like, I'm *so* looking forward to it. I can't wait to go through all that life throws at me, at us... with her and *only* her. Together. And knowing through it all, we got each other. That's really all I want, to be honest."

"Hmph," I huffed, leaning my head back against the headrest.

"When I realized I didn't want to go too long sleeping in a bed she wasn't in," he revealed with a nod. "That's when I *knew* I wanted forever with her."

"Forever is a long time, Dallas," I reminded.

"And thank God for all that precious time, right? To be so blessed." He grinned and patted my chest once. "I'm getting married, man, whew!"

I chuckled, feeling the infectious feeling he was giving off again.

"And I know many people don't think marriage is an accomplishment but for me and Ayanna." He whistled, then smiled. "It's a fucking victory, for real."

"That it is." I nodded.

As Dallas continued about having a good night and trying a few of the lounge's famous scotch, I wondered quietly, in that moment, could I ever be as excited and happy, and as sure and optimistic again about marrying Eryn the way I was once upon a time too.

# Twenty-One

**ERYN**

"I still can't believe how crazy and amazing of a day it's been," Ayanna voiced as she dropped herself onto the couch. We were in Ayanna and Dallas's suite, which was her suite for only the night. By tomorrow, when she and her new husband returned, she would be Mrs. Roque, and it would be theirs. Ayanna lifted her glass of champagne off the coffee table between us and tossed back what remained in the glass.

"Okay," Brooke, her best friend, said, taking the glass out of Ayanna's hand. "As maid of honor, it's my responsibility to make sure you don't walk down the aisle with a hangover."

I snickered.

"And seeing that we have to be up in literally only a few hours," Brooke added, "you've had enough."

"Yeah, girl," I said to Ayanna, "did you have to schedule your ceremony start time in the morning? We literally have to get up in the next five hours."

"Four now," Apryl corrected, taking a seat beside me. "I'm about to head out so I can get enough rest, and I would advise everyone to do the same."

This was the *crazy* Ayanna was referring to. It surprised me to see Apryl at the bachelorette party that was held in the hotel's ballroom where Ayanna was staying. The party was a simple dinner and gift exchange, like an extended bridal shower. Ayanna said she and Dallas agreed not to have any strippers at either of their parties and that they would rather keep things low-key the night before their wedding. Apparently, Apryl was flying out to Oakland to privately train Ayanna and initially met Ayanna when Apryl started photographing for Dallas's Pure Roque brand's campaign as a brand ambassador.

"We didn't really have a choice on the ceremony start time," Ayanna explained. "We wanted the rose garden at the Botanical Garden, and the only available slots were in the morning. Dallas would've accepted a ceremony at seven in the morning if it meant getting married among the roses. I wasn't about to argue with that."

I smiled, appreciating how they were staying true to their red rose wedding theme. Even the night before, when Dallas and Ayanna hosted their pre-wedding dinner in the same ballroom where Ayanna held her bachelorette party tonight. They had their wedding planner arrange a high-end dinner party surrounded by an abundance of red roses. The setup looked like a scene out of a movie. One long dining table for Ayanna and Dallas's family and guests to dine beneath two large gold picture frames that had red roses cascading around the edges from the top of the structure to the bottom. The way the decorators aligned the gold frames opposite each other, hovering over the lone long dining table, gave off a dope ass mirroring illusion. A line of red roses sat in glass vases between tall, cylindrical glass candle holders, putting everyone in a romantic mood. Even my ass. It was like sitting in a portrait. These two were all about red roses and what red roses signified, and it showed.

"It's still tripping me out to see you two sitting next to each other," Ayanna admitted. "I can't believe how small this world is."

"I know," I agreed.

"Dallas's best man, Jayce, is getting married to Summer, who, for the record, was way worse in college than who you met at the bachelorette party tonight."

I laughed. "I liked Summer."

"I do too," Ayanna concurred. "*Now*. Truth is, I wouldn't have known she was someone to like *now* if I didn't invite my former co-worker from my old job out here. Turns out, one of my co-workers, Lauryn, is married to Summer's cousin and that's why Summer was with Lauryn tonight. I knew about Summer and Jayce through Dallas but I had no idea Summer knew *my* Lauryn..." Ayanna pointed at me. "Who *you* also know."

"Well, I don't *know* Lauryn, per se," I corrected. "I literally just met her last month because, as Lauryn told you, *my* mother is *her* therapist."

"Yeah." Ayanna nodded. "Like what the fuck?! And you're Apryl's fiance's sister. What is really going on? This is all still trippin' me out, for real."

"I get it." I giggled. "The trippin' is definitely justified for you."

Ayanna had a couple of her bridesmaids and some women from her bachelorette party in her suite. They were here and there, either out on the balcony or in the kitchen where the drinks sat on ice.

"Are you ready?" Apryl asked Ayanna.

"To get married?" Ayanna asked. "Hell yeah!"

I smiled.

"This has been a long time coming," Ayanna added. "It's just so crazy that Dallas and I are finally *here*. The night before. And it almost didn't happen because of Dominick's lame ass."

"Let that be the last time we hear his name today and forever," her friend Brooke declared.

"Amen," I agreed. "Because his album did not come out today like he thought it would, due in part to that gag order on him and his label and he knows better to even mention your name in so much as a remix of a sneeze because a lawsuit will be soon to follow. He's weeping in a bush somewhere in Miami, just as sad as he is."

"Hello!" Brooke chimed in again.

"We have gagged and silenced him," I added. "We don't know him. Who is he?"

"And I *know* that's right." Brooke leaned over to high-five me, and I met her halfway.

"Y'all are too much," Ayanna said through her laugh. "Anyway, I'm excited to get married so Dallas and I can move on to the next step."

"Which is?" Apryl asked.

"Making some babies." Ayanna stuck her tongue out and they all laughed.

I felt a pang in my gut I swallowed back, forcing a smile.

"I want to give him *a lot* of them, too." She nodded. "Pop them out back-to-back. And I got you as my trainer, Apryl. So I know my snap-back will be epic every time."

"You are the one who is too much," Apryl expressed through her giggling.

I rubbed my lips together and tried to remain unaffected. I could be my vivacious self all I wanted, but the topic of babies always sent me to an uncomfortable place. Even when I tried hard for it not to. I tossed back the champagne I had left in my glass and stood to my feet.

I said, "I think I'm going to head to the hotel so I can get what little sleep I can get."

Apryl nodded and stood up as well. "Yeah, I'm going to grab a cab and head home to sleep. And as for you, bride-to-be, I'd suggest you do the same."

"Oh, you already know I'm on it," Brooke promised. "She's about to go to sleep right now. Hey y'all," Brooke called to the other ladies in the room, "y'all gotta clear out because the bride needs her beauty rest."

"'Cause I'm getting married tomorrow. *Ahh!*" Ayanna shouted, and all the ladies cheered. Including me. Because Lord knows I needed a reason to escape the feeling that washed over me.

———

It was like dying and going to heaven, surrounded by every rose known to man in every color God has allowed to grace the earth. When Ayanna said she would get married in a garden of roses, never did I imagine *this*.

The bridesmaids and groomsmen stood on opposite ends of the garden, Dallas already front and center. When they asked him if he wanted to walk down the aisle during rehearsals, he refused, wanting the aisle of roses to be reserved for Ayanna.

The day couldn't have been more perfect—bright and pleasant, with a sparkling sun and weather just right for mid-June, especially for a little after 10am.

I yawned, lifting the mini bouquet of blushing pink roses to my mouth to cover. Lifted my eyes in time to see Simeon looking my way. He winked, and that made me smile.

When we met in the living room of our shared suite hours earlier, he whistled as I walked out. The bridesmaid's dress—a graceful stretch crepe in a deep wine color with an off-the-shoulder neckline—fit like a glove. The split, extending from the floor to just above my knee, added the perfect touch of sexy to the ensemble.

Simeon and I matched, unsurprisingly. As a groomsman, he dressed himself in a classic wine 3-piece tuxedo. His silk black bowtie matched the tuxedo's black shawl lapel. The tuxedo had a slim-fit cut and gave him a sleeker and trimmer silhouette, which he honestly didn't need. Paired with a fresh fade and topped with his signature warm and spicy cologne, he was damn lucky it was too early, and I was too tired to see how easy it would be to get him out of his tux.

We'd been getting it on since the night of our hookup. Religiously. The way we just fell back into step, remembering our sexual choreography like we hadn't gone over a decade not seeing each other, was surprising to me. Especially when no matter how good it was, spending time with him that way, there was still the elephant in the room neither one of us wanted to touch, much less discuss.

That *thing* that happened between us that made over a decade pass. The major decision I made that had us not seeing or talking to each other in that time.

I couldn't keep my mind on that for too much longer. The environment and the sweet smell of roses too enamored me. They were in peak bloom and either swayed with the wind in nearby bushes or hung from vines that framed the altar. There were no seats allowed in the rose garden, so everyone in attendance had to stand. The Botanical Garden's wedding planner detailed all the restrictions and when I listened to her rattle all the "do nots" to Ayanna over the phone, I wondered why on earth did they agree to have their nuptials done there, especially given the early ceremony start time.

However, today, as I stood among her bridesmaids, all dressed in matching wine-colored gowns, with her maid of honor in the same design but in blush, and as I glanced ahead at the groomsmen in their coordinated attire, with Dallas in a stunning Italian-made white and burgundy floral three-piece tuxedo, it all made sense.

Especially when Ayanna appeared up the aisle. Just like with the other restrictions regarding what could and could not be at their garden wedding, the Botanical Garden planner ruled out a live band. So, to make up for it, Dallas and Ayanna hired an all-male black quartet. And the moment Ayanna's shoes touched the top of the rose-covered aisle, they began harmonizing "You" by Jesse Powell.

The moment Dallas saw her, he reached over to his best man, Jayce, grabbing Jayce by the lapel of his tuxedo jacket while Dallas brought his fist to his mouth to suppress a scream. That made us all laugh, both the ladies and gents in the wedding party and the wedding guests.

It was the perfect reaction. And he had every reason to express it. Because she looked like a dream come true. From head to toe, literally, she was the rose queen. Her stylist styled her hair in a slicked-up chignon that formed the shape of a giant rose. All hair. Underneath the sun, her designer wedding gown shimmered, catching the sunlight at every angle, competing with the twinkle in her eye she wore looking at Dallas. Her light ivory lace dress was absolutely stunning, and even that wasn't a fair description. Because with a sweetheart corset paired with an effortlessly flowing skirt, adorned with silver drawings of roses, she had us *all* in awe.

There were literal floral murals extending from the corset of her dress to the elegantly flowing skirt. The gown's train was subtle, the off-the-shoulder straps modest. Ayanna was simply a light and airy queen on her day. When she showed me her shoes the night before, after her bachelorette party, I knew then she wasn't playing with us. She wore an untraditional pair, too, red with the heel of her shoe forming an artificial red rose. The sequins and glitter on her dress grew more and more pronounced the closer she walked to the altar of roses, escorted by her father. The droplets of water on her red rose bouquet reflected under the sun's rays.

And Dallas didn't take his eyes off her once. Or had he stopped smiling. The second she arrived in front of him, he almost tripped over himself in his burgundy suede loafers, which sent humor around the garden. These two were truly in love, and it was a real treat to witness their connection.

Ayanna promised the ceremony would be a short one since everyone had to stand, and she wasn't lying. Because when it was time for them to exchange their vows, it felt like the ceremony had only started moments ago.

"Ayanna," Dallas started, "I knew there was something incredibly special about you when we met on our move-in day at Langston U."

Some guests shouted "*LU*," others echoing the call, making us all laugh, especially those of us who are Langstoners, young and old.

Dallas chuckled. "We started as friends, but I always felt a deeper connection, a spark I couldn't shake, baby. What I didn't know was my inability to ignore that connection, that spark, from the very beginning, was a sign you were who I wanted to spend my life with."

"*Aw*," I said low.

One bridesmaid in front of me, Mya, turned and said, "I know, right?"

I smiled and refocused forward.

"I remember those days," Dallas continued, "when you were hesitant about us taking the next step. You were cautious and hardheaded."

"Shut up," Ayanna mumbled.

We all laughed in response.

"But," Dallas said through his laugh, "I understood why, and you had a damn good reason, My Heart." He grew serious as he stepped closer to her. "But Yaya, my feelings for you never wavered. I held on to everything I had to stay patient. Because even in those moments when I thought, for just a split second, that we might miss our chance to move from friends to something more, I always knew we were meant to be together."

I could feel my tears pricking at the side of my eyes. I wasn't the crying type, but I swore in that moment, I would run my mascara listening to Dallas's vows.

"Your kindness, your down-to-earth personality, and your beautiful heart are only a few of the countless reasons I fell head over heels in love with you, Ayanna."

A tear escaped Dallas's eye and Ayanna caught it with her thumb.

"*Aw*, baby," she said as she wiped it away.

"Today," Dallas sniffed back another tear. "Standing here with you, I'm filled with so much joy and gratitude. I'm beyond geeked that I get to be your partner for life. And honestly, besides the perk of calling you my wife from today on, I can't get over how incredible you look in that dress, baby. Damn, you look good."

Everyone made their version of approval audible through cheers or claps, some even humor.

"I promise to always cherish you, hold you down for life, and stand by your side through every challenge life wanna throw at us. 'Cause I'm gonna be your rock, your homey, and your biggest fan, Mrs. Roque."

"They 'bout to make me mess up my make-up," I expressed in a whisper.

Ayanna's bridesmaids giggled in front and behind me.

"I can't wait to create a future with you filled with all the love, laughter, and dope adventures. I am honored, Ayanna, to be your man, your husband, your friend. And I look forward to every moment we'll share, My Heart."

I curved my finger at the knuckles to catch the tears welling in my lower lids.

"Dallas, my Dallas," Ayanna started. "From the time we became friends, you have been a constant source of joy and support in my life. Especially when I made the craziest, *wildest* decisions, you have always been there to support me and make sense of them."

Dallas nodded.

"Our journey from being only friends to this moment, here, in a rose garden, in front of everyone we love, has been filled with unexpected ass turns. But you know what?"

"What, My Heart?" He asked.

"Every step has brought us closer and shown me just how deeply in love I am with you."

"I love you too," he returned.

It was like no one else was there the way Dallas and Ayanna stared at each other. It was the most endearing thing to see.

"I'll admit it, since you already said it."

He laughed.

"I was hesitant at first. The thought of us becoming more than friends and possibly messing up the pure, genuine bond we created scared me. But as the days turned into weeks and the weeks into months, it became abundantly clear to me I couldn't imagine my life without you in it. Like, the idea of going even one more day without you by my side was a thought I couldn't get behind. I just couldn't bear it."

Dallas's smile grew wider as he nodded.

"Your patience, your unshakable belief in us, and your love gave me the courage to follow my heart. You've *always* seen in us what took me time to embrace, and for that, I am forever grateful for your stubborn ass."

Dallas tossed his head back to laugh.

"Your resilience is fine as all fine," she joked. "And you're already fine, so, you know, you're like triple fine."

"You're triple fine too, baby," he said, looking her up and down and licking his lips.

I laughed along with everyone else.

"Today, I am filled with a profound sense of happiness and peace that's running through me on repeat, like my favorite album. No skips."

"No skips," he repeated. "I feel you."

She giggled.

"Dallas, I promise to love you, cherish and support you with all my heart. I vow to be your biggest fan and your biggest supporter. Your partner in all things. I can't wait to spend forever with you."

I'd finally taken my eyes off the beautiful couple when I looked ahead of me to see Simeon staring right at me. The look in his eyes took my breath away, making the tears I tried to wipe away fall instead. He winked once more and my heart hammered a little harder. I twisted my lips to one side to keep back the other tears from falling. In that moment, listening to Ayanna and Dallas's vows, and meeting Simeon's gaze, sent a wave of emotions through me I'd never felt. Questions I never thought I'd have again.

They say weddings have a way of making those who attend self-reflective, regardless of marital status. Single women witnessing nuptials with their boyfriends often wondered if they would be next.

For me, I wish it were that simple. Because instead of asking if I would be next, I had a hard time asking myself, could it ever be me with Simeon or did I ruin that possibility when I made the decision that ended us?

# Twenty-Two

## SIMEON

"Whew, my goodness," Eryn expressed the moment we walked through the hotel suite's door. "That was ah-mazing. Wow."

I shrugged off the wine-colored tuxedo jacket I wore for the wedding and draped it over the armchair in the suite. Eryn and I were staying in a penthouse at the SoHi Hotel and Suites in Manhattan. The SoHi's penthouse was the perfect complement to the wedding we'd just attended. Our suite on the 33rd floor offered stunning views of the Hudson River and downtown Manhattan, including One World Trade. It was beautifully designed, with an L-shaped living space and a billiard table positioned in front of one of the sparkling floor-to-ceiling windows. If it had a taste, the spot would be absolutely delectable.

Eryn sighed as she sank into the couch in the penthouse living room. "I really should be exhausted after getting back so late from Ayanna's bachelorette party last night—and you keeping me up for the other half of it."

I chuckled.

"But I feel so energized." She beamed. "The ceremony was beautiful, but that reception. Oh, my God! Stunning."

"I know." I walked up to a nearby wall and leaned against it. "I'm still recovering from being so blown away."

*The moment the MC introduced the couple as Mr. And Mrs. Roque, Dallas and Ayanna—who'd changed out of her sparkling wedding gown for a sleek and glittering white midi reception dress—took their place at the center of the dance floor to dance to their wedding song, Ed Sheeran's song "Thinking Out Loud," over a rose monogram of their initials.*

*Dallas and Ayanna held their reception in the Garden's greenhouse. Upon entering, we were all met with vibrant tropical plants, exotic flowers, and lush greenery. Once the bridal party finished taking pictures, the wedding planner led us through a winding path that gave way to the most immaculate setup I've ever seen, and I'd seen plenty. A red rose oasis is the best way I could describe it. Two long mirrored tables, with glass plates shaped as roses, reflected the décor and added so much depth. The tables and rose-shaped glass plates paired well with the transparent chairs with white cushions. The sun shining through the greenhouse's glass was all the lighting needed to bring out the natural beauty of all the roses that surrounded us. And there were a lot. Red roses were the only flower present.*

*Even Ayanna's hairstylist styled Ayanna's hair in an updo with a bun that was shaped into a perfect giant rose. Roses filled the space, nestled in small vases around tall cylindrical candle holders, and clipped roses hung in glass globes from arching rose vines. But the real showstopper was the sea of roses covering Dallas and Ayanna's sweetheart table. The scent was incredible, and the whole scene felt whimsical, almost otherworldly. For those two hours in the greenhouse, with Ed Sheeran's "Thinking Out Loud" echoing off the glass walls, it was like I'd been hit by Cupid's arrow. The atmosphere was so enchanting, it was impossible not to get swept up in it. All I could think about was Eryn—getting her in my arms, like I was under a spell.*

*When it was time to join the bride and groom on the dance floor, I wrapped my arms around Eryn's waist and pulled her close. She rested her head against my chest as we swayed to the melody, and in that moment, everything brought me back to what I'd wanted since the day I first met her as a teenager at a farmers' market in Brooklyn.*

"Must be so nice to be as loved as Ayanna is by Dallas."

That pulled me out of my thoughts. I focused on Eryn to see her smiling to herself as she unstrapped the gold heels she wore.

"The way he looks at her and the way she looks at him." She giggled. "They're *perfect* for each other."

"Hmph."

I agreed wholeheartedly. I had literally watched those two grow before my eyes. I remembered traveling to Vegas for the Summer League and seeing him look like someone had stolen his puppy because she wouldn't come with him and refused to give their relationship a chance. I watched him nervously decide to return to New York for an interview with her. When I met Ayanna for the second time, escorting her to Dallas's room at the Four Seasons for his first interview with any publication, I knew they would leave that room as a couple. I've watched Dallas and Ayanna's love bloom like the roses decorating their wedding. But something about the way Eryn said it rubbed me the wrong way. It was as if she had never known the feeling of being loved by someone the way Dallas loved Ayanna.

"Like, I adored them before." She pressed her hand to her chest. "But now, I'm a *huge* fan. I literally can't imagine them being with anyone else other than each other—"

"You had someone who was as crazy *and* in love with you as Dallas is with Ayanna."

Eryn shifted her eyes over to me and stopped unbuckling her other sandal altogether. First, she jerked her head back, then she furrowed her brows, still staring at me.

"I'm sorry." I shook my head. "You said what you said and it just..." I pushed my back off the wall I leaned on next. "I mean, I agree with you, but you're speaking about their love as if you don't know what it's like. As if you didn't experience a love like that."

She scoffed. "Wow."

"Am I lying?"

She licked her lips, then glanced down again to finish unbuckling her sandal.

"No, you're not," she answered. "But the only difference is, the man who loved *me* so wildly eventually left me."

I swallowed.

"He left." She shrugged. "And was gone without a trace."

"After you lied by omission and kept something important from that man for your own selfish reasons—"

"You know what?" She stood to her feet and leaned forward to scoop up her heels. "I think I *am* tired."

"Eryn—"

"I'm gonna get some sleep."

"So," I said, turning to face her as she walked away toward one of the rooms in the penthouse. "That's it?"

I'd booked a two-bedroom penthouse suite shortly after Eryn's arrival in Oakland. I knew she would attend the wedding, and since we weren't intimate—and I'd promised myself we wouldn't be—I got the suite so she could have her own room and I'd have mine. But since we arrived, she's been sleeping with me. She stopped walking when she created enough distance between us. Too much distance. The most distance we've had in the last two weeks.

"We're just going to keep skating, huh? And not address what needs addressing?" I asked. "Are we *never* going to talk about what needs to be discussed, Eryn?"

She stared at me for a beat, then inhaled a deep breath, shaking her head next. "Maybe some other time, Simeon. Right now, I only want to go to sleep."

Eryn exited the room after that.

"Of course," I said to myself. "Always taking the lazy approach. Why am I not surprised?"

But how much longer can I accept that?

# Twenty-Three

**ERYN**

Ayanna's giggles traveled around the space, making me laugh along with her. We were at a photo shoot at For The Culture HQ. By we; I mean Dallas and Ayanna, of course, and Mykal Jones—FTC's current editor-in-chief, although she revealed her tenure at the magazine was ending. Also in attendance was a red-headed beauty, Juliette Hart, who I met at Dallas and Ayanna's wedding only two days prior.

Juliette was the journalist selected to interview the new Roques. It thrilled Ayanna to know it would be Juliette who would interview her, and Ayanna was happy to have Juliette attend her wedding since she knew Juliette when Ayanna worked as a journalist at For The Culture.

Juliette brought her boyfriend, Luke Lockett, as her plus one—the current men's basketball coach at my alma mater. Turns out, we all have that connection: Dallas, Ayanna, Simeon, and me. Luke was young and very handsome. Being at Ayanna and Dallas's wedding really made me realize just how intertwined our lives have become.

The prop designers and photographers at FTC recreated a wedding scene for Ayanna and Dallas's photo shoot. For this scene, the photographers put Ayanna and Dallas in front of a white wedding cake with roses that resembled their amazing wedding cake that had red roses cascading from the top of the cake to the gold cake stand that held it.

FTC's photographers told Ayanna and Dallas to interact with the cake for the photos and the two of them had fun with it, pretending to feed one another and purposely missing each other's mouths, getting cake on each other's faces and laughing about it.

"What do you think?" the photographer, Shana, asked as she showed me some photos she took in her camera's LCD screen.

I smiled and giggled at the snapshots. They looked natural, authentic, and extremely sweet. It was a fantastic idea scheduling Ayanna and Dallas to come in for the shoot two days after their wedding and one day before they flew out for their honeymoon.

They were still flying high from the romance of their red rose wedding. You could see the glow in Ayanna's cheeks and the twinkle in Dallas's eyes. It was perfection. Better than anything I could have masterminded.

With this piece of their media crisis strategy set in place, everything was complete. My job was done. The wedding was already the talk of the internet, and the official photos hadn't even been released yet. Dominick's record label had shelved his album, and both he and the label were under a strict gag order. If Ayanna's nudes ever saw the light of day—especially on an album cover—they'd be facing severe penalties, possibly giving up everything, including the pennies off their penny loafers.

In fact, the label's lawyers confirmed that their client had destroyed the nudes after Ayanna's legal team made it clear they were prepared to sue for invasion of privacy, defamation, and emotional distress.

America's new darling black couple were looking damn good in their magazine photos. I was feeling good. Accomplished. Everything was great... except for Simeon and me.

He stood far away from me, chatting with Mykal. He'd spoken to everyone at the shoot. Everyone except me. And that was partially my fault.

We hadn't spoken since that Saturday after the wedding and in the living room of the penthouse we shared. I refused to leave my room in the penthouse after I entered it that afternoon. When I emerged the next day, Simeon was nowhere to be found in the penthouse.

I hadn't seen him at all that Sunday, actually. This Monday morning was my first time seeing him at For The Culture HQ. And he had said nothing to me.

Mykal made her way over to me, her hips swinging from left to right and her engagement ring blinding me from afar.

"So?" she asked, clapping her hands once, then gesturing at Ayanna and Dallas.

"It's perfect," I commented. "Thank you for this, Mykal. For real. Setting up a mock wedding scene was genius."

"Oh, my God," she exclaimed, smiling. "It was nothing. We moved some things around to accommodate their story in our upcoming issue, but you guys are helping us more than we're helping you. The only magazine to have the story everyone can't be quiet about and their wedding photos that are absolutely to die for? Yeah, we are so grateful you thought of us. And I really mean that, Eryn."

"Oh, absolutely."

"Don't tell Ayanna this, but..." Mykal leaned in. "Girlfriend has me feeling like I need to rethink my whole wedding plan after that red rose affair. Is she kidding me?"

"It was the wedding of the century, right?"

"Oh, my goodness, and then some."

"It's going to be hard to top it, Mykal." I smiled slyly.

Mykal kissed her teeth. "Don't tell a soon-to-be bride that two months before her damn wedding. What's wrong with you?"

I hollered a laugh and covered my mouth, my eyes on their own, moving over to Simeon. He blinked away a moment later, lifting his phone to his ear to take a call while walking away.

Watching Ayanna and Dallas was so inspiring. And not in an envious way. In a truly inspiring way. Listening to the authenticity in their vows and knowing all they went through leading up to their wedding really put things into perspective for me. I would've loved something like that with Simeon, despite the only but biggest blemish in our relationship.

Unfortunately, after Saturday in the penthouse, I was sure we probably would never have that. He clearly didn't trust whatever it was we had now, and I simply didn't want to talk about what broke us. I snatched my eyes off his wide back as he approached FTC's elevator, likely to leave saying nothing to me.

"So," I said to Mykal. "Do I get an advance copy once the interview and photos go to print with the next issue?"

"Absolutely." Mykal nodded. "Here." She pulled out her smartphone and tapped her fingers on the screen. "Let me know where I can send your advance copy, and I'll have it to you right after we get back our first draft from the printer."

"Thank you, Mykal."

"I'll also send a link to the web article once it's published on our website. The hardest part of all this is going to be deciding what photos to go with because between the wedding photos and the photos they've taken today in the studio." She smiled. "I am having a really good problem right now."

"I love it," I expressed. "That *is* a very good problem to have."

If only all problems could be as good and easy as that one.

———

A streak of lightning, slicing through the night sky and splitting the night with a bright vein, suddenly lit up the room. The rumbling of thunder that followed close behind had me turning off my side and onto my back in bed.

The hotel's housekeeping left the heavy curtains opened after cleaning the suite earlier. The curtains hung open on either side of the ten-foot floor-to-ceiling windows, offering a clear view of downtown Manhattan. At that hour, One World Trade was all lit up, making the view outside resemble a blue-black painting.

I sat up in bed, balancing myself on my elbows, and watched briefly as water pelted the glass. I didn't bother checking the time on my phone.

It was clear it was late. But my throat was a little dry, so I decided to grab a bottle of water from the kitchen.

As soon as I opened my bedroom door, I noticed the lights were on in the living room. The closer I walked, I realized the lights were on in the penthouse where the billiard table was.

Simeon had taken a shot. The sharp, crisp clack of the colorful billiard balls colliding echoed around the space as he lifted his eyes to lock with mine. We had been avoiding each other for two days. Or I had been avoiding him?

After he left For The Culture to go wherever he disappeared to, I returned to an empty penthouse, alone, not seeing him for the rest of that day. Earlier, the next day, I left the penthouse bright and early for a spa appointment then met up with Apryl at the gym she trained at, only to hang out and for her to give me a quick session between her scheduled ones. When I returned to the penthouse that afternoon, Simeon was nowhere to be found. With nothing else to do since Ayanna and Dallas's interview was currently in editing and the newlyweds in Tahiti enjoying their honeymoon, I did my favorite thing in the world: sleep.

I got up around 9pm, ordered room service, ate, and brushed my teeth. After freshening up, Simeon was still nowhere to be found, so I climbed into bed, assuming that was it for the night. But, of course, Mother Nature had other plans for me.

I blinked away from Simeon's stare and entered the kitchen, pulling open the SubZero fridge to grab a bottle of spring water. We literally had exchanged no words since that Saturday after Ayanna and Dallas's wedding. We'd gone from not speaking for over a decade, to living together in his condo, in separate rooms, to hooking up every night after our initial hook up, to not even so much as saying bless you when one of us sneezed.

I left the kitchen and entered the living room area that was next to where the pool table was. Simeon stood upright again, polishing the cue tip of the pool stick with a cue tip shaper, eyes returning to mine.

With the view of downtown Manhattan as his personal backdrop and the man himself standing there wearing nothing but a pair of gray lounge pants slung low at his waist, I sighed at how defeated he made me feel.

I was dealing with a war inside of me. On one side of that war, I wanted to wave the white flag. Talk about whatever he wanted to talk about, which was the obvious. The obvious reason for us. But the other side of the war inside me didn't want to go back to a place that had me bed bound and in a depressive state for what felt like six years because he decided to leave.

Not one to spend too much time thinking, though, I took steps toward him and the pool table. His eyes left mine to drift down my body, focusing on my lace-trimmed white cami and short set. He licked his lips as he watched my legs close the distance between us.

I placed my water bottle on one edge of the pool table and walked my way over to him. In front of him, I tilted his head back to look at me in my eyes and he swallowed hard, doing as I wanted. The man was so damn beautiful. Even when visibly upset with me.

I knew we needed to talk, but I didn't care to do any of what would have to happen after the talk. The questions, the revelations. Having to rehash everything mentally and emotionally. The whole thing, in that moment, had me needing an escape pronto. Like always.

I wrapped my fingers around the slender structure of the pool stick and slid it out of his hand, which he allowed. I ran my fingers up his chest next, hearing him exhale this time.

I closed the distance between us, lifted onto my toes, and pressed my lips to his for a quick peck. It was when I brushed my lips against his, a second time, that Simeon grabbed me by the ass, palming both cheeks and using his grip to lift me high enough to sit on the pool table.

He pulled my hair out of its top bun and immediately buried his fingers into my strands. He held me by the head and parted my lips with his, snaking his tongue into my mouth soon after. He groaned the moment our tongues touched, kissing me with more vigor.

I leaned back on my hands, matching his energy and meeting his tongue thrusts. Our moans blended like a duet as I circled my hips in rhythm, feeling his hard-on grow against me.

I was breathing fast, my pulse racing, my nipples so hard they chafed against the fabric of my cami. I wanted him so badly I could almost feel him inside me, which is why I was moaning as if he already was.

Unable to keep my hands to myself any longer, I sat up, freeing my hands from supporting me, and slid one into the waistband of his lounge pants. He grunted in response.

"Uh-uh," he expressed on my lips next. "I have no more condoms on me."

The hour, like I said, was late, but this was New York City, which meant we could get condoms from anywhere that was open. Likely a pharmacy open 24/7. But in that moment, as hot and ready as I was, and as badly as I needed him between my thighs, who could bother with the work of stopping to get dressed and to go searching for some damn condoms?

"It's okay," I said on his lips between pecks.

He pulled away slightly. "What's okay?"

I wrapped my arms around the back of his neck to bring him close to me again. "We don't need them."

He jerked his head back. Simeon stared at me for a breath before removing my arms from around his neck. He stepped away shortly after, creating unwanted distance between us.

I inhaled a valiant breath, and it did nothing to calm the racing of my heart.

"How can you say that?" he asked, expression serious, brows severely furrowed. "How can you say that after everything?"

I kissed my teeth. "Are you kidding me right now?"

"Are *you* kidding *me*?"

And just like that, I went from being horny to being annoyed.

"I would think," he added. "After everything, you would never want to have sex without a condom ever again."

A streak of lightning ripped along the sky and a louder crack of thunder followed less than two seconds later, rumbling in the background. I remember learning that when thunder erupted shortly after lightning, it meant the storm was close. And it felt like that storm had arrived in the penthouse, too.

"You're never going to forgive me for what I did, huh?"

"You can't even say it," he spat low, balling his lips after. "You can't even say *what* you did—"

"Whatever," I interjected, shaking my head as I got off the pool table and made my way around it.

"Running, like always."

"Don't you give me that bullshit." I pointed at him, my chest heaving. "You're the king of running off without a word, so spare me the guilt trip."

Simeon shook his head and snatched the pool stick I'd leaned against the table. Without even a second glance in my direction, he went back to his hunched-over position, resuming his game exactly as he was when I left my room and came into the living room.

There was a lot unsaid, but what he didn't say to me was loud and clear. He blamed me for derailing our future. And he would never forgive me for pulling up something from its roots before it could grow.

# TWENTY-FOUR

**SIMEON**

I tightened my abs and engaged my core, slowly lifting my upper body toward my knees and curling my spine. I exhaled as I lifted, bringing my chest close to my knees before holding the position for a moment. Then, I inhaled as I slowly lowered myself back onto the penthouse's carpeted floor. I repeated the motion, continuing my sit-ups. Working up a sweat and getting my blood pumping, not only for the exercise but also for the relief.

I managed to get a little sleep last night after whatever the hell that was with Eryn. Because not only was I still pissed, but I also wanted her badly. It was insanely frustrating to be both angry and in need of someone at the same damn time.

"I'm headed to Brooklyn," she announced in front of me.

It was like she had materialized out of nowhere. Her hand rested on the telescopic handle of the rolling suitcase she brought from Oakland, her body clad in a vintage white t-shirt tied at the hem for a cropped look. Her hips swayed in a snug, cream-colored high-waisted maxi skirt as she approached the coffee table in front of me. She dropped the penthouse's room card on the table and added, "Here's the key."

I clenched my teeth to keep from saying what I really wanted to: that she was being ridiculous and still the same lazy Eryn who pissed me off so much that moving nine states away felt like the only way to cope with her lack of effort to do the damn work—the work of fixing something that had all the potential to be fixed. The work of seeing things from my perspective and not selfishly from only her own. The work of us healing, together. Because just like me, she hasn't forgotten. It probably drifts into her mind at random times during her day, or when something triggers her to think about it.

*It.*

Her decision.

Which she wasn't wrong for making, but she's wrong for not wanting to discuss it. I sat up completely, wrapping my forearms around my knees to catch my breath.

"If I'm being honest," she added. "I don't think I'm going to be returning to Oakland with you on Monday."

That made me arch both brows.

"New York isn't my first pick but, I'd rather stay here or go back to L.A. than to walk on eggshells with you wherever you are."

Always playing the victim. I let out a scoffing laugh and wiped the sweat off my face. She stood there for a moment, probably waiting for me to react, to push her to stay instead of running away. But we weren't in that place anymore. I used to chase after her because I thought she didn't realize what she was doing, that she had it in her to see things differently. But now? Now I see she's just been dodging the hard work, running from real conversations, from letting love be shown, not just spoken. I'm done chasing.

I didn't want to be the understanding one, like always. It felt like all it ever did was enable her, not help her. And I just couldn't do it anymore.

"If going to Brooklyn is what you want, Eryn," I started. "Go to Brooklyn."

She balled her lips at me.

"If returning to Oakland isn't what you want." I shrugged. "Then *don't* return to Oakland."

I pushed myself up to stand, using my arms for support, and she kept her eyes on me the entire time.

"You've been doing whatever you wanted, however you wanted, for so long, I didn't know there was any other option other than what Eryn wants."

I watched her chest rise and fall with each breath.

"Because what did you want for me to say?" I pressed my hand to my chest. "Don't go? Stay? Continue to be here with me, all so we can get back to just *fucking* every night and not talking about the shit that is clearly eating away at you? Is that what you want me to do?"

Her lips started trembling.

"Because, beloved, it's been eating at me too." I took a few breaths to keep the tears in. "But I don't want to be the only one who wants to *talk* about it."

She looked away.

"You won't even form the words to say what happened, and because of that, I don't want to say it either. I don't know what reaction to expect from you—and that's so unlike me but, fuck Eryn." I pressed my palms together. "I *want* a resolution. That's how *I* do things. Will it be pleasant? Likely not. Will it hurt a little to talk about? It might. But I don't shy away from things that are uncomfortable and you know that. I've only done that these past five weeks for you. So..."

I walked off, heading towards the kitchen, and feeling her eyes on me the whole time.

"If you want to go..." I continued. "Then go. Get to Brooklyn safely. Call me when you're ready to have a conversation or, shit, don't call me at all. I don't know at this point."

I turned to open the fridge to get a bottle of water. Before I could close the fridge's door, I heard the penthouse door close and when I turned to glance into the living room knowing what I would find, I saw, like I knew it, she wasn't there. She'd left. Like I knew she would do.

"Fuck," I spat low, squeezing the water bottle's body. "Fuck."

I placed the bottle on the granite countertop, then leaned my elbows against it, dropping my forehead into my hands. Unbeknownst to Eryn, I've been hoping for the day we could finally discuss what happened those few weeks before our college graduation.

I'd imagined and even dreamt about the moment we would finally talk about her decision and her lack of interest in involving me. I never told her how it all made me feel—how leaving New York when I did, and the way I did, was one of the hardest decisions I ever had to make. But I felt like she gave me no choice. What was I supposed to do? She rewrote our future. And like I said, until she was ready to talk about it, I wasn't moving any further with her in any capacity.

Those weeks before our graduation, I never imagined leaving college with her being my ex. Things have a way of changing, though. Often in unbelievable ways.

# Twenty-Five
## Then... Dewittville, New York - March 2007 – 16 years ago

**ERYN**

"It feels like we've been driving forever," I complained, my eyes focused out the windshield and, on the road, ahead of us. "I can't believe this is still New York."

We'd gotten off a highway so far back, I couldn't recall how long ago it had been. Simeon and I had left LU's campus at 9am that morning, and it was almost 3pm. My ass was growing numb from sitting so damn long.

"We're almost there," Simeon promised, glancing over at me. "I used to get anxious during our drives from here to Brooklyn and Manhattan too because of all the time it took."

Simeon and I were driving to his parents' farm, his childhood home. A place he didn't speak about often. At least not enough for me. On the surface, Simeon was not who I would imagine living on a farm, much less growing up on one. Even now, as he sat behind the wheel of his expensive Sedan, dressed in a designer cashmere sweater and wool trousers, Chelsea *boots maneuvering between gas and brake, I just couldn't see him living on a farm. But that's where we were going.*

*"Thanks for agreeing to take this drive and offering to come out here with me," he said, eyes focused. "It's your spring break, and you're sacrificing it to spend on a farm in forty-degree weather."*

*"When my boyfriend tells me he can't come with me to Florida because his father injured himself, so he has to go back home to help during his break," I started, "the reasonable thing for his girlfriend to do, who claims to love him, of course..."*

*He smirked.*

*"...is to offer to come with."*

*We were lucky, according to my roommate, who was also from Western New York. This time of year often brought with it heavy snowfall. Spring was only weeks away, but sometimes, Western New York would get unexpected snow shortly before spring arrived. New York City was a lot the same, so I comprehended what she said perfectly.*

*I imagined the trees that lined the roads were lush and green during the summer. But in that moment, they were bare, the ground brown and dirt-filled. I'd never been on a farm before. I was born and raised in Brooklyn, New York. The closest thing I'd come to being on a farm was in my head while reading a book that served as mandatory reading in school. A part of me was curious what it would be like staying on one. The other side of me was curious to see Simeon in that setting because I swore I couldn't.*

*We turned onto a dirt path road and drove through low-swinging metal gates. The road we drove down next blended into a semi-steep hill, and then more land and road awaited us.*

*"A couple of things," Simeon started. "One, this is not the city. At all. It sometimes smells like shit, and the roosters crow loud before sunrise, so the first time you hear them, it'll be jarring."*

*I giggled. "Nothing except an alarm clock or my mother knocking on my door has ever woken me, so this should be interesting."*

*He smiled. "Two, I'll be very busy while here, so you'll have to either hang with my parents or, if you want, you can hang with me." He shrugged next. "But a lot of the things I usually do aren't fun or pretty."*

*"Things, like...?"*

*"Things that cause chapped lips, rope burns, and sore muscles at the end of every day."*

*I stared at him. "If you're trying to make me feel like I made the right choice choosing Dewittville, New York, over Miami, Florida, Simeon, you are doing a terrible job, babe. The worst."*

*He chuckled and pointed his attention forward.*

*"I just want to get there already." I glanced out the passenger window at the large stretch of land bordered by thick wooden fences. "How much longer until we get to the farm?"*

*"We're on it."*

*I turned my head to look at him, then out of the window again. "What?"*

*"We've been on it for the last two minutes," he informed me. "We'll be in front of the house in about a minute."*

*"My eyes began surveying everything more intently—the patches of green and brown grass, the scattered pools of water here and there."*

*"This is all your farm?"*

*"Yup." He gave an acknowledging look. "All sixty acres."*

*My attention returned out of my window again. "Even the ponds?"*

*"Even the ponds." He smiled. "Bass, Bluegill, and Catfish live in one of the three ponds on our farm."*

*My jaw dropped.*

*"We sell a good bulk of them to the fish markets around the city."*

*"Simeon." I pinched his arm. "Are you kidding me right now?"*

*He glanced at me, then returned his attention back to the road. "What?"*

*"You didn't tell me any of this."*

*"I didn't think you'd be interested."*

*I twisted my head to stare out of my window again. "You thought wrong."*

*It didn't take long for us to pull up to a big red house. It was a contemporary home, two stories and huge. A few feet to the left of it was a tiny dove gray house that looked more modern than the big red one.*

*Simeon pulled up to the house and parked. He turned in his seat to face me. "Are you ready?"*

*I nodded, feeling completely beside myself. The moment we got out of* the car and stepped up the porch stairs, Simeon turned the doorknob and opened the door to absolute coziness. The air smelled of warmth and slow-cooked food.

Footsteps materialized less than a second later.

Mr. King, Simeon's father, entered the space. He was tall like Simeon, with a similar build but carrying a bit more weight around his stomach. We had crossed paths numerous times when Simeon would join them at the farmers' markets in Brooklyn and the neighboring boroughs. After Simeon and I started dating, I often stole him away from their vendor table so we could hang out wherever the day took us.

Today, though, Mr. King's arm was in a sling, hence why we were on the farm and not catching some sun on a beach in Miami. Honestly, the trip to Miami was more than a trip for a spring break for me. I wanted to see if Miami was for me. Simeon had applied to a sports management agency down there, and they promised him a job and financing for his MBA if he signed on with them. After graduation, I wanted to leave New York, but I wasn't sure if Miami was where I wanted to go. California was looking more interesting to me, especially since there was a PR agency out there that was the best in the country. But Miami wasn't a go for spring break, because Simeon had to return home, and that kind of sent me in a mild limbo on what the plan would be, what Simeon and my plan would be, after we graduated in two months.

Mr. King waved with his good hand before approaching.

"They're here, Regina."

"Oh!" a light voice said from the back of the house. "I'll be right there."

"Eryn," Mr. King said, taking my hand and holding it in his. "It's so good to see you again."

"Same." I smiled. "It's like I haven't seen you guys in forever since you stopped running your vendor table at the farmers' market."

"With Simeon in college," Mr. King started, placing a hand on Simeon's shoulder and leaving it there. "We have seen little need to drive all that way anymore."

Mr. King pulled his son into a hug and groaned a little.

"Take it easy, bossman." Simeon stepped out of the hug to look at his father. "Shouldn't you be in bed or something resting?"

"Oh, I'm about to send him back there now that you're here," his mother stated as she closed the space between us.

Mrs. King, or Regina as Mr. King referred to her as, was a tiny woman. I'm talking tiny. Literally reaching five feet by a hair, specifically her coarse curls that shaped her beautiful dark brown face like a beautiful cloud. Mrs. King extended her arms for her son first, understandably. She grabbed my hand in their embrace and pulled me close too, to wrap her arms around us both.

"I am so happy y'all came." She looked over at me. "Took his father having to sprain his wrist, after falling off a tractor, for Simeon to bring you here. Can you believe that?"

"I really can't." I smirked at Simeon and then focused on his mother again. "I also cannot believe how huge your farm is."

"Oh, baby, you haven't seen nothing yet," Mrs. King said. "Maybe by tomorrow, Simeon can give you a tour. It's not much to see this time of year, but there's still a lot to feast your eyes on. For now, I gotta get back in the kitchen and finish dinner."

"I'll come with," I said.

"Really?" Simeon asked at the same time as his mother.

Mr. King chuckled.

"Yeah." I nodded. "I mean, I won't know what I'm doing or anything, but I want to hang with the mama hen of the farm."

She chuckled. "Well, then come on."

"I'll bring the bags into my house, and will see you in a bit then," Simeon announced. "And Pa, you go upstairs and get some rest. I'll take a walk around and see what needs to be tended to."

"Yes, Vernon," Mrs. King concurred, looking at Mr. King. "I'll bring you some tea in a minute."

"Okay, then," Mr. King said as I walked away with Mrs. King. "Upstairs I go."

Their ranch-style house was like a house from a movie. I was a city girl, through and through. It's like I said. The closest thing I'd come to a farm was reading about them in books. The house was every bit of perfect, though. Outside their door and through the porch screen door that creaked a little as it opened and closed, was a beautiful view of all their land that seemed to go on and on forever.

*Inside was so pretty and vintage, with floral wallpaper in some rooms, antique modest furniture in the living room, and walls that seemed built but still maintained from the 1900s. In their kitchen, Mrs. King had all kinds of cooking appliances, gadgets, and gizmos. Equipment for things like making pasta, baking bread, and tools to make all the things I would watch my mother pile in a shopping cart during one of our market runs as a kid.*

*I said I would follow Mrs. King into the kitchen to help her finish preparing dinner, but the view from her kitchen's window of cows grazing in a fenced pasture far up ahead of us kept stealing my attention.*

*"Do they get cold standing outside like that?" I asked, turning to glance at her while gesturing at the group of cows on the other side of the kitchen window.*

*"Not really." She giggled. "Our cows and horses generate a significant amount of body heat. And when they're in groups like they are right now, they share the warmth of each other. Besides the several measures we take to protect their well-being, their thick hides and natural body fat are like a heating blanket for them whenever they're out like that."*

*"They sleep out there?"*

*"They sleep in the barns on bedding made of straw and wood shavings." She winked at me. "The straw and wood shavings offer insulation and help keep them dry and warm."*

*I smiled and nodded. "It's like I'm living in a painting right now. If I were you, I would never leave this house."*

*She chuckled as she kneaded the dough. She told me the dough would be dinner rolls tonight.*

*"Do you make everything y'all eat?"*

*"Everything." she answered.*

*"And when do you go to work?"*

*She chuckled. "This is my work, Eryn. The farm."*

*I furrowed my brows.*

*"Today we're eating these rolls, but sometimes, I make enough to sell to a supermarket in bulk so they can put it on their shelves so you can buy 'em."*

*"Hmph."*

*"We tend to our cows out there to get their milk and to make cheese,*

*and we tend to our vegetable crops and our fruit trees so we can harvest them, then drive them out to the city—"*

*"To sell at farmers' markets," I finished.*

*"That's right." She agreed with a head motion. "So pretty city girls can approach our table and hit on handsome farm boys like mine, then steal him away from working that table every weekend shortly after."*

*I tried tucking my lips into my mouth to hide my smile.*

*Mrs. King smiled while dusting her hand over the long butcher's block she worked over. "Can I have some honest girl talk with you, Eryn?"*

*I took a seat on the lone stool opposite her. "I love girl talk."*

*"Well, hopefully, you love this one."*

*Mothers were important to me. I loved mine and admired her too, although she frustrated me. But regardless of my relationship with my mother, I understood the power the matriarch of a family wielded. Quiet as kept, they were the real bosses. So, I knew I needed to get in good with Mrs. King. She was the mother of the man I planned to spend the rest of my life with.*

*"You're a sweet girl." She held up a finger. "I mean woman. Because I am sure you are doing womanly things with Simeon."*

*I parted my lips to say something, but she stopped me with the raise of a hand.*

*"I don't need you to confirm or deny, baby. I said that more so for myself so that I can address what I want to address with you the right way."*

*"Okay..."*

*"I'm not gonna mince words with you, Eryn. I don't want you two having sex while you are on this farm."*

*"Oh, wow." I sat up in my seat on the stool and pressed my hand to my chest. "That's the girl talk you want to have. Okay. I did not come prepared for that. At all."*

*She snickered. "That's the girl talk I need to have with you."*

*I inhaled a deep breath and let it out slowly through my mouth. For a small woman, she sure didn't act small.*

*"Now, baby, Simeon may have built that house y'all are going to be staying in over there..." She pointed over my shoulder. "But you two are*

*still on my land, and I would like for you to behave yourselves respectfully while you are here."*

*"Hold on." I raised a hand. "Rewind." I pointed over my shoulder in the direction she pointed. "Simeon built what house?"*

*"That little gray one to our left."*

*My jaw dropped. "He built that?!"*

*"Well, yes," she responded with a brief head bow. "His father helped him with the tiny house's framing, the rafters to support the roof, and the plumbing, but yes, Simeon built it from the ground up when he was seventeen. He didn't tell you that?"*

*"No!" I shrieked. "Are you telling me he built that house with his actual hands? Like, the hands on his body?"*

*Mrs. King hollered a laugh, and it was the sweetest thing. "Yes, Eryn. Your boyfriend built his house. Your boyfriend, not yet your husband. And that is why I would like for you to respect my one and only rule while you are staying in his house and on my land during your week here. Do you understand?"*

*I blinked erratically and shook my head in disbelief. I quickly forced my attention back on the conversation we were having out of respect for Mrs. King.*

*"Keep my legs closed and lock it up tight." I snapped my fingers together. "Got it."*

*Mrs. King stared at me and only blinked.*

*"No sex and no jokes on the farm." I smiled. "I got that too."*

*"You have a wonderful sense of humor." She turned to the large drop-in sink to rinse the flour off her hands. "And you're charming, charismatic, and extremely beautiful, young lady. I can see why Simeon has fallen for you as hard as he has, but I am being very serious with you, Eryn. And I am not playing with you." She turned to point at me.*

*I threw my hands up in surrender and lowered and raised my head quickly.*

*"No sex," I repeated. "I promise. You have my word."*

———

*The bed moving woke me from sleep. Simeon and I had only returned to his tiny gray house three hours prior, after we spent most of the night at a bonfire with his childhood friends, who were also home for spring break. A night of drinking and making s'mores over an open fire was a good time I didn't even know I needed.*

*The week was ending with Simeon and me scheduled to return to campus at Langston University the following day. It had been a week of me sleeping in and joining the Kings on their porch to sit under a snuggly blanket and drink coffee while having a few laughs.*

*Mrs. King had warmed up to me and had made me also promise to return over the summer so I could see the orchards and their strawberry field. She promised to bake me a strawberry shortcake if I came back. And she had me at strawberry shortcake.*

*When I turned off my side to face in Simeon's direction in bed, he was up, barely able to catch his footing but still approaching his bathroom. Too tired to ask any further, I returned to my spot on my pillow. A few minutes later, he pressed his lips to my forehead, waking me again.*

*"Today, I need to tend to the horses' stable," he started. "But first, I'm going to wax the tractor. The one my father tried to wax but fell off."*

*"Are you for real right now?" I peeked over at the alarm clock on his night table. "It's five in the damn morning."*

*He gave me a half smile.*

*"We leave tomorrow, and you've been working every day since we got here." I lifted the covers on his end. "Just get back in bed and go to sleep for a little."*

*"Uh-uh." He shook his head. "That was my whole reason for coming here. Tend to the farm since my father can't and set things right so he can get another few days of rest once we're gone. You sleep." He leaned forward again, and this time left a kiss on my lips.*

*That one sent some heat between my thighs. It was the first time he'd kissed me on the lips all week—intentionally. After I told him I didn't want to have sex while visiting his parents, we consciously kept things G-rated, including no kissing on the lips. It had been forehead kisses for the past few days... until that morning.*

*"I'll be back in a few."*

*Sleep was the last thing on my mind after he left.*

*The house he built was truly beautiful. It was small and resembled your standard tiny one-bedroom apartment in the city. With high ceilings and high-end furniture, though, and top-of-the-line appliances. In the bathroom was a stand-in shower and marble floors. It was like he picked this house up from Manhattan and dropped it on the farm. It was so different from the farmhouse and so on-brand for Simeon.*

*Instead of going back to sleep, I climbed towards the headboard to peek out the window behind it, which faced the front of the house. During our week at the farm, I always seemed to wake up at just the right time—right when Simeon was finishing his farm work for the day. I'd never gotten up this early before that morning, so I never actually watched him work.*

*He moved around the tractor parked outside his parents' home like a seasoned farmer—starting this, cleaning that. He got up under the vehicle, lying on the ground as if he wasn't the neat freak he usually was. I watched as he pulled himself up with one arm, then hopped onto the tractor's giant wheel in his black rubber work boots, balancing himself to wax the top of the machine. After a few minutes, he hopped back off the tractor and walked out of sight.*

*After that, I paid the bathroom a visit to freshen up because, suddenly, after watching him and getting kissed on the lips, I wasn't sleepy anymore. I stood under the showerhead Simeon installed that had water cascading out like rain. I finished up and stepped out to the sink to brush my teeth. We were leaving the farm the next day and curious if we could cut down on how long we spent on the road getting up here, I finished brushing my teeth and washing my face, and tasked myself with searching up some quicker routes on my phone before the trip the next day.*

*When I returned to the bedroom, with only my towel around me, and found my phone on the nightstand beside my side of the bed, I peeked up just in time to see Simeon riding a horse. I leaned my head back, staring out in front of me, my eyes tracking him in complete disbelief. Tilting my head to one side, I watched as he sat upright with a straight back, holding the horse's leather reins in a gentle grip. He steered the horse by gently pulling on the reins, his voice and the sounds of him clicking his tongue faintly audible through the thick pane windows. I stood frozen, witnessing a man I called my boyfriend for almost five years, riding a horse like a seasoned jockey, and I did not know he knew how to ride a damn horse.*

*"What the...?" I blinked. "Am I really seeing this right now?"*

*The whole thing had my jaw so far from my upper lip, my lips were getting dry.*

*"Who is this man?"*

*And how can I have him inside me right now?*

*Because I promised his mother I would keep my legs closed to her son on her farm. And I'd done well with keeping that promise these past few days. But that was before I saw him ride a horse. And as odd as it might sound, it was the sexiest thing I'd ever seen Simeon do. Which was saying a lot because Simeon had done some very sexy things.*

*After galloping a few times out of sight, Simeon halted the horse and had it stand still for a few beats before he dismounted it. I watched him walk the horse around for a bit, running his hands down its body in such a gentle way. Simeon was talking to it while caressing before walking completely out of sight, guiding the horse with him.*

*I had to take a seat on the bed after that. Staying on the farm, living in the house he built, watching him ride a horse and be this man I did not know he could be. Simeon was amazing to me before we visited his parents' farm. He was smart and diligent at being the best at everything he did. But here on the farm, watching him obviously just be himself... I knew he would not only have to be my husband. He'd have to be the father of my future children.*

*He opened his house door a few minutes later, stomping his rubber boots on the mat outside. As soon as he entered the bedroom, he was pulling off the Langston U hoodie he wore outside and tossing it to the floor.*

*"Oh, hey," he greeted, stretching his arms high above his head as he approached the foot of the bed. "I thought you were still sleeping."*

*I said nothing in return. I just crawled his way, watching as a slow smirk appeared on his lips.*

*"What are you doing?" he asked.*

*I didn't answer, and I didn't stop crawling until I was in front of him, placing my legs on either side of him, caging him between them in front of me.*

*My hands were at the belt buckle he wore over his jeans, undoing them.*

*"Eryn?"*

*"Hmmm?"*

*I undid the buckle, and I hurried on to unbuttoning his jeans.*

*He chuckled.*

*I was unzipping his fly when he asked me, "What's happening right now?"*

*I pulled his dick out of his pants and leaned forward to kiss the tip, and he moaned. I didn't delay after that. Sliding his soft erection into my mouth and immediately starting oral.*

*"Shit." He groaned, then chuckled, then groaned again. "What the hell did I do to deserve this?"*

*Everything.*

*Simeon ran his fingers through my flat-ironed bob haircut. "I thought you told me no sex, beloved?"*

*I did. And I didn't tell him it was a promise I'd made to his mother. Like I said, I simply told him that out of respect for his parents, I didn't want to have sex while they were around. And I stayed true to that—until I saw him on that damn horse.*

*I pulled my lips off him and released my towel from around me. Gripped him by his forearm to encourage him to lie with me when he gave some resistance.*

*"What?" I panted.*

*"I was kind of relieved you said no sex because I forgot the condoms at my dorm when I was packing," he told me, his eyes scanning my face. "I don't have any here."*

*That gave me a moment of pause. I moved my eyes off his and thought about it. Did as much thinking as someone would do in that moment, with my legs spread wide, his hard thick dick in full view, and, well, me very horny at that point.*

*"It's okay." I signaled with a head nod, pulling him towards me. "It's okay. We don't need them. Come here."*

*Simeon stared at me for a moment. The smirk he originally wore on his face and in his eyes was long gone. He blinked a few times out of his stare and swallowed really hard, but he eventually obliged. Taking his position over me and lining his erection with my warmth.*

*We both gasped when he worked the first inch in. Then we moaned together when my walls adjusted to him and he slid all of himself inside of* me. *We kept our eyes on each other for what felt like the whole time until he stroked me into a trance that had me unable to do anything except for focusing entirely on coming.*

*And I felt it. Everything.*

*"Oh God!" I cried out. "Mmm, I love you so much."*

*"Shh, I love you more." Simeon pressed his mouth against mine.*

*Beyond feeling the mounting pressure building between us, I felt the moment our relationship transformed, the moment everything felt permanent. Most of all, I felt and heard when we both arrived at the point of no return at the same time. That never happened until that morning.*

*"Simeon," I whispered. "Oh my God, I'm coming—"*

*"I'm coming too. I feel it too," he whispered back, shuddering uncontrollably with me.*

*That was the day everything changed, the day our relationship took a completely different trajectory.*

## ERYN

I peeled open my eyes and exhaled in relief as I recognized my surroundings. I don't know what I was expecting to see when I opened my eyes, especially when my childhood room was where I fell asleep the night before.

I'd avoided my mother, who tried to stop by my room the night prior after she realized I was home. But it was the next day, a Thursday, and minutes before noon. And as predicted, I needed what? That's right. Coffee.

No longer in the same space as Simeon, I tasked myself with fetching my caffeine. It wouldn't be the perfect cup like he always made, but it would do. Anything was better than nothing.

I opened my bedroom door carefully, not wanting to make too much noise. The plan was to tiptoe my way down the stairs and take careful steps into the kitchen. Because the coffee machine would make the most noise brewing coffee, I decided I would gather the creamer and sugar from ahead of time so I could dump those sweeteners in the mug and dash my ass back up to my room without being noticed.

Except when I walked into the kitchen, my mother was sitting at the kitchen table, her beautiful eyes already searching for me as I turned the corner to enter the space. I jumped back, slapping my hand on my chest.

"Ma!" I exhaled. "Damn. You scared me."

She giggled. "I should be the one scared. I didn't know you were here."

I blinked out of our stare and made my way to the coffeemaker.

"I only knew you were back in town after Everett told me he'd attended a wedding near here and wanted to stop by to say hey since he was with Apryl."

"Hmph." I opened the compartment to place a tiny coffee container inside of it.

"He told me the wedding was for a couple of your clients."

"Did he now?" I approached the fridge without making eye contact.

"How has the work been, anyway?" she asked, lifting her mug of tea to her lips. "How has it been working with Simeon?"

I rolled my eyes at the mention of his name.

"Done," I replied. I poured creamer into my mug and kept my eyes on the cup. "Our working together has ended, so we're done."

"*Aww.*" She sighed. "I was hoping there would be more to you two reuniting than business."

"Well..." I tried like hell to bite back the tears. Inhaled and exhaled deeply, refusing to turn and face my mother.

"Either way," she started again, over my shoulder from her seat, "I'm proud of you, Eryn."

I squeezed my eyes shut.

"You went through something tough out there in Los Angeles," she added. "Most people would've struggled to keep going, but *you* did. You picked yourself up, accepted Simeon's offer to work together on his client's situation, and you did great. You did good."

"Ma, please," I whispered. "Just... stop."

She said nothing in response.

"Stop trying to say all these nice things about me…"

"But what I'm saying is true," she insisted. "And you should hear it. You *deserve* to hear it."

I spun around to face her and blurted, "I had an abortion in college."

I locked eyes with her wide pair.

"Two weeks before graduation, I had an abortion." I threw my hands up. "Are you still proud of me?"

My mother tried to recover from her shock. She tried to use her slack jaw to say something, anything, but while her words wanted to come out, she couldn't say anything.

"Simeon hates me for it. So, *please*, stop *hoping* there could be anything more than business between us. Because unless I can undo the abortion and put that baby back inside me, he and I are done—forever. Okay?"

My mother was a cool and calm kind of woman. She'd heard it all, from people from all walks of life as a practicing psychotherapist. But nothing could prepare me for the look of shock mixed with sadness shaping her expression. And the moment I realized her look was because of me, because of what I revealed, I gasped so loud, my reaction echoed around the kitchen.

I couldn't believe I'd said it.

Because the abortion—the secret I'd been keeping from everyone except Simeon, a decision I made without thinking it through that had been eating away at me like a flesh-eating virus—was finally out.

And the result was my mother, who looked like she'd just heard the worst thing in her life. My stomach knotted so tight and my throat was closing to stop the bile from rising.

"Oh, my God." I slapped both of my hands to my mouth. When the tears began building in my eyes and I could no longer hold my cry back, I dropped my head into my hands and shook my head, covering my eyes with my fingers. I was fighting it all back, like I'd been fighting back, remembering what I'd revealed when my mother's arms wrapped around me, and she leaned my face against her chest. I couldn't hold anything back after that. So, I cried like I'd never cried before, and she held me tight through it all.

———

"I regret it," I whispered, staring down at my pink bedding. "If I could take it all back, I'd do it *so* fast, Ma."

I lifted my eyes to look at her and she sighed.

In our hands were mugs of tea. I was drinking tea. So you know I was feeling bad.

"I knew something wasn't right," she recalled in a calm tone. "After your graduation, I *knew* something wasn't right. You were never as close to me as Everett but, there was still some level of openness you had to me. Now, *you* were always a closed book." She giggled softly. "Sometimes I'd feel like I'd need a crowbar to get into that head of yours." She gestured at my head, and I scoffed a laugh. "But something told me everything was not okay after you graduated from LU. And I just knew it wasn't only the breakup with Simeon... which was shocking and so sudden, yes. I just could not understand what and how to get you to tell me."

It was her idea to bring me back to my room. Promised she'd prepare me some tea, and I didn't bother protesting. Drained is what I was. Telling my secret I've held in for so long was draining. It felt like physical labor, not only saying what I did but mentally, in a flash, remembering the entire process from finding out I was pregnant at LU's student health services, receiving the information where I could end the pregnancy, and actually going through with it.

The day of the abortion was horrible. It poured rain, the skies grayer than usual. The clinic workers were amazing, including the doctor who performed the procedure, but I wasn't prepared for the rush of feelings afterward. The emptiness. The regret I couldn't shake. And the unforgiving city I would have to live in, carrying all of that. I went to the clinic alone and took a cab back to my dorm. And because of the rain, traffic was bad. So, I was stuck in the heart of New York City, centered in a sea of honking horns and fussing drivers, surrounded by gray skies, pelting rain, and steely buildings, feeling every bit of horrible. I was right in the thick of rush hour, surrounded by the hustle and bustle of people moving on with their lives, while mine felt like it had come to a screeching halt. I couldn't change my circumstances. I couldn't change the flow of traffic or the fact I'd done something irreversible. That moment, sitting in the backseat, wanting to be anywhere else and feeling anything but that awful emptiness, I was helpless. The feeling clung to me like a stain. The doctor advised me to rest for the remainder of the day, but sitting upright in traffic, cramping in pain, left me feeling broken in the cab's backseat. Inside and out. I had done something I desperately wanted to undo, and New York felt like a silent witness to my sad story. The city showed no remorse, no care for my inner turmoil. There was too much going on for anyone to notice my pain, or anyone else's for that matter, I guess. I wondered how many others in this city that never slept were dealing with pain no one noticed. In a city so big and busy, I felt utterly lost and alone. That feeling persisted for six long years until I finally gave up and left New York. I just wasn't in a place quiet enough to process the hell I had created for myself. That day marked the moment I fell out of love with my hometown. It was when I wanted out of the feeling and the city for good. I never wanted to feel that way again.

Often, when the memory of the abortion resurfaced in my mind, I'd go out for a drink in L.A., meet a guy, and add to my body count, even though I never found true satisfaction in the interaction. But it was a distraction, and it distracted me long enough to forget that I had done something I immediately wanted to undo, something I deeply regretted.

"I can counsel thousands and thousands of people." My mother shook her head. "But my *own* children and their problems have been my biggest challenge. Mostly, the challenge is in figuring out what they don't realize." She reached over to lift my head by the chin. "They don't realize that more important than the thousands and thousands of success stories I've heard from clients after they sought therapy with me, my children's lives, no matter how old they are, are my most important and greatest work in this lifetime. And I'm always up for whatever kind of work that is. Regardless of how big or small they think it is."

I blinked in response.

"Eryn, you have been punishing yourself for a decision you made over a decade ago. Are you aware of that?"

I dropped my head. "I am."

"I could go on and on about how you should have come to me, but you knew this already. Didn't you?"

I nodded slightly.

"But you didn't come to me because you thought I would've impeded the plan you had, and I likely would have because we would have done the work of figuring out what would be the best way to handle your situation. And I don't mean focusing on if you should do it or not. At the end of every day, that is your choice and your choice alone. What I mean is us analyzing what you were considering back then and figuring out healthy ways for you to accept whatever decision you came to. We would've weighed the pros and cons and I would've supported you in whatever decision you made after that. Without judgment, and you know this. Because it would've been your decision, Eryn. *Yours.* But to you, all of that would've been—"

"Too much work," I finished.

"What you *believed* would've been too much work, but my love." She smiled sweetly. "The work would have been worth it even if you arrived at the same decision you ended up making those few weeks before graduation. At least you would have arrived there confidently and possibly with less regret after going through with your decision."

I twisted my lips to one side.

"Regret won't get you anywhere, Eryn, except depressed," she said, shaking her head gently. "It's done. What happened is done. You had the abortion. It happened, and now you need to move forward from there." She caressed the side of my face with her soft hands.

"How, Ma?"

"By doing the work of healing now." She gave a subtle head gesture. "You've got to acknowledge your emotions, practice self-compassion, and be receptive to love, starting with love from your mother."

I smiled.

"Do a lot of self-care, both physical and mental." She nodded. "And focus on the future because the past is done, Eryn. It's done, my love. And believe it or not, you are a better person because of your past."

I had been avoiding this time with my mom, too afraid of doing what I ended up doing, which was revealing the abortion. And yet, for the first time in a long time, I was feeling better.

"I see why your clients love you so damn much."

She snickered. My mother took my hands and held them in hers.

"You can heal physically from just about everything. But healing mentally is a deeply personal and lifelong process," she explained. "It's self-work. You'll go through much of that process on your own, but I'm hoping you will let your mother, who does this for a living, help you by recommending strategies to support your emotional recovery. Eryn, you should know by now I have plenty of strategies I'd be more than happy to share with you. But you have to *talk* to me, my love. And you have to be ready to put in the work."

"I know." I squeezed her hand. "And I'd love your help, Ma, thank you."

"Thank you for finally letting me in."

"I'm sorry for only calling you on Mother's Day and your birthday."

She nodded. "I appreciate that apology, Eryn. I've really missed hearing your voice, especially since I don't get to see your beautiful face as often as I'd like."

"You always seem to have the answers, and it can be a little intimidating."

She tilted her head to one side and her salt and pepper curls caught the light from my furry light fixture above my bed.

"It's always like you push one button and things get fixed." I shook my head. "It's as if you have a mental Rolodex of solutions to every problem known to man. I've been dealing with these feelings for so long I've learned to cope with them. You just heard about it and within the hour, you have me feeling like I can feel happy again."

"I've lived a lot of life and have made enough mistakes that I can lock the lessons in a vault in my mind and access and share it with my daughter at will so she doesn't have to make the same mistakes and learn the same lessons I already had to learn." My mother pressed her hand to her chest. "I may not have gone through what you've had to go through, but Eryn, the ebbs and flows of life have no distinction."

"What do you mean by that?"

"Life is a series of trials and the challenge of moving personal mountains, my love. For you, it's an abortion. For me, it was losing my mother at too young of an age to remember who she was." She took my hand again. "But I've learned that although our ebbs and flows are unique to our lives, the process of healing really is a one size fits all. Healing in every capacity requires one important thing, regardless of what that healing journey entails."

"And what's that one important thing?"

"Work, my love." She smiled. "You cannot take the lazy way and attempt to get around your problems. You must find the resolve within yourself to *work* through them. You understand what I'm saying to you?"

I smiled back at her. "I understand you are superwoman, and I don't think I can ever be that."

"Why would you want to be my brand of superwoman when you are your own?"

I rolled my eyes playfully.

"Eryn, you are the most big and bold human I have ever met. And I have met many people. I am enamored by your spunk and how much you aren't complacent, even when it's frustrating to me. But in this world where there are people who are constantly telling women like you to shrink yourself or to be everyone else besides yourself, you need the type of fire you naturally have pumping through your veins to get you through this life. You may not get through it unscathed, but the diligence is there within you. You just have to tap into it and show up and allow it to show up too in all areas of your life. Because that's where the actual work is."

"Hmph."

"Now drink your tea and get some rest," she instructed as she stepped off my bed. "I have a client in about an hour and I need to destress and decompress after all of this."

"I'm sorry, Ma."

"Don't you dare apologize, Eryn." She pointed at me. "Like I told you, you and Everett, even with him in his 40s and you in your late 30s, are still my babies. And as long as I have breath in me, I'm going to be there for you. I am *here* for *you*. Please remember that and never forget it."

She was gone a minute later, and the air was suddenly easier to inhale after the talk we had. I peeked over at my phone and considered calling Simeon but decided against it. At that moment, I wanted to do the first recommendation from my mother.

Acknowledge my emotions.

So, I did. I let myself cry and release everything. Finally, I cast off my burden instead of carrying it in secret.

# Twenty-Seven

**SIMEON**

I turned the steering wheel to the right to guide my rental in front of my parents' home. My childhood home. The moment I turned off the path and drove through the low-swinging metal gates at our farm's entrance, I immediately felt nostalgic.

It's funny. When I was living there as a child, I often dreamed of living a life bigger than the farm. And as I got older, and finally got a taste of being in the city whenever my parents would bring me to the farmers' markets to sell our goods every weekend, my love of the big city continued to trump my love of my family's farm in our small town. But now in my late 30s, as I touched the heels of my 40s, and have lived off the farm for so long, I've grown to really love this farm. Absence really does make the heart grow fonder.

Summer was always one of the most beautiful seasons to experience here. Autumn was a close second. The transitioning of the leaves on the sea of trees that extended as far as the eyes could see was truly breathtaking.

I needed the drive I took up here. I even left earlier than usual, before daybreak, only so I could get out on the road and out of the penthouse I was now in alone. So many times, I had to fight myself from calling Eryn. For someone I'd gone so long without speaking to, we'd only reconnected weeks ago and I couldn't get her off my mind suddenly again.

I grabbed the manila envelope off the passenger seat and pushed open my door, stepping out a second later. The moment my designer leather tassel loafers hit the ground, I felt them sink into something much softer than the usual dirt road. I recognized the pungent odor instantly—earthy and unmistakable. It clung to the air and everything around it, now including the bottom of my shoe.

I clicked my tongue in frustration and shut the car door, glancing down to see I'd stepped right into horse manure. I scraped my leather sole against the dirt, swiping my foot back and forth, trying to get as much of it off as I could. "Shit."

"Literally," my father joked at the same time he pushed the house's screen door open.

I chuckled at that while shaking my head.

"Now you knew better than to wear them fancy ass shoes out here." He jogged down the stairs, wearing his usual sly grin. "What? You've been gone for so long you done forgot the horses love to gallop around here and drop their load when the sun is high and bright like this?"

"Of course not, bossman," I answered, extending my hand for a handshake. And like always, he accepted before pulling me in for a warm hug. I hugged him back, and we both patted each other's backs in our embrace.

He pulled away long enough to ask, "Where's Eryn?" He peeked through my rental's windshield. "Is she in the car?"

I scratched the back of my head. "No, Pa. Eryn's not in the car."

He cringed. "Oh boy."

"Hey!" my mother greeted through the screen door before pushing it open. She took quick steps down the stairs, smiling the entire way. "I knew I saw a car pull up. Where's my girl?"

*Damn, I should've told them she wasn't coming.*

"I didn't bring Eryn with me, Mama."

Her smile morphed into a frown. "*Aw,* well, maybe next time?"

I smiled as convincingly as I could, but I could not tell the lie with my mouth.

My mother sagged her shoulders in defeat and kissed her teeth. "Well..." She sighed. "Will you at least stay for lunch?"

"Of course, Mama," I replied. "I'll stay for lunch."

"You're *damn right* you will." She kissed her teeth again. "I told you to bring that pretty lady here, and you didn't. Staying for lunch is the *least* you could do."

My father snorted. "He looks great, though. Don't he, Regina?"

"He looks incredible, and it would've been nice to see Eryn standing right beside him, Vernon, so I could've seen how incredible she looks too." My mother focused down on the ground and told me, "Go to the back of the house and hose that off before you step *into* my house."

"Will do, Mama."

"*Mm-hmm.*" She extended her arms, and I walked in between them, needing to bend my legs at the knees to match her height. "It's good to see you, baby."

"Good to see you too," I said before stepping out of our hug.

"Come on," my father gestured for me to follow him between the gray house I built and our family home as he led the way to the back of our family's house. "You should've told me before you got here that you weren't bringing Eryn. Your Mama was really hoping to see her."

I was really hoping to see her, too.

As soon as we made our way to the back of the house, I handed my father the manila envelope and reached for the long green hose to clean the bottoms of my loafers.

"Those are the documents I told you about concerning the market in Greene Gardens." I focused my attention on aiming the spray of water at the bottoms of my shoes. "I've looked through everything and have had my lawyers look through their proposal too, but nothing moves or gets agreed to until you okay it."

"Son, I trust your judgment, but I'll look through everything when I get a minute."

"Cool," I replied, continuing to work.

"What I want to get into is what's going on with you and Eryn?"

I inhaled a deep breath and let the air go through my mouth. Because since she left the penthouse four days ago, I hadn't heard from her. We had a flight scheduled for the following evening and her words about not returning to Oakland have been echoing in the corner of my mind and getting louder as the hours progressed in my chronograph.

"We randomly hear her when we call you a few weeks ago, after not hearing you mention her in over a decade. You say you and her were only working together, but now I mentioned her and it looked like me just saying her name knocked the wind out of you. What's going on?"

The bottom of my loafer was looking brand new again, clean of horse shit, so I twisted the valve on the hose to turn the water off. I stood upright again to look my father eye to eye. "You want the short story or the long one?"

"I want whatever story that's gonna take me to the root." He arched a brow. "You know what I'm saying?"

"I know what you're saying, Pa."

He released a hearty laugh. "So then give it to me. Let's take a walk," he suggested with a pat on my back. "I want you to see what we've done with the orchards."

Everything I'd ever eaten from birth and until the night before I moved off the farm and onto Langston U's campus, we grew on this farm. If I wanted pizza, I had to pick the tomatoes, the onions, the garlic, and snip the basil. I even had to milk a cow and bring the fresh milk to my mother so she could start making the mozzarella well before any of that other stuff got made. We made burger buns from the dough kneaded with the flour we ground from wheat grains we plant in the fall and harvest in late spring and early summer. Birthday cakes, popcorn, potato chips, you name it. If I wanted it, the ingredients for it had to be harvested, picked, and prepared right here on the farm. And on a fixed schedule.

It used to drive me mad living like that. I wanted so badly to experience what it was like to want something and just have it—no planning, no scheduling, just instant gratification. Silly, but it was how I felt. Our farm was massive, stretching for miles, but there were neighboring farms scattered across the landscape. Kids my age lived on those farms, growing up just like me, so I always had peers to vent to. Some of them saw nothing wrong with living that way. A lot of them had never left Dewittville. But I had ventured beyond our small world and seen so much more. After experiencing city life, my dreams of being a part of that world wouldn't let me rest.

I'd spend so many nights escaping into my imagination, making a home in the city. Any city, honestly. Because from my perspective, any and everywhere else was better than Kings Farm. The stupidity.

At 38, I could appreciate the farm, and all it was worth. Grateful, I had enough sense to use my knowledge I got in my studies at LU and in Miami when I earned my MBA at a local university, to help my parents grow within the farming industry.

We had at least a dozen farmhands now who helped tend to the farm so my parents could rest more and not work every day. I'd also put together a team to manage the day-to-day communications with buyers and reps whenever I was unavailable. It has been through my guidance and my suggestions that had made our farm one of the top farms not only in New York State but in the country. These days I was very proud to call this place home.

On our way to the orchard, we passed by free-range chickens, our small greenhouse, and our garden full of rows and rows of vegetable crops.

"So, talk to me," my father started. "What's going on?"

"Do you remember that one spring break, two months before I graduated from LU when I drove up here with Eryn to help manage the farm after you'd fallen and sprang your wrist?"

He confirmed with a head motion. "Yes, I remember the time vividly. You thrilled your mother bringing a girl home."

I smiled at that.

"I remember your mother being so dang happy Eryn loved this farm." My father exhaled, then laughed. "Told me Eryn was the one because if a woman loved a man and his farm, she would have to become his wife."

"Hmph, well." I scratched my head. "Eryn and I conceived a child during that trip, Pa."

My father stopped walking to turn and face me.

"And she didn't tell me we did," I revealed. "Or that she ended the pregnancy. I had to find it out on my own."

My father blinked twice in response. "How did you find out?"

*I'd pressed my lips into Eryn's neck for the second time when she giggled and finally pushed me away.*

*"Would you stop it?"*

*"I took my final exam of the semester and of my college life today." I leaned in again to kiss past her hands to get to her neck. "I most definitely cannot stop."*

*She giggled again, scooting away this time.*

*We were on her bed, killing time, until it was close to the time our movie started at the cinema we planned to visit that night. I hadn't seen Eryn in a week, and I missed her. We were both studying and taking final exams, so our availability was minimal. That was why I invited her out for a movie to get us in the same place and at the same time.*

*I smoothed my hand over her thigh, aiming to nestle my fingertips between her warm legs. But she stopped me.*

*"I can't," she said low, pointing her eyes to her lap.*

*I chuckled and leaned forward a bit to meet her eyes. "And why not?"*

*"I'm bleeding... down there," she answered, still avoiding eye contact.*

*I took a deep breath and released it. I'd never considered chasing red lights as we used to say back then, but I had been missing her so damn bad. I was willing to look past it only that once. Plus, I'd dealt with messier situations working on my parents' farm, so it wasn't a big deal to me at that moment.*

*"I don't mind if you don't mind." I smirked. "We'll be wearing a condom, anyway. Let's put a towel down. It's only a period, anyway, right?"*

*"It's not my period." She glanced over at me. "I had a... a procedure."*

*"A procedure." I blinked twice. "What kind of procedure?"*

*"An abortion, Simeon."*

*I pulled my hand back so fast.*

*"And the doctor who did the procedure recommended I wait at least two weeks before having sex again to prevent infection."*

*I held my hands up in front of me when I asked, "You had a what?"*

*She stared at me for a moment, not blinking. Not reacting.*

*I blinked a few times, sure I had to have misheard her. Because there was no way she would have done something like that without first letting me know she was pregnant.*

*She ran her hand through her hair. "Please don't be mad."*

*"Please don't be mad?" I jumped up out of my seat. "Wait, are you serious right now? Did you really have an abortion, Eryn? I... I didn't even know you were pregnant. How could you not tell me you were pregnant?!"*

*She said nothing.*

*"Tell me you're joking." I locked eyes with her. "Just... please."*

*"I'm not."*

"Oh, my." My father placed his hand around his thick waist. "Is *that* why you left for Miami shortly after y'all's graduation from LU?"

I nodded. "It was like a knee-jerk reaction. I applied for the internship back in January, not really expecting to get it. So when they called in February, it caught me off guard. Honestly, I didn't think I'd accept the offer either. I told them I was still considering it in late April. But when she told me she had the abortion in May, I just—"

"Left?"

"I left," I confirmed. "I called HR at the sports agency in Miami and accepted the job."

"Without talking to her about leaving?"

"I mean, I told her about their interest in hiring me when they first reached out that January, but we never discussed what my decision would be. So yeah." I gave a knowing look. "I left without talking to her about leaving. Without talking to her about what she did. We have never discussed the abortion since the day I found out about it. Not even after reconnecting recently."

"What?!" He shook his head. "That's unlike you."

"She blindsided me back then." I shook my head. "I didn't know how to react to her revealing that and since we've reconnected, she won't even say what she did and, out of concern for triggering something in her, I haven't said or mentioned it either. Her reaction when I mentioned having an investment in the diaper company I'm a silent partner in was one reason I haven't pushed to discuss what needs to be discussed."

My father exhaled a long, measured sigh. "That's a lot of avoiding, Simeon. I don't like that."

"Not more than I don't like it, Pa. Trust me"

My father's blowing air out of his mouth made his lips vibrate. "Well, it was her choice to have the abortion, and she was well within her right to make that choice."

"And it was her decision to keep everything a secret from me."

"So, you retaliated her choosing that option and not letting you know, by you leaving abruptly?"

I looked away.

"Because she had the abortion and hadn't told you she was with child, you retaliated by leaving New York abruptly. Am I right?"

I twisted my lips to one side.

My father and I continued walking, the scent of the nearby orchard trees heavy with fruit filling the air. The whinnying of our Clydesdale and Shire horses lifted my spirits a bit. I didn't enjoy stepping in their shit, but I loved riding them. I just wished I'd dressed to ride that morning.

"So, what?" My father continued as he walked beside me. "Is that why you didn't bring her home today?"

"We got into an argument a few nights ago." I created a visor with my hand to get a look at the orchard my father wanted to show me, my eyes falling on the vast amount of land we owned a little further up. "She got up the next day and told me she was going to Brooklyn to stay with her mother until the flight back to Oakland. But in the same breath, she said she wasn't sure if she would be returning to Oakland."

"Because you still hold her decision against her?"

"Okay, may I ask whose side you're on, bossman? Because it's sounding like it's not *mine*."

"No." He smirked. "You may *not* ask me that."

I scoffed a laugh.

"I mean, I might come off a little biased here. Because I kind of feel for Eryn." He gestured subtly. "You have a way of punishing people with your absence. You sure did it a lot with your mother and me."

I shook my head and refocused in front of us.

"When you told your mother and I that you had applied for

entrance at Langston U instead of applying to the local community college up here where you'd been taking pre-college courses, we expressed our disappointment and you built that gray house beside ours and only allowed us to see you at the dinner table every night and no other time throughout the day."

I tucked my lips into my mouth.

"When you arrived at LU and told us your plans to study Sports Management and not Agricultural Business, and we told you we weren't okay with that, you retaliated by only calling us to let us know when you would come home for the holidays."

I stopped to turn to face him. "So you *are* taking Eryn's side?"

"No," he answered.

"Sounds like it."

"Some animals sound the same," he retorted. "That doesn't mean they are."

I stared at him for a moment, and he burst into laughter.

I chuckled at his attempt.

"Look, I'll say this," my father began. "I'm not taking anybody's side. I like Eryn, but you're my son, and you're my son, but I really like Eryn, Simeon."

"Okay..."

"If an undiscussed abortion is the worst thing, you two are dealing with and it is what is keeping you two apart for all this time? You can *talk* about it." He nodded. "You two can at the very least talk about *that*. Come on now."

I focused on him.

"Y'all can't undo any of it, but you *can* discuss it, and your hurt feelings and your problems can reach a resolution. I'm sure of it." He nodded. "And the Simeon I know and raised can do at least that, right?"

I shrugged. "I guess."

He smiled next. "Plus... your mother has always wanted a daughter and Eryn fits the bill, Simeon. I mean, come on. You know your mama doesn't like everybody."

I laughed out loud, and he joined in.

"If it wasn't for the difficult pregnancy and delivery your big ol' body put on that little lady in our house back there, she would have wanted a whole stable of children." He grinned. "Your mama likes your ex-girlfriend. A lot. And so does your Pa. The least you can do is have a conversation where y'all discuss everything. And if after that you see things can never be what you feel they can be for you to see a life with her again, then let her go and move on. Who can tell you anything after that?"

# TWENTY-EIGHT

**ERYN**

"Hey Pops," I said into the phone as I made my way to the elevators.

"Hey there, my angel."

I blushed. My father had been calling me angel from the time I was a little girl, begging him to read me a book before he left to catch a flight to jet-set around the world for some business meeting in some faraway land. And the nickname has not lost its endearing quality of warming my heart or making me blush whenever I heard him say it.

I pressed the call button for the elevator and stepped back to glance up at the floor indicator. I was back at SoHi Hotel and Suites, as per Simeon's request, both curious and eager to know why he'd asked for me to come back here.

*"Eryn," he said into the phone after calling me two hours prior. "Do you think you can meet me at SoHi's penthouse so we can talk?"*

It had been a couple of days since I revealed my secret to my mother. Since that time, I'd experienced the relief of no longer carrying that heavy load around anymore. It also gave me time to think. About Simeon and me. I'd retrieved the room key from the front desk. He asked me to. Plus, to access the penthouse floor, I needed to scan the card before selecting the penthouse's floor button.

"What did I do to be so lucky to get a call from the famed Craig Peters this evening?"

He chuckled, and I smiled.

"I'm gonna be in L.A. in the middle of July and would love to see my daughter, that's what."

"I'd love to see you, too."

The elevator chimed, and the doors peeled apart.

"Oh, you're not home?"

"No," I replied, entering the elevator and immediately scanning the card and pressing the penthouse floor button. "I'm not in L.A. either. I'm in New York."

"Really? Visiting your mother and your brother?"

"No, although I did that, too." I sighed, turning to check myself out in the elevator's mirrored wall. I adjusted one of the straps on my jumpsuit before facing forward again. "I had to attend a client's wedding last week. And if you can believe it, she even put me in the wedding party."

"That's lovely."

The elevator shot up floors the numbers in the floor indicator window, switching with speed.

"Well, where are you headed now? I hope I'm not slowing you down."

"You can never do that, Pops." I smiled. "In fact, speaking with you is helping with keeping me cool, calm, and collected, like you."

He snickered.

"I'm on an elevator, heading up to see one of your favorite guys in the world."

"Your brother?"

The elevator doors peeled apart, revealing the metal core door of the penthouse.

"Nope, Simeon."

"Simeon?" He shouted, elated. "Get out of here!"

I approached the door and scanned the key, and the door opened to the living room. Simeon sat on the couch wearing a slim-fit white tee and black trousers, barefoot.

"Tell him I said hi and that it's been too long."

Simeon lifted his head and locked eyes with me.

"You can tell him yourself if you want to."

"I absolutely do." My father chuckled. "Get him on the phone."

I did as instructed and walked the phone to Simeon. His expression was even, brows a little curious.

"It's my dad."

His face lit up, and he was up on his feet, taking the phone out of my hand.

"Mr. Peters," he said. Then chuckled. "You're not lying about that, sir. It's good to hear your voice. What you been up to?"

I removed my quilted designer shoulder bag and placed it on the coffee table, watching Simeon speak casually on my phone with my father like they'd spoken the week prior when they hadn't spoken to each other in over a decade, to my knowledge. It was always like that. Simeon fit like a puzzle piece everywhere he went, but with my family, Simeon always seemed like he was the missing piece. It was always natural for him to hang out with my brother and my father whenever my father wasn't catching a flight to some country whose name I couldn't pronounce correctly sometimes. Simeon does not know how hard it was to explain his sudden absence after college.

"Your dad said he'll call you tomorrow," Simeon told me, placing my phone on the coffee table beside my bag.

"Cool."

I was back at the scene of our last blow up. This time it was almost 9pm and my head and heart were a little worse for wear.

"I visited my folks today at the farm in Dewittville."

My brows went up. "You went to the farm?"

He nodded. "They were a little disappointed I didn't bring you with me. Mostly my mother. She wanted to see you."

"I know all about that kind of disappointment when people are expecting to see someone and they're not there and they have questions you can't answer."

He clenched his teeth, tightening his jaw.

"Why'd you call me back here, Simeon?"

"I told my father why we broke up."

Shock was the first feeling I felt, then concern.

"And he sided with you, even though he wouldn't say it." He shook his head. "He told me if that was the worst thing we were dealing with, we could talk it over and so that's why I asked you to come here. So we can talk."

I said nothing. Just waited. Simeon fell silent too, and soon the silence was getting awkward.

"Well." I shrugged a shoulder. "Start."

"No, *you* start."

"*You* invited me back—"

"And I'm asking you to take the initiative." He folded his arms. "Show me you're capable of not sitting back and letting me do all the work, like always."

I sucked my teeth.

"It was your choice that started it all anyway, so..." He shrugged. "It's only appropriate."

"You abandoning the relationship started it all, Simeon."

"I *left* because you got rid of our baby and didn't let me know there was a baby to get rid of before you did it."

"What was I supposed to do? *Hmm?*"

"Tell *me*, for one." He poked at his chest with each word spoken.

"So, you could've talked me out of it?"

He blinked in response.

"So, you could tell me everything would be okay, and we would figure it out?" I scoffed a laugh. "Give me one of your Simeon fucking King affirmations on how everything happens for a reason, and we'd be okay? So, then years later, when I fuck up dinner yet again or forget to pay an important bill, or something smaller than that because I was irresponsible as fuck, you can have a distant thought that makes you question if you made the right decision telling me to keep a pregnancy neither of us planned?"

"Eryn—"

"Your mother told me the day we visited the farm not to have sex on her land."

Simeon reared his head back.

"And even though I knew, and she acknowledged, that we would stay in the house you built, still, I told her I would respect her wishes." I rolled my eyes closed. "I promised and gave your mother my word I would keep my legs closed to her son on her farm."

Simeon exhaled, then pinched the space between his eyes.

"The only reason my absence disappointed your mother today, why she even wanted to see me, is because we didn't show up on her farm a few months after visiting all those years ago with me sporting a pregnant belly. Because do you *think* she would not have been able to do the math, Simeon?"

He said nothing, just stared.

"Do you honestly believe she wouldn't have been able to put two and two together?" I shrugged a shoulder. "I'm sure she would eventually accept it all at some point, but there would always be that one area of contempt. It would be in her eyes whenever she looked at me. In my heart of hearts, I know that question would always loom and there would either be a lack of respect or trust, or shit. Both. Definitely, she would've wondered at least once. Did this girl tell me one thing and then do another? Which... I did."

I bit at my bottom lip. "So, I fixed it."

"No, you did what Eryn always does," he interjected. "You made a big decision and then told me about it after. Like always. You did it with tickets to Cancun, only telling me you bought tickets after buying them. You did it with the tattoo, telling me to write 'Simeon's' only to show up a day later with it tatted on your thigh. And then you did it with the abortion." He sighed. "If we didn't meet up that night, if I didn't insist we see each other and catch a movie, you would have never told me you were ever pregnant. Would you have?"

I looked away.

"Would you have?"

I couldn't answer.

"But the thing is..." He started pacing. "I knew you were."

I focused on him.

"I didn't know for a fact? But I knew, Eryn. I *knew* when we made love in my house that we'd done something different. Us doing it without any protection wasn't the only thing that made our time that morning different. I *felt* something, Eryn. Something deep down within me that let me know what we did that morning?" He shook his head. "Was nothing like the other times we'd made love."

I swallowed hard.

"Then I had a dream, a month later." He nodded. "I was back on the farm and there was a baby crying in the apple orchard. I followed its voice to where it was laying. But when I got close to it, I couldn't see its face. Couldn't tell if it was a girl or a boy, nothing. Because I couldn't see it. I couldn't make out the baby's face. Something blurred my vision the closer I got to them. And now I know why I couldn't see them. Why I couldn't look into their eyes."

I folded my arms over my chest.

"I told myself after that day at the farm and after that dream that if we conceived a child, yes, I would have altered my plans completely. I would have forgotten about sports management and lived whatever life we needed me to live for *us*."

"Exactly."

"And *that* would have been fine, Eryn," he insisted.

"No, it would not have been, Simeon." I shook my head. "You applied for that internship in Miami and hadn't turned it down after they made you an offer. A really *great* offer. You kept that offer hanging around. It had become a fear of mine. Because I knew I didn't want to go to Miami. I knew California was where I wanted to be. In my heart, I just knew our last year at Langston would have been our last year, period."

"And *that* was the problem, Eryn."

I furrowed my brows.

"Right there." He jabbed the air with his pointer finger in my direction. "Your mindset."

"What are you talking about?"

"It wasn't *your* decision to have the abortion that upset me. It was your mindset. You always take the easy way out."

"There was nothing *easy* about that, Simeon."

"You did the things you were comfortable executing—"

"Comfortable," I mocked. "Wow."

"And you didn't consider the other options."

"Options." I felt my bottom lip trembling as I tried to keep the tears in. "You abandoned the relationship. You just left! You told me you were taking the job two days after I told you I had the abortion and the weeks leading up to graduation and after it, you stopped calling me. You just stopped. You ghosted me. You vanished."

"Because you got rid of my baby!" he shouted, then inhaled a stuttered breath. "You got rid of something *we* made together. In love."

The vents and us both breathing heavily were the only things audible in the living room.

"I was pissed, shocked, too young to truly wrap my mind around what you did and *why* you did it." Simeon ran his hand down his trimmed beard. "Your decision. God, *your* decision. It hurt me to my core. But a part of me felt like I had no right to feel hurt because it was your decision." He squeezed his eyes closed. "So, I did what you do. *I* made a decision, then I let you know about it after the fact and I didn't bother to care for your input. Then I left. I moved to Miami, took the internship, and had the agency finance my MBA at a university in Florida. I busted my ass making them money, bringing in clients, trying to live the life I always dreamed of... but none of it mattered after a while because I didn't have you. And even now, over a decade later, that feeling hasn't changed."

I stared at him without moving.

"Every deal I've closed, every city I've traveled to, every investment, all the money I've made, it's all been things to do, distractions to take part in. Because I couldn't shake missing you. I just..." He pressed his hand to his forehead. "I wish you would have let me show you how *much* I loved you. I wish you had let me do the work, let me be there for you because you didn't have to go through that alone, Eryn. You didn't have to, beloved. I would have been there for you, no matter *what* you decided. I swear on my *life*, I would have."

Even from a distance, his words hit me with such force I could feel every single one of them.

"I realize that now," I admitted. "I realize I didn't have to go through it alone. And maybe... maybe I didn't have to go through with it at all. Because the more I thought about how hard life might have been with a baby we didn't plan, I also thought about how I could have made those tough days special for you. Just to show you that you made the right choice—that going through with the pregnancy was the right choice. Because we loved each other, and we *would've* figured it out."

He acknowledged with a head bob. "We absolutely would have."

"After you left, and everyone kept asking, 'Eryn, what happened between you and Simeon? Why did you guys break up?' I felt like I couldn't say anything." I pressed my trembling lips together, trying to hold back the tears welling up in my eyes. "I kept dodging their questions and making up abstract reasons that made little sense because admitting why you left would mean admitting I had the abortion. And telling them that would mean confessing that I regretted it the moment it was done."

His shoulders sagged.

"And then I'd have to tell them I regretted having it every day since I went through with the procedure and kept it a secret because not only was it a decision I didn't really think through but that decision caused the love of my life to stop loving me. And..." I inhaled a deep breath through my mouth. A tear escaped, and I refused to wipe it. "The only way to cope with keeping the secret and all the shit that came with it was to search and find distractions, just like you. Making my career my baby. Moving to Cali and assuming the identity of anyone but myself." I wiped away my tears, but they kept falling. "Because I was so exhausted, just waiting for the day I'd finally be okay again, like all those other women who had abortions and moved on with their lives, thriving. But I kept waiting, and waiting, and waiting." I pressed my hand to my chest, tears streaming down my face. "And still, I'm waiting—waiting to stop regretting it, waiting to feel like myself again."

Simeon walked up to me and used my arm to pull me to him. He wrapped his arms around me, holding me tightly against his chest, and I broke down completely.

"I'm so sorry. I had no idea," he whispered against me. "I didn't know you went through all of that." He held me tighter. "You didn't have to do that alone. You didn't have to do any of it alone. I'm so sorry."

"I'm sorry too," I said back.

I cried into his chest and he held me tighter, pressing his lips into my hair and leaving soft kisses against my strands. He let me let out everything against him without interruption, only holding me close.

"You're okay," he murmured against me, holding me closely. "It's all okay."

When I'd cried all I could, Simeon cradled my face in his hands and gently tilted my head back so I could look at him. He wiped the space beneath my eyes with the pads of his thumbs. When our eyes met, I noticed he had tears in his too.

"I have never stopped loving you, Eryn. Not once," he confessed, then sniffed back his tears. "And believe me..." He closed his eyes for a moment, a tear escaping. I caught it with the side of my hand, then gently caressed his face. "I've tried, dammit, I have *tried*, but you've never been easy to shake or replace."

With his next breath, he lowered his lips to mine, and I met him with a kiss, melting into him and his embrace as we parted our lips in unison. I wasn't sure if it was the moment or the surge of emotions and energy between us, but after a few caresses of his tongue against mine, I wanted more. A lot more.

"Simeon," I whispered against his lips, "I need you right now."

A second later, I was in his arms, being carried to the bedroom where we spent our first couple of nights in the penthouse before Ayanna and Dallas's wedding. In the room and on the bed, with downtown Manhattan glittering through the floor-to-ceiling windows, I watched Simeon pull off his shirt and step out of his trousers as I slipped out of my jumpsuit.

We weren't apart for long. But as soon as he joined me in bed, he pulled me close and crashed his lips into mine. I had tears in my eyes the entire time we kissed, my feelings cycling between wanting him and simply being grateful to be here... in whatever it was, but knowing I was there with him.

We kissed for what felt like forever. Our clothes were off, but for the first half an hour we volleyed from kissing to cuddling to caressing and him simply holding me. But I kept feeling his erection, and it was enticing me. So, as we spooned in bed, my eyes just a little heavy, I turned in his arms and rolled myself on top of him.

And Simeon, without saying a word, moved me into position to receive him. No condom. I pressed my palms against his chest and pulled back slightly, meeting his eyes as the realization hit me. "Are you sure?" I asked.

"Absolutely," he told me, flashing a perfect white smile I could see in the dimly lit room. And the moment I allowed him to guide me in a seat atop his erection, I tossed my head back, pressed my hand into his abs, and rocked and circled my hips until he was completely inside of me. I dropped my view to watch him watching me. How we'd effortlessly moved into our seamless choreography of making love. Just like that.

Moving slowly because that was the only way I could move full of him, and moving slowly so I could take my time, because what was the rush? Because I dreamed of this from the moment he stopped calling me. Being with him again and getting another opportunity to do it all over again from scratch. Make love and make a life with a man I knew was *the one* at first sight.

Simeon groaned and gripped my waist when I'd worked us into a rhythm. He sat up in bed and pulled at my legs so he could turn us, placing me beneath him, never disconnecting. Like always.

He grunted with each stroke, and I matched his sounds with cries of my own. Soon those strokes, like always, hollowed me, filling me to the brim with kinetic energy. Making me tingle everywhere I had nerves. Causing me to tremble and for my skin to prick and pimple with goose-bumps. I dropped my jaw as my eyes rolled back, surrendering like always to his power. His diligence. His persistence. I was gone out of my mind when he whispered, "I love you," in my ear. "I love you so damn much, Eryn."

He grabbed my jaw a second later to turn my face towards him, then pressed a kiss into my lips, sending me on a ride of iridescent views with my eyes closed. I swore I could get used to this. I prayed I could strike gold twice.

# TWENTY-NINE

**SIMEON**

I lay facing Eryn in bed, watching her sleep. Observing as her chest and breasts lifted and fell gently as she inhaled and exhaled. Her eyes, even when closed, were so beautiful. She looked soft, vulnerable, lying there looking like a dream come to life for me.

I smiled to myself when she inhaled deeply and let her exhale escape as a moan. My dick firmed a little at the innocent sound, wanting to be closer to her in that moment. But I decided to wait for the right time.

I watched the sunrise through the floor-to-ceiling window. I had drawn the curtains open with its remote control when I stirred awake half an hour prior. Instead of getting out of bed, I watched the sunrise and turned over to face Eryn to watch her do the thing she loved to do and did well. Sleep. And damn, was she a sleeping beauty? One I wouldn't mind awakening with a kiss in that moment.

But she needed the rest. I had kept her up practically all night. Day was breaking when we finally drifted off to sleep. I only managed two hours of rest. Too excited, maybe, especially about what I wanted to ask her. The question seemed random, almost immature after finally having the talk we'd been avoiding for weeks—years, actually. But something inside me craved this new direction.

I had dreamed of the day we would finally talk again, hash out everything, and speak our peace. I never knew Eryn was facing what she faced. On the surface, she seemed okay with it all, like the abortion was just something to get done and over with, then move on from. But knowing she had been carrying all that emotional weight on her own, telling no one, didn't sit right with me. It didn't seem right for her to do it by herself anymore, especially when she shouldn't have had to carry it alone to begin with.

I would have been there for whatever decision she went with if she had told me she was pregnant the moment she found out. She was right, though. I would have done everything to talk her out of it. But in the end, I would have respected her wishes. Because I wanted *her*. For the rest of my life.

Our flight back to Oakland was for six that evening. Eryn had voiced plans about not returning with me to Oakland, which stung a bit. She said she wasn't sure about returning to L.A. either. And I wanted us to bypass California altogether.

Her eyes blinked open, and they focused on me. A sweet smile spread across her lips and she moaned, writhing her body beneath the covers as she inhaled an abundance of air and let it out the same way. Her attention was completely on me when I told her, "I want to marry you, beloved."

Her brows shot up, and a huge smile spread across her face. "Well, good morning to you, too."

I chuckled while moving closer to her to pull her to me. "What do you say to that?"

"I'd say," she started. "I did a damn good job last night."

I leaned forward for a kiss and she tried to pull away.

"I just got up."

"I don't care," I replied, pecking her once on the lips.

She moaned and kissed me back, pressing her hand to the back of my head, then pulling away for a bit.

Eryn focused on me, and then she blinked hard. "You're serious."

I nodded.

She dipped her chin a bit to look at me under her long lashes. "You want to marry me?"

"I *really* do." I caressed the side of her face with the back of my hand. "Do *you* want to marry *me*?"

A smile pulled at her lips before she was moving her head up and down. "I *really* do."

"Great, then let's do it." I pulled the covers off me and stood to my feet.

"What?" Eryn sat up in bed. "You mean… right now?"

"Of course not." I grabbed the hotel robe that lay on the armchair in the room.

"Oh." She sighed, relieved. "Okay."

"I was thinking either Wednesday or Thursday."

Her jaw dropped. "Of… *this* week?"

I smiled. "Yeah."

She hollered a laugh that made me laugh too, even though I was serious.

"Simeon, where? This is New York," she reminded. "To get an appointment to get married at city hall takes weeks."

"I wasn't thinking city hall."

"So, *where* were you thinking?"

I winked. "Vegas, baby."

She stared at me for a moment and then released an excited scream that had me laughing from my gut.

She was up on her knees, holding the bedding up against her naked body. "Wait, are you serious, Simeon? Or are you playing?"

"I'm very serious and I am not playing at all."

"Even after *everything*?"

"Even after everything." I walked up to her and cradled her face in my hands. "I want you. I want *this* for the rest of my life. You're *it* for me. I'm done with all others. You're my final choice."

Her eyes moved back and forth between mine.

"For so long I have searched for you in women I've dated, which was completely unfair to them. I have dreamt of starting over. With you. But, beloved, what we'll create won't be from scratch, though. It'll be from experience and knowledge. Our love is so seasoned. It's ready. *I'm* ready."

She smiled up at me.

"The night before his wedding, I asked Dallas how he knew he wanted to marry Ayanna and why he thought marriage was necessary and he said something that reminded me of what I felt the first time I spent the night in your dorm room at LU."

"What did he say?"

"He said he knew he wanted to marry Ayanna when he realized he couldn't stand the thought of waking up without her or going to sleep without her by his side."

Eryn pressed her hand to my chest and over my heart.

"I don't want to go another night or another morning without you," I told her. "I want to wake up to you, like I did this morning—watching you sleep, marveling at you as you do your favorite thing in the world, and giving me all the more reason to rest a little more too. I want to do what I wanted to do over a decade ago. Eryn, I want to make you my wife."

"Oh my God." She giggled.

"So will you marry me, Eryn?" I smiled, seesawing my head from left to right. "Sometime this week?"

"Yes." She affirmed with a head tilt and threw her arms around me. "Let's go to Vegas, baby!"

# THIRTY

**ERYN**

I gasped the moment I walked through our hotel suite's door. "Damn!" My eyes fell on the setup at the bar from the entrance. The name of the hotel we were staying in appeared in big bold letters with a script version sprawled on top. Both writings decorated the wall behind the bar.

Simeon insisted I walk into the suite with my arms swinging, and he promised to bring our bags inside. That gave me an opportunity to take in all the beauty our suite offered. The pure white bar chairs sat in front of the bar counter made of black marble. A bucket of champagne sat waiting on ice for us to uncork.

I turned to glance at Simeon, who simply watched me take in the space. I'd only been to Vegas once. It was with co-workers at the first PR agency I worked at, and it was for our work retreat. The hotel we stayed in was okay, but this one totally trumped it by so much.

I stepped into the spacious living room and glimpsed the view of all the Vegas attractions. The patterns and color scheme of the suite looked heavily inspired by Italy's Lake Como. The decor gave off a calming and luxurious vibe and was very easy on the eyes.

Before arriving at our suite, Simeon and I stopped by the Clark County Marriage License Bureau as soon as we landed in Vegas. The bureau was the only marriage license bureau in the country open from 8am to midnight, so when we stopped by their office that afternoon, we could get our license after pre-applying online through the bureau's website. It only took our presence, our IDs, and $102 paid by credit card to get our license.

To get married. We were getting married, and my mind was still spinning at only the thought.

If we wanted to get married at that hour, we totally could. But Simeon and I planned to tie the knot the next day. He insisted we wait a day after our arrival because he wanted to take me somewhere first.

When we broke the news to our parents that we were running off to Vegas to elope, the response was not what I expected. I thought Simeon's parents of all people would've been the most against it since they seemed so traditional. But they were excited and couldn't wait for us to get back so they could celebrate with us. My mother, father, and Everett simply expressed the same collective reaction, which was, "It's about time."

Even though we had changed our flight and boarded our private plane to Nevada, and were now standing in one of the most famous hotels in Las Vegas, I still couldn't believe Simeon and I were about to go through with this. It was crazy that just a few days ago, I was unsure if we could ever get back to where we were.

A part of me was still unsure, but I'd done plenty of things in my life that didn't feel half as right as this and did them anyway. This just felt right. I loved Simeon, and ever since we reconnected, life had been exciting again. I mean... look at what we were doing now.

"Ready to step out?" he asked, walking up to me. He wrapped his arms around my waist, and I coiled my arms around the back of his neck, holding him extra close.

"I don't know." I smiled. "Are you going to tell me where we're going yet?"

He shook his head. "No, not yet." Simeon slid his hand down to take mine, interlocking our fingers together. "Let's go."

I thought he was going to take me far, but it seemed we weren't even going to leave the hotel. We stopped in front of a high-end jewelry store. But not just any jewelry store. The famous store that had its name in a movie title.

"Ready to pick out our rings?"

That made me lose my breath. The store was lit under bright lighting and furnished in long counters and gleaming glass displays. Everything sparkled from the rings in the display cases to the chandelier glittering overhead.

A sales associate, all smiles and eager to help, greeted us. "Congratulations, by the way," she said to both of us. "I'm Tatianna, and I'd be happy to assist with your selections today. Do you know what you're looking for?"

"Let's work on finding something for the bride," Simeon offered. "Whatever she wants, it's hers."

Tatianna looked at me with arched brows and a huge smile.

"Girl, I know," I said. "I still feel like I'm dreaming."

She laughed.

Tatianna escorted us to a display case that had beautiful rows of bracelets and earrings made with precious stones like rubies, emeralds, and, of course, diamonds. And when we arrived at the case that had rings on display, the overwhelm hit me like a fast-moving train, knocking the wind out of me.

There were so many to choose from. Enormous stones, tiny ones, princess cut, pear shape.

"Can I get you glasses of champagne as you peruse?" Tatianna asked.

"Pretty please," I told her, my heart beating harder than my pulse in my neck as my eyes kept scanning in front of me. "Thank you."

I knew I agreed to come to Vegas with the understanding Simeon and I would get married. I knew it when we deplaned the jet and took a black car to the marriage license bureau. But everything wasn't real until I saw the rings in the case and couldn't decide which ring was mine.

*Could I wear a wedding ring? Did I even deserve one? Was I marriage material after everything?*

I pressed my hand to my chest, hoping to get a grip.

"Are you okay?" Simeon asked beside me.

"*Umm...*" I exhaled.

"Here." Simeon took my hand for us to sit in the cushioned robin's-egg blue armchairs that were positioned opposite the ring displays. "Let's sit."

Tatianna returned with our glasses, and the moment I took a flute from her hand, I gulped the sparkling wine down without pausing, feeling it tickle the roof of my mouth and bubble against my tongue on the way down.

When I finished, I realized both Simeon and Tatianna were staring at me—Tatianna wide-eyed and Simeon with a boyish smirk.

"Okay." Simeon chuckled, turning his attention to Tatianna. "If you could be so kind as to bring us another glass, please."

Tatianna nodded at Simeon, then glanced at me and winked. "I'm on it. I'll be right back."

"Take your time," Simeon insisted.

I took a deep breath in, inhaling traces of glass cleaner and a merriment of shoppers' fragrances, including mine and Simeon's. I let all the air I held in go through my lips.

"What's happening right now?" he asked. "*Hmm?*"

I turned to look at him. A part of me wanted to keep what I was feeling inside, but that went against the promise I made to Simeon as we made love in the Manhattan suite. When we had our heart-to-heart. Keeping it all in would go against the promise I made to myself, too.

*"Promise to tell me everything," he whispered in my ear as he thrusted slowly in and out. I moaned in response, widening my legs so he'd go deeper. "Promise me no matter how you believe I'll take what you'll tell me," he whispered. "Promise you'll still tell me."*

"Are you sure you want to do this?" I asked him as I turned in my seat to face him. "With *me?*"

He sat attentively and listened.

"Like Simeon..." I exhaled, running my fingers through my hair. "I have *so much* work to do on myself. So much unlearning and unpacking.

The decisions I've made from having the abortion to sleeping with my boss only so I could get promotions at my job."

He bit his bottom lip.

"Do you really want *that* in a wife?"

He cracked a smile, then chuckled lowly. "You're not supposed to tell me about the flaws before the marriage, you know that, right?"

I laughed, slapping my hand to my mouth when I realized I was too loud.

"I'm supposed to find out all that stuff, after, but." He shrugged. "I guess it's unlike Eryn to do anything to form and that's why, yes, I want *this* and I want all that *you* are in a wife. Absolutely."

I stared into his eyes.

"I've got some good news and bad news for you." Simeon turned more to face me. "What do you want first?"

"Definitely the bad news." I gave a quick nod. "Let's just get that one out of the way."

He hollered a laugh. "Okay," he started. "The bad news about all this is, we've seen the worst in each other." He winked next. "But the good news about all this is we've already seen the worst in each other."

I dropped my head and laughed.

Simeon lifted my head by my chin. "What's done is done, and I don't care about any of the things you did when you weren't with me. And it's like I told you, Eryn." He smiled. "You don't have to do any of the hard parts of life alone. I'm *here* and I want to be *here* for it *all*. I'm never the type to run from a little work, anyway. You know that about me. I welcome it. Always will."

Simeon pressed his hand to my face, then ran his thumb over my lips.

"Eryn, I can't say it enough. You are *it* for me. In every sense. No one else even comes close."

"Same." I kissed the pad of his thumb, watching as he bit his lower lip. "No one compares to you."

He nodded. "My sentiments exactly. No one else has ever had the woman I have, and they never will. And no one has ever had the man you have. They never will either."

"Are we ready?" Tatianna asked as she returned to us. She placed the new flute of champagne on a table nearby.

I nodded while holding my attention on Simeon. "Yes, we are."

I was up on my feet, leaning against the cool glass, browsing through the case in search of a ring that seemed like me.

After scanning two rows of beautiful gems, one ring winked at the light differently than the others. It mesmerized me and it was love at first sight.

"Tatianna, can I please see this one?" I asked, pointing at the ring.

She pulled it out and held it in her white-gloved hand. It was simply beautiful. Rose gold, with so many diamonds, I couldn't decide which to focus on first.

"This is a rare four-carat diamond engagement ring with a rose gold halo setting. As you can see, the smaller diamonds appear on both sides of the central halo and the main stone is oval-shaped and prominently set at the center to enhance its brilliance and the sparkle of the side diamonds. The gallery..."

Her words went in one ear and out the other. I was so enamored. The rose gold gave the ring a warm and romantic hue that was taking my breath away. It was my favorite color of gold. Loved it so much I had my Range in L.A. detailed and spray-painted rose gold.

"I love it," I said to Tatianna and turned to look at Simeon. "This is the one."

Thinking I'd lock eyes with him standing beside me, he was down on one knee instead. And that brought the biggest smile to my face. I lifted my gaze for a moment to notice the few patrons in the jewelry store were focusing on us.

Simeon tugged at my hand so that I would focus on him and when I did, he was smiling so big I could count all his teeth.

"Eryn Peters."

"Yes, Simeon King?"

"Will you give me the honor of getting you coffee every morning for the rest of my life?"

I tossed my head back in a laugh.

"Will you marry me tomorrow?"

I nodded, then said, "I absolutely will."

He stood to his feet and drew me in for a kiss, wrapping his arms around me, making me feel like the luckiest woman in the world. Simeon pecked his lips off mine long enough to ask, "How soon can we have this sized and adjusted, Tatianna? We get married tomorrow."

"Half an hour to two hours, max," Tatianna replied with a smile. "We're used to last-minute requests. This *is* Vegas."

Simeon and I snickered.

"Perfect," Simeon replied, glancing over at me. "I'd like to have our rings engraved. Is that okay with you?"

I exhaled to keep the tears in, nodding quickly. "Absolutely."

Simeon closed the space between us to place a soft kiss on my lips. "Cool," he said on them. "Tatianna," he added, focusing on our associate, "let's get the matching wedding band for the missus." Simeon brought me in front of him so he could wrap his arms around my waist and hold me from behind. "And when she's happy, let's focus on a wedding band for me. In rose gold, of course."

"Of course." Tatianna blushed. "Yes, let's get back to work, then. So." She gestured inside the glass display case. "This is our selection of rose gold women's wedding bands..."

Her words were going in one ear and out the other, again. I was going to have to ask her to repeat herself. Because Simeon had me caught up on the idea of being a missus. But not any missus. Mrs. Simeon King. And I could get used to that.

———

Simeon and I didn't return to our hotel room until one that morning. While our wedding rings were being sized and engraved, he and I did some quick shopping, picking up some last-minute wedding things like a bouquet of faux white roses and a tiny veil from a local gift shop.

The lively entertainment scene had us not realizing we'd been walking for hours in Vegas's July heat. We spent a lot of our time checking out some of the famous casinos. At first, I thought we were checking them out for the sights alone. But apparently, it was to gamble.

*"How much money did you change for chips?"*

*We returned to our hotel and checked out the casino on the lower level.*

*After visiting a few of the other famous ones along the strip, Simeon refused to let the opportunity pass before trying his hand at a game.*

*I wasn't the gambling type, to be expected. But there was something about being in Vegas that made it feel okay to try my luck.*

*I wasn't the one gambling, though. Simeon was. Which is why I waited off the line when we stopped by the cashier's cage - or the cage, as I heard people in line call it - for him to change his money for chips at the casino.*

*The space was buzzing with energy. This was one of the more upscale casinos on the strip. With high arching ceilings, flashing lights and what seemed to be thousands of backlit gambling machines.*

*The music playing competed with the warble of slot machines and the dinging of alarms whenever someone won.*

*"100K," Simeon answered beside me as we made our way around the large room.*

*"What?"*

*"I changed 100K for chips."*

*I reared my head back and grabbed his arm, forcing us both to stop walking.*

*"Excuse me?"*

*People moved around us, making their way around the casino as I stood still staring at Simeon.*

*"Why'd you take out so much?" I blinked when I realized something else. "Wait, you had 100K hanging around to withdraw like that?"*

*He smirked, then winked, moving his eyes off me to survey the room.*

*"Simeon, are you rich?"*

*His eyes lowered to mine.*

*"It's not something you have to answer but... you know..." I moved in closer to him. "Are you? Rich?"*

*"I told you I do well. And now..." His smirk grew into a wide grin. "...we do well. We do very well, Eryn."*

*I peeked down at his hand, that was balled into a fist. The chip was in that hand. A $100,000 chip fit in the palm of his hand, just like that. He was palming my yearly salary.*

*"And I'll show you how well we do in due time. For now..." Simeon*

*took my hand with his free hand and interlocked his fingers with mine, lifting the back of my hand to his lips to kiss. "Come on."*

*We threaded our way through tables and casino patrons, passing security guards and players seated on stools wearing intense expressions as they focused down on playing cards, dice, and casino chips.*

*"Pick a table," Simeon said to me, drawing my attention away from all that was happening around me.*

*I'd been to Vegas once before, with colleagues at my first PR job in L.A., but we never visited the casinos. There was something both exciting and nerve-wracking about this place.*

*I pointed at a long rectangular table with rounded ends. "That one."*

*He followed my gesture and smiled. "Why that one?"*

*I shrugged. "I like the guy's hair who's standing over it. I don't know."*

*Simeon chuckled. "Okay. Then let's go."*

*We arrived at an empty spot at the table I chose that already had at least twenty other people standing all around it. The table had high padded rails which most of the twenty people standing around leaned on while throwing dice.*

*"What's this called?" I asked. "What are they playing?"*

*"It's a craps table," Simeon answered, guiding me to the table with him. "They're playing craps."*

*"Well, crap doesn't sound nice, now does it?"*

*He laughed. Simeon guided me in front of him and wrapped his arms around my waist. His warm and spicy scent settled in my scent space, making me want to say, "fuck this crap and let's get back to our room."*

*Besides the twenty people around us, there were four men in casino uniforms working on that one table.*

*One worker who stood on one end of the table made a signaling sign with his hands and then gestured at Simeon. In response, Simeon placed his 100K chip in a space labeled Pass Line.*

*"How do we play?" I asked.*

*"We place our bet and roll the dice," he answered in my ear, making me shiver. "Our bet is seven."*

*"And if we don't roll a seven?"*

*"Then we don't win."*

"Okay, so..." I turned my head to glance up at him over my shoulder. "How much are you betting?"

"We," he corrected, emphasizing his words with a smile. "... are betting it all, beloved."

I turned in his arms this time to get a better look at him. "Excuse me?"

He smiled. "We're shooting for even money."

"Even money?!" I shouted. "What the hell is even that?"

Simeon focused above my head and nodded, refocusing on me after. "It's time for the come-out roll."

"Huh?"

I did not know what he was talking about and strangely, that made me more nervous but extremely curious, too.

Simeon leaned forward to scoop up the two dice off the green table. He rattled them a few times in his palm, then brought his fist level with my lips and said, "Blow the dice for me."

I couldn't help smiling at that. "What if we lose?"

"What if we win?"

"Seems too risky, no?"

"Sometimes..." He caressed my chin with his thumb. "The risk is all worth it."

"Sir," someone called behind us.

"Look," Simeon started. "If we lose, then we lose. And if we win, then we win. But at least we're trying either way, right?"

I stared into his eyes, my heart beating a little faster. "Is this still about craps?"

"Sir," I heard a second time behind me. "Your roll."

Simeon focused on me. "Our roll."

I inhaled a deep breath and let it out hard through my lips.

"Do you trust me?" he asked me next.

I locked eyes with him and nodded. "I do."

"I trust you too." He grinned. "So blow this real nice for me."

I smiled and did as told and turned as Simeon tossed the dice on the table.

My eyes watched as the dice bounced and wobbled on its cubed sides until they both stopped. One displaying five dots on its face and the other only two.

*"Seven, winner! Even money!" The dealer closest to us shouted, pointing at Simeon and me, wearing a brief smirk, before he focused on the other players at the table.*

*I gasped and turned to look at Simeon in shock. "You won?!"*

*"We won." Simeon wore the biggest smile on his face and it was more of a rush seeing his sexy smile than winning.*

*"Just like that?"*

*"Just like that," he confirmed*

*"How much?"*

*"Double what we bet," he answered. "Even money. Two hundred thousand." He pulled me to him and pressed his lips to mine. "We're having fun tonight, good girl."*

And we started that fun sightseeing and acting like big kids in an adult version of Disney Land. We felt every bit of the dry heat the Mojave Desert offered on the sixth day of July. But with the dazzling strip that at night looked better with its neon lights on, we hadn't realized it was so late. We only became privy to the hour after we returned to our hotel suite at 1am.

And we didn't go to sleep when we got there. No, we swallowed down two bottles of champagne dressed in the hotel suite's robes and watched the infamous Bellagio water fountain from our window shoot water up about 460 feet into the air. I marveled as the water danced in intricate patterns, tonight illuminated by beautiful, colorful lights.

Simeon and I made love against that floor-to-ceiling window, christening every part of that suite instead of getting the rest we needed.

By the time we arrived for our wedding appointment at the Little White Chapel, the next day, we were *so* tired. But still very excited. Simeon rented a vintage white convertible as our wedding car for the day. The bellhops at our hotel snapped photos of us in front of the iconic vehicle. We'd only gotten two hours, maybe three hours of rest, but the adrenaline coursing through our veins was enough to keep us wide awake.

We spotted the iconic chapel sign that was shaped like a stylized white wedding bell as we turned off the I-15 North ramp. Once we were inside and had confirmed our information and handed over our marriage license, a gentleman escorted us into the chapel, and the entire view melted my heart.

I've always imagined being married, but never the wedding. I only knew that I wanted to love my husband with everything in me and know my husband wanted to do the same. And I was happy to know I'd gotten back the man I've always seen myself living forever with.

Inside the chapel, the ambiance was charming and intimate. They decked the interior out in white and pastel colors. White and red floral arrangements complemented the elegant white drapery, adding to the ambiance that the soft lighting provided.

One question asked on the website where we made the appointment was if we wanted a traditional ceremony or a civil one. We, of course, chose civil, too excited to get this part done with and to start our lives together.

Our officiant was the chapel's owner. An eighty-something natural blonde who was more vibrant and spunkier than me.

Simeon and I exchanged our vows—quick ones that we'd written hours before in separate rooms of our suite. That was the rule. We wanted to hear each other's vows for the first time at the chapel. Simeon's idea.

"Go ahead, groom," the officiant said to Simeon.

"With pleasure," he began, his eyes locked on mine. "Eryn, I have waited so long to say these words to you. Even during our time apart, my love for you never wavered. I carried you with me in my heart, always hoping we'd find our way back to each other."

He paused, taking a breath. "Standing here today, I can hardly believe that dream is real. To call you my wife, to make you Mrs. King, is a privilege I don't take lightly."

I smiled, feeling the sincerity in every word.

"I promise to love you without end, to cherish you, and to give us the life we've both always dreamed of. A life filled with love, laughter, and everything we once thought was out of reach. From this moment forward, and for the rest of our lives, I'm yours, Eryn."

He nodded once at our officiant, sealing the vow.

"Short and oh so sweet. I love it." she commented then gestured with a wrinkled hand. "And now the bride."

"Thank you." I smiled. "Simeon, from the moment we met, I knew you were special. My heart has never stopped yearning for you, even though I tried like hell to make it stop. But the truth is, I've always loved you, and I will continue to love you until my very last breath. I am so incredibly grateful for this second chance with you—to love you unconditionally and to hold on to the dream of our forever, now and always. I promise to cherish every moment, to learn from our past, and to build a future together that's even stronger than the dream we once had."

"Very lovely, my dear," the officiant said with a blush. "You two are just beautiful. And now, we've arrived at the end of this ceremony and the beginning of your journey together." She smiled. "By the power vested in me by the State of Nevada, I now pronounce you husband and wife. Handsome sir..." She looked up at Simeon. "You may kiss your beautiful bride."

I laughed giddily as he closed the space between us and took me in his arms. Simeon turned with me and imitated a dance dip, leaning me low enough to press his lips against mine in a kiss.

Just then, the sound of slot machines chiming behind us and a high-pitched ringing echoed around the space, startling me.

Simeon helped me back to my feet, and we both glanced behind us at a Vegas-style casino sign, its red 777 flashing on and off.

He and I looked at each other and laughed.

"This is so Vegas," I acknowledged with a giggle.

"And so is your wedding date." The owner smiled. "You two have gotten married on one of the luckiest days of this year. July 7, 2023."

I arched a brow.

"When you add up 2023," she explained. "The year as one number adds up to 7, making this day 777. Congratulations you two. You've hit the jackpot!"

Simeon and I looked at each other. Just like how we won at the craps table rolling a seven, we were winning again. This time for life.

"Well, that's an excellent sign." He beamed.

"Excellent indeed." I wrapped my arms around the back of his neck. "I love you."

"And I love you." He pecked my lips and on them added, "Always and forever."

# THIRTY-ONE

**SIMEON**

"Simeonnnn!" Eryn shouted in front of me, digging her fingertips into the back of my head. "Oh, my God, oh my God. Ooooh!"

I tightened my grip against her lower lips, rubbing the pad of my middle finger against her clit as I thrusted into her from behind. I inhaled and exhaled the saltwater air through my mouth, grunting as I delivered the last of my strokes between her thighs.

We made love in an all-white macrame-style swing bed that hung from a sturdy gold wire attached to the villa's back porch awning. We were in Belize on a private island resort that was only open to one guest party at a time. Eryn and I were the guests that week. We were staying in one of their one-story villas that we had all to ourselves. A seven-person staff kept us fed, our villa cleaned, and the grounds around the property kept. They weren't there at that hour, though. It was just Eryn, me, and a beautiful view of the blue, green turquoise ocean in front of us.

A stretch of white sand extended as far as the eyes could see. Beyond that was the hazy view of a neighboring island in the distance. Our footprints were still visible in the wet sand closest to where the shoreline of the ocean kissed the earth. Eryn's bathing suit, which she'd taken off before we ended up in each other's arms again, lay beside one of the leaning palm trees, shading part of the sand a few feet away.

Eryn and I had been in Belize for the past two days, with five more days to explore the island. And every day, we did just this. Made love everywhere. Anywhere there was a surface strong enough to hold us up, we were on it. Today it was the patio of our villa on a swing bed.

The frame around the mattress rocked back and forth with my movements, assisting with gliding me in so deep I could feel Eryn's walls fluttering and quivering uncontrollably. Her body vibrated against me, her moans traveling around us, and there was no one to hear us for miles and miles.

I pressed my lips into her hair and thrusted the last of my deep strokes into her, grunting and shuddering, refusing to breathe, too concerned about ruining the rhythm we'd created.

The way I saw it was, if I died from lack of air, at least I'd die the happiest man who had the most epic nut of his life.

I caught my breath against her, feeling her breasts rise and fall against my arm.

"Oh, fuck, Simeon. Dammit!" She panted in front of me. "You are a relentless beast, I swear. Unhand me at once."

"Never." I pecked her shoulder while smiling. "You're all mine now and I'm *never* letting go."

She moaned, then giggled. "I don't think I can take any more of this."

"Can you still feel your legs?" I whispered into her ear.

"What?" She laughed. "Yes. Why?"

"Well, if you can still feel them, that means I have more work to do." I grinned. "Which means we're far from done."

She bumped me away with her derriere, and I chuckled.

"Crazy ass." She turned in my arms to face me and threw her arms around the back of my neck. "I love that."

"I love you."

"And I love you." she smiled. "So damn much."

This was our impromptu honeymoon. Just as unplanned as our wedding. We ended up returning to Oakland to take care of a few things, including instructing my PR interns on how to assist Dallas and Ayanna with promoting their For the Culture interview.

Once we completed everything, Eryn and I were on the next flight to Belize for a few days of sun, sand, and sex on the beach. A beach only steps away from our villa's back door.

I knew there was a lot more that came with marriage, and I looked forward to learning what all those things were. For now, though, I was enjoying the perk of being married to a woman I truly loved and loved fucking, too.

I was getting the ultimate thrill, making love to her on a private beach where the only signs of life that could hear her sex cries were the seagulls walking about and the random tortoises sunbathing on the sand.

I pecked her lips again as I smoothed my palm down the curve of her ass. Only the feel of her skin against my hand was getting me hard again.

"*Mmm,*" she moaned against my lips before breaking our kiss. She peeked down between us and tossed her head back in a laugh.

I bit my bottom lip, smiling and pulling her close to me with my grip.

"I don't know if you know this," she started, "but you have a really big dick."

I smirked. "I've heard."

"And while I'm flattered, my husband is so turned on by me he's ready to go moments after he and I just went." Eryn pressed her hand to my chest. "I'm going to need a short refractory period. Because she is tender. To the touch."

I chuckled.

"Plus, not all of us grew up on a farm only eating the things organically grown there."

I feigned surprise with my brows. "That's news to me."

She fought back her smile. "I know, right? Shocking."

I snorted.

"So, I'm sorry," she continued. "We don't all have the stamina of a damn Thoroughbred. Nor are we used to dealing with men hung like one. I'm gonna need a short refractory period, big boy."

"Well, short refractory, like, what?" I squeezed her ass. "Two more minutes. Ten?"

"Half an hour, maybe an hour."

"Hmph." I nodded. "Well, I guess we can talk in the interim."

She giggled. "I mean, I would hope so since we *are* married and all now."

Eryn turned to lie in my arms, and I snuggled up behind her, interlocking our fingers together. Our silence allowed the soothing swish of the waves crashing into rocks in front of us to fill our sound space.

Our impromptu wedding in Vegas and now our honeymoon in Belize came at us fast. I honestly wouldn't have had it any other way, though. But there *were* things to talk about.

"Speaking of being married," I said in her ear. "There are some *married* things we need to discuss."

"Like?" she asked softly.

"Well, *like...* are we calling Oakland or L.A. home when we leave from here?"

"Oakland," Eryn answered swiftly. "You have an incredible office space and an amazing team at KSM. I wouldn't ask you to up and leave them like that."

"Okay," I replied. "On that note, we've already established on the flight over here that you will work with me at KSM."

"With you, not *for* you," she agreed. "*Mmm-hmm.*"

I smiled. "Will you be working from home or at the office?"

"Hybrid," she replied. "Some days in the office, most days from home."

"And whose home in Oakland will we be calling home? My condo or the apartment you loved at first sight?"

"Your condo, *duh.*"

I chuckled.

"That loft-like condo is everything and is one reason I said yes to marrying you if I'm keeping it real."

I slapped her ass in reaction.

She burst into laughter. "I'm only kidding... a little."

I laughed.

"Traveling," I continued. "How comfortable are you with it?"

"I'm looking forward to it." She nodded. "I know you are a seasoned traveler, so I hope that includes us visiting your parents a lot in Dewittville at the farm. At least once a month. Maybe twice?"

"We can visit the farm and my folks as many times a year as you wish."

She did a little dance in place, and I snickered.

"I'd like a short hotel getaway in the city whenever we're in New York, too," she added. "It'll give me an opportunity to check in with my mother and Everett."

"Done," I agreed. "And how about actual vacations? How many times a year works for you?"

"At least once," she answered, clearing her throat after. "Preferably in early May. If possible."

"Because of the—"

"Yes, because of the abortion," she confirmed. "If I can get away for a bit, around the anniversary, that would be cool."

"Done."

I swallowed hard because of the thought discussing that elicited. I made her promise to never shy away from addressing the uncomfortable with me. Whatever it was, we could do the work to make it less unpleasant. So, I was about to take my advice.

"How about children?"

Eryn turned her head to look at me over her shoulder before she turned completely in my arms to face me. When she wanted a better view of me, she sat up in the bed swing to look into my eyes.

I held her stare with me for a beat, running my hand up and down her bare thigh. "If I can just come right out and say it, beloved, I would love to have children with you. I would love to have all my children with you and only you."

Her eyes moved along my face.

"I know we never discussed children and having them when we were younger, which I imagined contributed to your decision."

She nodded.

"But I *want* children, Eryn." I focused up at her. "But if you don't, I understand—"

"I want them too," she replied, a smile gradually pulling her lips up. "At least three."

I sat up excitedly and pressed my palm to my chest. "I want three too."

"For real?"

I nodded, licking my lips. "Wanna get started?"

She hollered a laugh. "Sure."

I was moving in when she placed a hand between my lips and hers.

"In half an hour to an hour, nigga, damn."

I laughed.

"I already told you she is sore."

"*Aww.*" I leaned in to kiss her neck. "Well, it's my duty to lick her better. Come here and let me get to work."

I wrapped my arm around her waist and Eryn screamed then giggled as I threw her to the swing bed mattress.

I pecked her once against her lips and whispered, "Good girl."

I could definitely get used to this.

And because of my diligence, I actually could.

Thank God for do overs.

# EPILOGUE

## OAKLAND, CALIFORNIA - 1 YEAR LATER

### SIMEON

"Aisle 7," I mumbled, making my way outside of the aisles with my eyes pointed above them at the aisle signs. "Aisle 7."

"So, what do you think, Simeon?"

I was on the phone while at the pharmacy, trying to do two things at once. I was getting out of my car when my client Leo Vanguard called with an idea for his latest venture.

Leo was one of my newest clients. Ambitious and hungry to grow and expand outside of basketball. He was an excellent center for the Bronx Ballers, who had a lot of attention on him because of how he'd been playing the game, and he'd been obsessed with figuring out how he could capitalize on the attention the moment he got it.

"*Uh*," I said, scanning the aisle signs above my head. "What do I think?"

He chuckled on the other end of the phone. "Is now a good time, man?"

It wasn't, but I would never tell a client that. Come on.

"It's always a good time for you, LV," I promised.

The moment I found aisle 7, I turned into it, my eyes immediately searching the shelves.

"You want to start your own line of umbrellas." I made a shrugging expression with the sides of my lips. "Okay, I love the idea. But why umbrellas?"

"People always need them, right?"

I nodded while smiling. "That's true."

"And you told me a good investment satisfies needs or solves problems."

"Also true," I repeated.

I stopped in front of the shelves lined with various boxes, each promising the same results. Letting out a breath, I hunched my 6'3" frame down a bit to browse through the options.

"So, I'm guessing the sneaker line idea we've been hashing out in those New York meetings is off the table now?"

"Sneaker lines are so 1990s and 2000s," he groaned. "See, I like what you did with Dallas. The nutritional line thing?"

"Dallas did that on his own, LV. I just helped him along."

"Well, help *me* do something like *that*."

Speaking of Dallas, he and Ayanna were living in marital bliss. With Eryn's help, the two have been able to maintain a healthy public life, with boundaries. They hadn't and wouldn't share details about their relationship outside of the For The Culture interview. And this has made people more curious and enamored by them.

Dallas's brother, on the other hand, had become a running joke and a source of funny memes over the past year. After the label shelved his album and eventually dropped him, Dominick posted an apology video to his social pages. Along with the nudes he claimed to have—which brought hordes of women after him for perpetuating misogyny—Dominick's ex-girlfriend added fuel to the fire by confirming Ayanna's experience with him. Unlike Ayanna, who kept her silence, Dominick's ex was eager to spill the tea. His ex-girlfriend spoke to any media outlet that would listen, revealing how Dominick cheated on her multiple times and even gave her an STD. Every time he posted anything on social media, think pieces and online video commentaries flooded the internet. The guy didn't have a choice but to do something. And the apology video was *that* something.

Eryn disagreed.

The moment Eryn saw it, she wondered who his PR was and why did they hate Dominick so much? Because as Eryn put it, "No one in their right mind, not even someone fresh out of their first semester of intro to public relations, would *ever* advise this man to do this."

People online had turned the video of Dominick apologizing into the internet's latest joke. In the talking head video, Dominick had somehow made it all about him and blamed his serial cheating on Ayanna and the several other women he dated after her on his alleged sex addiction. Clever content creators took that one video and chopped, screwed, remixed, and made a parody song out of it.

It was the epitome of secondhand embarrassment.

Out of respect for their parents, Dallas called Dominick to let him know he accepted the apology. But that's as far as Dallas is willing to take it. He's hopeful that his brother will make a genuine change soon, but he's not holding his breath.

And Dallas has lived in peace ever since.

"But Dallas is Dallas, LV." I picked up a box and turned it over to its back to read its writing. "His nutritional products line has done numbers because he literally went to school and majored in chemistry to know how to formulate nutritional products."

Leo sighed on the line.

"You're still shooting blanks in the dark, but that's okay." I placed the box back on the shelf, deciding against it. I reached for another box when I said, "I love the umbrella idea. But maybe, let's find something you genuinely like and see what we can do with that."

"Well," he started. "I like Legos."

I lifted my gaze off the box in my hand to focus in front of me. "Legos?"

"Yeah, man." He chuckled. "I love building them in my free time. I made a Back to the Future-inspired car earlier today."

"Okay." I nodded. "I think we could do something with that."

My sports management agency, KSM, has expanded in ways I didn't initially imagine. The year prior, I only had three clients, but after hiring four agents to work under KSM, my roster of three clients has expanded to eighteen. And growing.

The company's name was getting around the NBA, and my team was growing beautifully. Especially once Eryn joined officially and improved the way we did PR. She was the reason I was at the pharmacy today.

*"I haven't had my period in over a month," she said matter-of-factly as she sipped the coffee I brought to her.*

*She'd just gotten out of the shower and taken a seat on her side of the bed with the towel still wrapped around her.*

*I turned to face her.*

*I was only dropping off the mug to her before heading out to the office. It was a Thursday, and she usually only came into KSM on Mondays and Fridays. Since getting married in Vegas the year prior, I'd reduced my office time to four days a week, Mondays, Tuesdays, Thursdays, and Fridays.*

*So, I had every intention of leaving her the coffee and heading into the office, but her comment changed some things.*

*We hadn't been actively trying, but we had been active. We were newlyweds who just celebrated their one-year anniversary a month prior. To the day.*

*I took one look at her and arched both brows. "Do... you think...?"*

*She smiled, then let a little laugh escape her lips. "As much as we've been going at it? Maybe?"*

Instead of driving into the office, I drove to the pharmacy and now I was holding a pregnancy test box in my hand, sure this was the one I was going to go with.

Since the conversation Eryn and I had on the swing bed in Belize, babies had been on my mind. Like I said, we weren't trying. But I'd be lying if I said I hadn't been intentionally making love to her frequently, all the while patiently waiting for Eryn to tell me she's late.

Her words were like music to my ears.

I hoped that they weren't only words and were the start of a new chapter in our lives. Because although the chapter we were in was better than any chapter I could have dreamt up, a new one would be exciting and a dream I would love to bring to life.

"Let's set up a video call for Monday," I suggested to Leo, turning to leave the aisle and to walk to one register. "I want to explore this Lego idea. I could so see you having your own special edition set."

"Yeah, boy!" Leo shouted on the line. "Really?"

"Really."

The cashier signaled I could approach her register, and I didn't delay.

"I'll be in the office for a phone meeting on Monday, so I'll have my assistant confirm the appointment time, okay, LV?"

My other phone meeting on Monday was about the partnership between Kings Farm and Bryant Greene's community-building project at Greene Gardens. My parents and I finalized the agreements, shook hands, and toasted with champagne. Plans were underway for Kings Farm to supply produce, dairy, and some baked and jarred goods to Greene Gardens' only supermarket. Surprisingly, Kings Farm was outperforming my investment in Good-Vibes... which, I must add, was thriving wonderfully as well.

"Cool," Leo replied. "Monday it is. I'll wait to hear from your assistant then."

"Sounds good." I placed the box on the cashier's counter. "We'll talk then."

"Good morning," the cashier greeted with a smile as she scanned the box. "How are you today?"

"Optimistic," I replied as I slid my credit card out of my wallet. "I'm positive today will be an extraordinary day."

"It just started though," she insisted.

I nodded. "Which makes it the perfect time to set that intention and decide you want that kind of day. You should try it." I smiled. "It works."

---

**ERYN**

"Hey, Ma," I said into the phone as I took a seat on the lounge chair.

It was a beautiful day out in Oakland, like most days, so I decided outside on the patio would be my office for the day.

The sun was out, not high just yet, so I figured I could get some work done and get some vitamin D at the same time.

"Hey, you!" My mother replied. "Is everything okay?"

"Everything's great." I smiled. "I had some time between phone calls, and I figured I'd call you only to say, hey."

"Oh! *Aww*, wow, Eryn." She giggled. "I love that, thank you. I love a good just-called-to-say-hey phone call."

"Good."

"How's Oakland?" she queried.

Oakland was amazing. Life after returning from Simeon and my honeymoon in Belize has been transformative.

I mean... I was calling my mother to say, *hey* for goodness' sake. And it wasn't her birthday *or* Mother's Day.

Once I finally did the work to unpack all the emotional baggage I'd been carrying—like that bag lady Erykah Badu sang about—holding everything inside, life started to feel so much lighter.

Necessary days of journaling and meditating have helped a ton. Confronting my feelings instead of avoiding or ignoring them, as obvious as it might sound, has really made a world of difference for me.

Having Simeon as my husband helped as well.

He left the condo in a hurry earlier, promising he would be back. It was Thursday morning, his in-office day, so I figured I'd see him later.

"Oakland is good, work is good too."

"And Simeon?"

"Amazing." I grinned. "Like an endless dream, as always."

A week after we returned from our honeymoon, Simeon signed the lease for the office floor above his at KSM to house the PR division of his company that I was now running as my own. I wasn't close to hiring a full team of PR agents yet, but he gave me his PR interns to help manage his clients and any others I brought in—including many of my old clients from Opal Sands.

So many of my previous Opal Sands clients called asking me where I was now because wherever I was, they wanted to be too.

I now had half of the clients I worked with at Opal Sands now calling me at Eryn King's Public Relations Agency, better known as EKPR, to provide PR for either their company or for them. But my most successful and favorite clients were, of course, Dallas and Ayanna. After working on their scandal, Dallas asked if I could manage his PR, and Ayanna wanted the same for her wig line of products, and I, of course, said yes. Besides being favorite clients, they were good friends. Like my little cousins, I sincerely loved being around.

"That's great to hear," my mother replied. "You know, I cannot stop thinking about your vow renewal ceremony you had on Simeon's parents' farm last month. Oh, my love, it was beautiful."

After getting married in Vegas, Simeon and I decided we would do something special for our one-year anniversary by holding a vow renewal ceremony where we could invite our friends and families to celebrate with us.

Although our parents hadn't made a fuss over us flying to Las Vegas and eloping, we didn't want to leave them out entirely.

So, we asked Simeon's parents if it would be okay to host a ceremony and reception on their farm with a small group of fifty people, and their answer yes was flying out of their mouths before we could get our question completely out of ours.

A small rustic wedding beneath the setting sun in Dewittville, New York. I really loved his parents' farm, so I was elated to have our vow renewal there. People couldn't stop talking about the food, which was made by a caterer who used only the fruits and vegetables grown on the farm. Mrs. King's recommendation. And it was a brilliant one.

I smiled big. "That food was amazing, right?"

"So good, Eryn," she concurred. "How's work?"

With my previous Opal Sands clients now with me at my agency, things were looking fantastic for me. Even though the agency was in its infant stages, its potential for growth was very clear. I knew it would take a lot of work to make it happen. And I was up for the job. Especially after getting a call from Brielle Chadwick a few months ago.

*"Hi, this is Lana from Opal Sands, calling to speak with Eryn Peters."*

*"Respectfully, it's Eryn King now," I said into the phone. I was sitting*

*at my desk in my brand-new office at EKPR and only took the call because the number looked familiar.*

*"My apologies," Lana said. "I'm calling on behalf of Brielle Chadwick."*

*My brows shot all the way up.*

*"She would like to set up an appointment with you to come into the office for a meeting to discuss a potential new employment offer with Opal Sands."*

*I scoffed. "A potential new employment offer with Opal Sands? Seriously?"*

*"Yes, Ms. King."*

*"Mrs."*

*"My apologies, again."*

*"Please tell Brielle if she wants to set up an appointment with me, that she can call me to set it up herself," I said into the phone. "Because I would love to speak with her personally."*

*"One second, Mrs. King."*

*I was grinding my teeth back and forth at the mention of that woman's name.*

*I hadn't thought of her or Richard in so long. I honestly forgot they existed. But since she wanted to make herself known, I'd give her the special attention she ordered.*

*"Eryn," Brielle chirped as she got on the line. "Eryn King, huh?"*

*"Mm-hmm," I replied.*

*"Congratulations."*

*"What can I do for you, Brielle?"*

*She cleared her throat. "Well, I hope a lot. In fact, I'm hoping some things are about to change because of this phone call between us."*

*"Are you now?"*

*She giggled. "Look, I let my emotions impede business when I fired you last year."*

*"Uh-huh..."*

*"It was obviously not the best decision and I'm sure you aren't too proud of your reaction to it all, either, right?" Her voice went up an octave. "We both can admit it wasn't our best moment."*

*"Again, I'll ask," I said. "What can I do for you, Brielle?"*

"*We want you back, Eryn.*"

"*We?*" *I questioned.*

"*Richard and I have discussed it, and we have decided you are an asset to Opal Sands.*"

"*Really?*" *I challenged.* "*I'm shocked.*"

"*We know that quite a few of our clients have left because you left, and we think we can let bygones be bygones for the sake of Opal Sands.*"

"*Well, there's that, but I would imagine having to show daddy he bought an entire company only to see it tank close to a year after the acquisition doesn't feel too good, right?*"

"*Eryn...*" *She sighed.* "*It really wasn't anything personal.*"

"*Brielle,*" *I retorted, mocking her high-pitched voice.* "*It was all personal, and you know it. Don't play a player.*"

"*Eryn—*"

"*Girl, cut the shit,*" *I interjected.* "*You fired me because my brother moved on and got engaged to a wonderful woman, I must add. A woman you could never even touch the heels of on your very best day.*"

"*Excuse me?*"

"*Oh, mamas, you're excused. Believe that, okay?*" *I replied.* "*Because the only reason I wanted you on the line was so I could tell you to kiss my entire ass, including the asshole, hoe.*"

*She gasped.*

"*Because I would rather clean the Hollywood sign with a toddler's toothbrush on the first day of my cycle in seven-inch stilettos than bring my black ass back to Opal Sands. So you can take that appointment you're trying to set up with me to discuss a new job opportunity and shove it up your dumb ass—without lube.*"

"*You—*"

"*And if I were you, I would put in a help wanted ad for a new front desk employee, because I'm taking Gina too. So, you're gonna need a new receptionist.*" *I laughed.* "*And that's just the start. 'Cause baby girl, by the time I'm done with Opal Sands, the only things left in that office working for you will be the printer and the fax machine. Maybe. I might take that shit too. Because God forgives. I don't. God is in fact still working on me, so in the meantime, while I'm working on being a better person, Brielle? Fuck you, hoe.*"

*"You stupid bit—"*

*"Bloop!" I shouted. "Bye, bitch. Have the life you deserve."*

It wasn't the most mature way to handle things, I know. And I'm sure if Simeon were there, he would say the same, but I wouldn't be me if I didn't at least get my lick back, just a little.

Besides, I considered Brielle and my phone call a consolation prize for not being able to at least pinch the bitch in the conference room the day she fired me and Richard stopped me from beating her ass.

I've changed since then, but I was also still a work in progress. And I was finally up for the work.

I should thank Brielle, though, for being so horrible. She was one of the major reasons my previous clients came banging down my door to work with them instead of her.

Maybe I can send her some blank DVDs wrapped with a big red bow so she can have a fresh batch to record her latest sexcapades.

"Work is fantastic, Ma," I replied. "Thanks for asking."

"Great," she said. "I'm so happy to hear that, and Eryn? I'm so very proud of you, my love."

I peeked over to my right when I heard the patio door slide open. Simeon appeared with something in his hand.

"There you are," he said as he walked closer.

"Hey, Ma." I smiled. "I gotta go. Simeon is back home when he should be at the office."

"Okay, my love, we'll talk later," she told me. "And let Simeon know I said hello."

"Will do. I love you."

"Love you more, Eryn."

"Ma said hi," I told him when he took a seat beside me. "What are you doing back here?"

"I bought this."

Simeon held the box in my view. It was a pregnancy test.

"You went to the pharmacy instead of work?"

He nodded. "Do you think you can take the test? I mean... do you *want* to take it? Right now? Pretty please?"

I giggled as I placed my laptop onto the lounge chair cushion and stood up from my seat, taking the box out of his hand.

"Let's go."

After our conversation in Belize about children, Simeon has not brought it up since.

But we've been making love. Frequently. And not once with a condom, so I knew it was inevitable.

I didn't expect it to take a year, though, and I would be lying if I didn't wonder, even for a moment, if my decision in college was causing the delay.

I walked into our en suite, and Simeon waited outside of it.

"Come on." I gestured with my head into the bathroom.

"You're cool with me coming in?"

"Babe, of course." I winked. "Let's find out together."

I ripped opened the box and removed the test stick and walked it to the toilet room in our bathroom to pee on the absorbent tip.

Following my mother's advice and her strategies, I have gotten to a place of peace and acceptance about my decision.

I could admit, I didn't think it through back then, having the abortion in college, but I knew also that things happened for a reason.

I didn't love having to go so long being without the love of my life. But it seemed the time apart really helped us to grow individually and to live lives on our terms... either for better or for worse.

We were back together again. We took our second chance and ran with it. And I had a feeling that the best was yet to come.

After I was done, I laid the test stick on the bathroom's vanity and washed my hands in the sink. I peeked up in the mirror to see Simeon stretching his neck a little to read the test stick at a distance as it did its thing.

I dried my hands and approached him, stepping into his view of the test stick to press my lips to his.

He moaned against them while circling his arms around my waist to pull me in closer.

Simeon pressed his forehead to mine, and we stood there, not saying anything.

I was ready. So very ready to make this man a daddy, because I knew he would be an excellent one.

No matter what that test said, I would do everything I could to give him a baby. Even if that meant us purposefully trying, starting that morning.

Simeon was so amazing I wanted to give him the world, and everything else he wanted in between.

He wasn't like any other man on this planet. I'd been with a good amount of them and understood I lucked out by getting another chance to make a life with a man worth making a life with more than once.

We inhaled a deep breath together, and I took his hand for us to approach the vanity to read the test together.

And when we got within inches of it, I gasped when I read *PREGNANT* in the test window.

"You're pregnant," Simeon staged whispered so loud, it might as well had not been a whisper at all.

I looked at him and he looked at me and we screamed at the same time.

Simeon had me in his arms less than a second later, pressing his hands to either side of my face and cradled my head in his hands.

"We're having a baby," he sighed against my lips. "Oh, my God. Thank you."

"Congratulations," I whispered back, placing several kisses on his lips. "You deserve."

"*We* deserve," he said back.

And all I could do in that moment was thank God for second chances. I was so grateful for the rarity, to course-correct and get another spin of that wheel of fortune, getting it right this time.

To be *so* blessed.

The sequel of our love would be better than we'd ever imagined it would be.

With dedication and effort.

And I was up for the task and more than willing to do the work to make all our dreams come true.

At last.

**THE END.**

# FINAL WORDS

Dear Reader,

The final author's note for this series. "Sentimental" fails to fully express the emotions rolling through me as I write this. Thank you so much for joining me on this journey and for reading the final story, *Sloth*. This ride has taken five years to conclude, and I couldn't imagine a better way to end it.

First, if you read *Gluttony* when it was released in January 2023 and have been waiting patiently for Eryn's story since then, thank you so much for your patience. Many of you were eager to read her story, and you had to wait through an entire book (*Wrath*) to get it. I would be remiss not to express my gratitude for your loyalty and understanding.

Writing Eryn and Simeon as the final vice and virtue was such a pleasure. We got to see how characters from my earlier books, who were once searching for love (or running from it) and found it in my book world, played a role in bringing Eryn and Simeon back together. We also saw how both Eryn and Simeon were different yet still the same, especially in how they responded to their personal crises. Simeon, in particular, was an inspiration. To him, obstacles were opportunities, and problems were possibilities. He was flexible and knew how to adjust on a whim. It was refreshing to see how he found solutions through his lens. I never realized how attractive diligence truly is... or how powerful it is to embody that trait in one's character.

I loved Eryn's zest for living in the moment, for better or for worse. She didn't hesitate to act, and while that may have led her to make a decision she later regretted, her openness to new experiences is what makes her so magnetic. And honestly? Eryn and I share the belief that when things aren't working out, a nap is and will always be the remedy, lol.

Regardless of how Eryn and Simeon handled their sudden upheavals, one thing was clear: the shocks to their realities in Chapters 1 and 2, which seemed like the end of their worlds at the time, turned out to be the best things that could have happened to them individually.

For those who read *Wrath*, you might have noticed that both Eryn and Lauryn found themselves in similar situations. They were each faced with mirrored dilemmas and stood at significant crossroads in their lives. Both were also heavily influenced by the mothers of the men they loved... though, one far more negatively than the other. I won't spoil *Wrath* for those who haven't read it, but this parallel was intentional. The sins sloth and wrath share many similarities, even though they may seem quite different on the surface.

Sloth can often lead to moments of wrath due to unresolved tension either in the person being slothful or in those affected by their inaction. For Eryn, her habit of disengaging and avoiding deeper emotional truths often made her resentful, even angry, whenever Simeon's name came up. Had she and Simeon not reconnected, it's likely that she would have crossed over into wrath. We saw hints of this in *Gluttony*. Both sloth and wrath are ways of escaping reality... one through inaction, the other through destructive overreaction. That's why they sit side by side in this series. While sloth tries to avoid confronting life by doing nothing, wrath seeks to force control through anger and destruction. Both can be devastating in their own ways, whether through passivity or aggression.

When deciding how to draw parallels between these two vices, I wanted to show what would have happened if Lauryn had made a different choice. A choice that Eryn ultimately made for herself.

Another aspect of *Sloth* is emotional apathy, which was highlighted in Eryn's relationship with her mother. If you've read my previously published stories or other books in this series, you're already familiar with Dr. Liz Peters. You know she's so lovable that it's hard to imagine anyone not liking her. Enter Eryn.

Eryn was, in a sense, denying herself the love of her mother. She kept herself from being vulnerable, refusing to put in the effort to connect deeply. She disengaged on purpose, avoided her mother and her own emotions, and neglected the work it takes to maintain a meaningful relationship. It's a side of sloth that isn't often spoken about, and seeing this dynamic between Eryn and Dr. Liz evolve—especially when Eryn finally opened up about what had been weighing on her heart—was beautiful to witness unfold on the page. Dr. Liz remains one of my favorite side characters, and we're not done seeing her yet!

I'm going to miss this series so much! It was a creative challenge to research the seven deadly sins and their opposites. It was tough at times to brainstorm and create scenarios that showed rather than told how they aligned with their vices or virtues, but I learned so much. All in all, it was truly a joy to bring the saints and sinners of *Love is Cure* to life on the page.

Although this chapter has ended, I have plenty of plans ahead and more stories to tell. After all, this is Volume One for a reason.

If this is your first book by me and you enjoyed it, welcome! You're officially a Brookelynite! To my readers who have been with me from book one or even further back, thank you from the bottom of my heart. Seven whole books. It wasn't easy making them, but it sure was worth it. Thank you for trusting my pen.

I'll see you at the end of the next book!

Love,
BK

# CHARACTER CAMEOS



**Brielle Chadwick**
Gluttony

**Ayanna Dale**
Forbidden: An Anthology
So This is Love

**Dallas Roque**
Forbidden: An Anthology
So This is Love

**Dominick Roque**
Forbidden: Anthology
So This is Love

**Everett Peters**
Gluttony
Glimpses

**Dr. Elizabeth Peters**
Last Comes Love
Ebb & Flow
Meant to Be
Lust
Envy
Ready or Not
Gluttony
Wrath

**Lauryn James**
Wrath

**Apryl Wilde**
Gluttony
Glimpses

**Bryant Greene**
Greed

**Manny (Kuts Kings)**
No Fraternizing series

**Summer**
Pride
So This is Love
Glimpses
Wrath

**Jayce**
Pride
So This is Love

Glimpses
Wrath

**Juliette Hart**
When Luke Met Juliette
When Life Gives You Sunsets

**Luke Lockett**
When Luke Met Juliette
When Life Gives You Sunsets

**Mykal Jones**
Envy
So This is Love
When Luke Met Juliette

# Story Extras

**Eryn mentioned how she and Simeon met when they were teenagers now experience it for yourself.
Download Sloth's prequel!**

Type this link into your browser to receive a copy of Sloth's prequel (you will need to join my mailing list since this is a BK Insiders exclusive)

-

https://dl.bookfunnel.com/ieow75lvdl

# Book Club Questions

1. What was your first impression of Eryn?
2. What was your first impression of Simeon?
3. How did your impression of Eryn and Simeon differ from what you first thought of them when they appeared in Gluttony and So This is Love, respectively?
4. What did you think about Eryn's relationship with her mother, Liz?
5. Do you agree with the decision Eryn made in the weeks leading up to her and Simeon's college graduation?
6. If you had to choose, whose side are you on—Eryn's or Simeon's?
7. Who was right and who was wrong?
8. What was your favorite moment in Sloth?
9. What did you think of Ayanna and Dallas's wedding?
10. What did you think about how the story ended?

# About Brookelyn Mosley

Brookelyn Mosley is a captivating voice in the world of black romance literature. With a gift for weaving heartfelt narratives and steamy encounters, she invites readers on journeys of love, passion, and self-discovery. Through her compelling storytelling, Brookelyn celebrates the beauty of black love and explores the complexities of relationships with authenticity and depth. With over 40+ titles, her stories resonate with true-blue readers, touching hearts and inspiring conversations about love, identity, and resilience.

### Connect With Me Online!

**Twitter:** @brookelynmosley
**Facebook:** http://facebook.com/brookelynmosley
**Facebook Reading Group:** Brookelynites Book Lounge
**Instagram:** @Brookelynmosley
**My Website:** BrookelynMosley.com